Praise for the Novels
of Jo Beverley

A Lady's Secret

"Well-matched, charming protagonists banter beautifully as they play a game of double deception. This cleverly plotted story rewards readers with a captivating blend of thrilling adventure, steamy sensuality, and gratifying emotion, as well as a surprise link to some of Beverley's earlier titles. Another flawless Georgian gem." —*Library Journal*

"With wit and humor, Jo Beverley proves a wonderful eighteenth-century romance starring two amiable lead characters whose first encounter is one of the best in recent memory. The tale is filled with nonstop action. . . . Jo Beverley provides a tremendous historical."

—*Midwest Book Review*

"Jo Beverley's writing is usually a cut above the crowd, and *A Lady's Secret* is no different . . . a book to enjoy." —Curled Up with a Good Book

"Beverley's attention to historical detail is as good as ever . . . delightful."
—*The Romance Reader*

Lady Beware

"Jo Beverley carries off a remarkable achievement in *Lady Beware*, the latest and possibly last in her Company of Rogues novels. . . . It is the unusual combination of familial comfort and risqué pleasure that makes this book a winner. . . . No doubt about it, *Lady Beware* is yet another jewel in Beverley's heavily decorated crown." —*The Romance Reader*

"[E]nchanting . . . a delightful blend of wit (with banter between Thea and Darien), intrigue (as evil lurks throughout) and emotional victories (as love prevails in the end). . . . Watching Thea and Darien spar is entertaining, and watching them succumb to the simmering love and passion is satisfying." —*The Columbia State* (SC)

To Rescue a Rogue

"Beverley brings the Regency period to life in this highly romantic story [with] vividly portrayed characters. [Readers] will be engrossed by this emotionally packed story of great love, tremendous courage, and the return of those attractive and dangerous men known as the Rogues. Her Company of Rogues series is well crafted, delicious, and wickedly captivating." —Joan Hammond

continued . . .

Jo Beverley

LORD WRAYBOURNE'S BETROTHED

A SIGNET ECLIPSE BOOK

SIGNET ECLIPSE
Published by New American Library, a division of
Penguin Group (USA) Inc., 375 Hudson Street,
New York, New York 10014, USA
Penguin Group (Canada), 90 Eglinton Avenue East, Suite 700, Toronto,
Ontario M4P 2Y3, Canada (a division of Pearson Penguin Canada Inc.)
Penguin Books Ltd., 80 Strand, London WC2R 0RL, England
Penguin Ireland, 25 St. Stephen's Green, Dublin 2,
Ireland (a division of Penguin Books Ltd.)
Penguin Group (Australia), 250 Camberwell Road, Camberwell, Victoria 3124,
Australia (a division of Pearson Australia Group Pty. Ltd.)
Penguin Books India Pvt. Ltd., 11 Community Centre, Panchsheel Park,
New Delhi – 110 017, India
Penguin Group (NZ), 67 Apollo Drive, Rosedale, North Shore 0632,
New Zealand (a division of Pearson New Zealand Ltd.)
Penguin Books (South Africa) (Pty.) Ltd., 24 Sturdee Avenue,
Rosebank, Johannesburg 2196, South Africa

Penguin Books Ltd., Registered Offices:
80 Strand, London WC2R ORL, England

Published by Signet Eclipse, an imprint of New American Library, a division of Penguin Group (USA)
Inc. Previously published in a Walker edition. Published by arrangement with the author.

First Signet Eclipse Printing, October 2009
10 9 8 7 6 5 4 3 2 1

Copyright © Jo Beverley, 1988
Excerpt from *The Stanforth Secrets* copyright © Jo Beverley, 1989
All rights reserved

SIGNET ECLIPSE and logo are trademarks of Penguin Group (USA) Inc.

Signet Eclipse Trade Paperback ISBN: 978-0-451-22833-8

The Library of Congress has cataloged the hardcover edition of this title as follows:

Beverley, Jo.
Lord Wraybourne's betrothed/Jo Beverley.
p. cm.
ISBN 0-8027-1051-4
I. Title.
PS3552.E864L67 1988
813'.54—dc19   88-12147

Set in ITC New Baskerville Roman
Designed by Alissa Amell

Printed in the United States of America

PROLOGUE

I<small>T WAS THE</small> most talked-about and yet the most tedious betrothal of the year.

The announcement in the *Morning Post* of April 12, 1813, of the forthcoming marriage of the Honorable Jane Sandiford of Carne Abbey, Gloucestershire, and David Kyle, Tenth Earl of Wraybourne of Stenby Castle, Shropshire, and Alton Street in London sent gossips from Edinburgh to Bath scurrying to their favorite meeting places. The ancient lineage of both families was traced. The enormous wealth of both families was assessed. Then the topic was found to have been sucked dry.

What was there to say about two such eminently correct people? Lord Wraybourne was an intelligent, well-educated man of thirty-two, admired by all levels of society. He handled his fortune responsibly, played his part in the Lords without aspiring to political leadership, was an excellent host and an amiable guest. If his manner was detached that was only to be expected from one of his lineage and betokened a proper acceptance of his place in society.

Miss Sandiford was the only child of Sir Jeffrey and Lady Sandiford. The lack of aristocratic station was not mistaken by the knowledgeable as a sign of lower status. The Sandifords were one of the oldest families in the land and one of the richest. In recent generations the family had been the epitome of starch-stiff rectitude, and despite their meticulous attention to charitable works, sober, dutiful living had led to even greater prosperity.

It was true that few people had met the young lady, for she had been educated at home and the Sandifords did not entertain. She had not yet made her debut even in nearby Cheltenham, which was unusual for a girl nearing twenty. Nonetheless, it was only the most daring and absurd scandalmonger who suggested she might be deformed or mentally defective. Anyway, shrugged the practical, what would that matter when her portion was bound to be immense?

Thus the gossips were forced to abandon the topic for the moment to discuss, according to their tastes, the new use of stiffer fabrics in evening gowns or the preparations being made in Portugal by the Duke of Wellington to finally put paid to the upstart Corsican. Curiosity about Miss Sandiford would be satisfied in time. Lord Wraybourne was a leader of fashion and would surely bring his wife to Town in due course. Then, at first or second hand, all would be able to assess Lord Wraybourne's betrothed, the new entrant to the ranks of the ton.

≈ 1 ≈

LADY SOPHIE KYLE looked across the breakfast table towards her brother, Lord Wraybourne, who was hidden behind his copy of the *Times*. Her delicate finger indicated an item in the *Morning Post*.

"Well, David. I see your fate is sealed in print." Though her tone was light, her pretty, heart-shaped face reflected distaste. "I still think it is a dreadfully dull way to choose a bride. Why, even Mama and I have not met the girl."

"Her name is Jane," commented her brother, looking up from the far more interesting news of the Spanish War.

"We have not met Jane," Sophie persevered. "David, when are we to meet her?"

Lord Wraybourne laid down his paper with a sigh. "At the wedding, most probably."

"Well, it's to be hoped she'll be *there* at least."

Her brother grinned. "Minx! You know what I mean."

She returned his grin, and her face lit up. He could see why she had already broken hearts when, at eighteen, she was only just preparing for her debut. She was not easily daunted by her brother's manner, even though he was more than ten years her senior. Strangers might find his smiling reserve intimidating, but his family and friends knew better.

"It's outrageous!" she continued. "First you announce you're marrying this girl of whom no one has ever heard and, if you please, after meeting her once, *and* for the most cold-blooded reasons such as money and ancestry. Then you do not even introduce her to your family. Really, David!"

"All that without a breath," he said dryly and quite unmoved. "Amazing."

"Stop being so provoking. Why are we not invited to Carne at least?"

His lean features expressed satirical amazement. "I thought to spare you. Believe me, you, above all people, would not find it to your liking, Sophie. Prayers morning and evening, plain food and a lack of good fires."

From long experience Sophie could tell he was beginning to lose his patience. After all, it was not the first time she had taken him to task about his betrothal.

"Well, I'm thinking of the poor girl herself," she defended.

"Jane is a year older than you, Sophie. She has no complaints about the arrangements. Once we return from our marriage trip you will doubtless see all you wish of her."

Sophie tossed her head, causing her mass of auburn curls to dance. It was a mannerism which proved effective with many an admirer but had no power over her brother.

"I can see you're feeling stuffy," she said saucily, "but I must tell you that I am disappointed. You could have married any one of a hundred eligible hopefuls."

"A hundred?"

"At least," Sophie insisted. "All my friends at school were smitten when you came to visit me and there were three great heiresses among them, you know."

"I am sure all the other brothers had the same effect."

Sophie let that pass, though she was amazed at how little he appreciated his attractions. The two of them were very alike. The blue eyes and auburn hair which made her a beauty turned his firmer, fine-boned masculine features handsome. Her daintiness was in him a lithe, athletic grace which could stir the most alarming sensations within a young maiden's breast—or so her friends had said. Nor did his habit of treating people with exquisite and impersonal courtesy detract. Even his way of hiding stronger feelings behind heavy eyelids did not cool the ardour with which he was received. Letty Fenwick-Stacy, one of her particular friends, had declared in fact that it drove her wild.

"What of Mrs. Danvers?" Sophie queried with a fair assumption of innocence. "I quite thought you would offer for her, though I'm glad you didn't, for she's too sarcastic for me. However, I know Maria had great hopes her bosom-bow would become her cousin."

She was amused to see her brother's heavy lids drop

over his blue eyes and his lips twitch slightly. Not for the first time Sophie wondered about his relationship with the ethereal widow. He was not about to enlighten her.

"I thought you were to ride out with Randal and his sisters? You'll be late. If you have something you wish to say, do so and be on your way."

Sophie stood abruptly. "It is only because I care for you, David. What of Love?"

"Been reading Minerva Novels again, poppet?"

"It is not only between the covers of a book that love exists. David, you will regret this cold-blooded choice."

Lord Wraybourne flashed his sister a sweet smile. "I know you care, Sophie, and I thank you. But this heat is all misplaced. You'll like Jane. She's good-looking, well-bred, and intelligent. She'll make me an excellent wife."

"But you don't love her and she doesn't love you!" Sophie wailed.

"Love will grow," said Lord Wraybourne firmly, then added with impatience, "Really, Sophie. Anyone would think you were in love yourself with this ardent advocacy of the state. I hope you haven't been foolish, my dear."

Sophie colored up. "Heavens, David, you know I'm determined to make a brilliant match. Where would I have met such in Bath? And why would I be hiding my conquest from you?"

"Precisely what I was wondering."

Sophie flounced to the door. "I know well what you're doing, brother mine. Attack is the best form of defense, but one day you'll realize I was right."

Lord Wraybourne was left to shake his head at the

slammed door. It would be restful when Sophie moved into the house of their cousin Maria, Lady Harroving, who was bringing her out. But he wondered whether she had not become a little too lively in her manners in recent years. She had lived in Bath with his mother, who had removed there on the death of the ninth earl two years ago. But his mother, in her grief, had become a recluse. He feared she had not watched over her daughter as well as she might.

He compared Sophie with Jane Sandiford to the latter's advantage. Jane was the most composed young woman he had ever met. She was never impetuous, her voice was always well-modulated, and her words considered. She exhibited no extreme emotions. She would be a restful and congenial companion.

He smiled slightly as he thought that Miss Sandiford might prove to be more. There were dozens of well-bred eligibles around but none had intrigued him like Jane, with her lush figure beneath schoolgirl gowns and the quickly veiled flashes of humor and passion which would light her serious eyes.

He put these tantalizing thoughts away and returned to the problem of his sister. Heaven help the man who married Sophie. But he did know that man would be socially acceptable, at least. Sophie had high standards. He had hopes his friend Lord Trenholme would come up to scratch and be accepted, for he would be able to control her and he was a kind, intelligent man. But there was nothing to be done until the Season started.

Thankful for tranquillity, Lord Wraybourne settled back to his newssheet. But he had merely glanced at the editorial when his peace was invaded again, this time by his uncle Henry. Mr. Moulton-Scrope was a dignified man with a tidy estate in Berkshire and a position in the Home Office. He also had his own fine home in London but no one would have suspected it from the way he commanded the butler, Harper, to bring him some ale and beef.

"Excuse me calling so informally, David. I need to speak to you and I'm tied up all day. Thought I'd breakfast here." Mr. Moulton-Scrope flipped up the tails of his coat and settled his ample form into a chair as the butler laid a place.

"Should eat a good old-fashioned breakfast, David," he announced, and launched into his favorite subject: how the ridiculous eating habits of the younger generation were going to ruin the country.

"How can we raise a nation of fighting men on little morsels of fancied-up food?" he demanded, cutting into the excellent rare beef which Harper had brought up from the kitchen especially, his lordship having no taste for it at breakfast. "Look at you. A strip of wind!"

Even as he spoke, Mr. Moulton-Scrope knew his description was unfair. It was true Lord Wraybourne was not of a large build but his was the slenderness and grace of muscles, not frailty. Mr. Moulton-Scrope had seen him fence, his favorite sport, and knew him to be a formidable opponent.

Lord Wraybourne was too wise to be drawn into an old debate. "What can I do for you, Uncle? I have my secretary and my estate manager from Stenby waiting."

"I need your help with a little problem, David."

Lord Wraybourne was surprised. In the tight circle of Society he and his uncle encountered one another frequently but they could not be called close. Mr. Moulton-Scrope was deeply involved with the political machinations of the day and took his post at the Home Office with great seriousness. Neither David's duties as a landowner nor his social life meshed with his uncle's tastes at all.

"If I can help you, Uncle, I am yours to command."

"Excellent," replied the older man with disquieting satisfaction. Lord Wraybourne wondered if he would have been wiser to have been noncommittal.

But Mr. Moulton-Scrope pressed on. "There's someone loose on the town attacking young women. Young ladies I should say, I suppose. Overwhelms 'em, takes 'em somewhere, has his way, and dumps 'em. Nasty business."

"Very! How is it I have heard nothing of it?"

"Well, it isn't a matter the families would want in the broadsheets. In fact, I suspect there may be more victims than the three we know of. It's only because of contacts with the families and rumors that those are known. And all in confidence."

"Are you saying these are women of our class?" Lord Wraybourne was astonished.

Mr. Moulton-Scrope shook his head. "No, no. Our young gels don't go about unescorted. No, these are more of the middling class. They do an occasional errand alone. In fact, one victim is a music teacher and goes about her appointments every day. But still ladies. They do not deserve to be so attacked."

"I doubt any woman does, not even those who offer

themselves for money. But forgive me, Uncle. I do not see how this can affect me."

Mr. Moulton-Scrope watched his nephew withdraw himself while remaining quite pleasant on the surface. It was a nasty habit. It must be the way his lids shielded those deceptively lazy eyes. It was because he knew Lord Wraybourne was never lazy and had a powerful and perceptive brain that he was seeking his aid.

"You did say you would help," he reminded.

His nephew sighed. "I knew I would regret that."

"The two previous victims of which we have knowledge were attacked before Christmas. We thought we'd seen the last of it but now there's another. And the devil of it is, the latest victim is the daughter of one of Prinny's favorite musicians. Believe me, royalty do not like to think of violent assault in any way connected to them. Orders have come down that the miscreant must be found."

"What of Fielding's Runners? Is this not their kind of work?"

"Hah. They are thief catchers! This is too delicate a business. For the sake of the young ladies there must be no talk."

"Then what will be done if the man *is* caught? A trial will reveal all."

A disconcerting hardness was seen in the older man's eyes. "The letter of the law is not always the way to spell justice."

"You alarm me, Uncle."

"Nothing ever alarms you. You're a damned cool fish, David, but you're one of the cleverest men I know. You also like to mix with the artist set. Your mother is always complaining you'd rather spend time with a bunch of philosophers than searching for a bride."

"Quite true."

Mr. Moulton-Scrope was distracted for a moment. "Should apply yourself, my boy. Past thirty. Need to set up your nursery. Besides, it might get Selina from drooping around Bath mourning your father. It's been two years."

Lord Wraybourne took up Sophie's paper and pointed to the social notices with one long, perfectly manicured finger.

His uncle choked. "The Sandiford heiress. Well done, my boy. Well done indeed! I didn't know she was on the Town."

"She's not. I met her in Gloucestershire."

"Do the Sandifords entertain then? I thought it was against their principles or something. I met them once at a devilish dull do. Something to do with succoring ex-slaves. Couldn't help feeling that if I was a blackie I'd think twice before accepting succor from such as they."

"Lady Sandiford has a *stern* view of life," agreed Lord Wraybourne with a slight smile.

"What about the daughter? You know what they say about daughters ending up like their mothers."

"Are you trying to make me cry off?" Lord Wraybourne asked in mock fright. "And abandon all that money?"

"Ha! Laugh if you like, my boy. Sermons are damned uncomfortable bedfellows even if they're printed with gold leaf."

Lord Wraybourne's lids drooped even lower, as if to hide

amusement. "How very poetic, Uncle," he murmured. But he was seeing large dark eyes set in creamy skin and a mass of rich ebony hair hanging in a simple braid down to his betrothed's waist. That hair already disturbed his sleep.

"But enough of your business," declared Mr. Moulton-Scope, ending any hope Lord Wraybourne had of deflecting him. "You're old enough to make your bed and make the best of it. I want you to go about your artist and donnish friends and see what you can find. Other victims, rumors, other gentlemen who move in those circles."

"You suspect a gentleman?"

His uncle nodded. "The victims can tell us very little. When they recover consciousness they are in the dark. But they all agree that their attacker was clean. Now you know how uncommon that is outside of the upper class, despite the influence of Brummell. Sometimes think he should be honored for that, a title maybe."

"I'm afraid the Marquis of Bath is already spoken for. Lord Wash, perhaps?"

Mr. Moulton-Scope chuckled. "Aye, that's a good one. No chance, of course, now he's fallen out with the Regent. Man's a fool. Forgot. He's a friend of yours."

Lord Wraybourne did not seem concerned. "I do not insist that all my friends be considered totally admirable."

"Just as well when Ashby's one of them. Boy's a reprobate!"

"Lord Randal is nearly thirty, Uncle. He was only a few years behind me at Eton."

"Then he's old enough to know better. Too much time on his hands. He's the sort who'd be well off at the war. I was surprised to see him escorting Sophie as I arrived. You need to watch him."

"Randal?" Lord Wraybourne was astonished. "He's like a brother. The Kyles and Ashbys have run together for generations. I grant he's not husband material but he would never let any harm come to Sophie. I trust him implicitly." There was a firmness in his tone that was a warning. Mr. Moulton-Scrope heeded it and returned to his business.

"Well. What were we saying? Brummell, Bath, ah yes. Our man is clean. He also reeks of lavender water and has soft hands. Likely a gentleman."

"A clerk? A music master?" prompted Lord Wraybourne.

His uncle shook his head. "There's something else. He called each woman by name. He whispered so they couldn't recognize his voice but he knew them. Was nasty in what he said too, though none of them can think of any man with cause to hate her. The point is that they were chosen victims but trapped in an opportune moment—when they took a shortcut by a secluded path or when caught in a sudden fog."

"Watched, you mean," said Lord Wraybourne thoughtfully. "So an employed person is not possible. They have too little free time. An unemployed?"

"Uses a carriage, my boy. A clean one too. Look at the timing as well. Up for the Little Season playing his nasty games. Home for Christmas. Back again now ready for the Spring Season. It's a gentleman and we want him."

Lord Wraybourne played idly with the Kyle ring, his crest cut into a cabochon ruby. "I do not relish the role of spy. I cannot see why you have come to me for this."

"We suspect there may have been more attacks, hushed up to protect the gels' reputations. You already have the entrée to that group and you have a way with you that gets people to trust you. If, as we suspect, the villain is a gentleman who mixes with these people, who better than you to sniff him out? You have a mind like a mantrap."

"Mixing your hunting metaphors, Uncle. I was anticipating being rather busy in the next few weeks. Sophie's making her debut this Season."

"Does that mean Selina's coming to town? Do her good."

"No, my mother won't come. As you say, she is still mourning my father. Maria is to do the honors."

Mr. Moulton-Scrope choked on a piece of bread. "My Maria?" he exclaimed, amazed at the thought of his daughter in this role. "Good God, she needs a bear-leader herself! Ten years married and four in the nursery, she should have some decorum but she barely keeps on the right side of scandal."

"Sophie can look out for herself," said Lord Wraybourne unconcernedly. "She's been unofficially out for years. But I was expecting to be busy keeping an eye on her, receiving a multitude of offers for her hand as well as preparing for my marriage. It is fixed for June."

Mr. Moulton-Scrope set himself out to persuade. "I'm not asking a lot, David. You *like* to go to readings and *soirées* and such. Just keep your ears open. Take Sophie. It would do her good."

Lord Wraybourne laughed. "She would likely run away from home first."

Mr. Moulton-Scrope shook his head. "She needs a tight rein, David. Selina has neglected her the last little while. I've heard of her on the town in Bath while still a schoolgirl. Don't *you* start indulging her. Find her a strong older man for a husband. One who'll keep her in hand or she'll bring disgrace on us all."

Lord Wraybourne's face had set in hard lines. "Sophie will never disgrace her name."

Mr. Moulton-Scrope met hard blue eyes and was surprised to find himself blustering. "Well, I didn't mean . . . Lovely girl . . . I only mean . . . Damn you, David, stop doing that. You look just like your father and he always scared me to death!"

Lord Wraybourne relaxed and laughed. "I'm sorry. I'm just feeling the weight of sudden responsibilities. I don't need your problems too. You really have nothing to go on, you know."

"Of course, I know! It's like looking for a needle in a haystack. I'm just thrashing around in the hope of finding something, anything to go on. If you keep your eyes and ears open you may hit on something . . ."

". . . or end up with a needle in the rear," interrupted Lord Wraybourne dryly.

"Or that. At least I can trust you. You could never be responsible for these kinds of acts and you'd never use perfume, thank God." He suddenly looked very tired. "David, I don't know what to do or what to look for but I need you to help me do it."

Lord Wraybourne's fine features lit with genuine amusement. "How can I resist such an appeal? I'll be your eyes and ears, Uncle. And if I see anything that could be a needle I'll report back to you."

"Needle, pin, bodkin—anything with a point to it, boy . . . anything with a point."

Mr. Moulton-Scrope hummed a light tune as he strolled on his way to his office. He hadn't been at all sure he could get his nephew to assist him. He always felt a little ill at ease with him, never knew what to make of him. Some people made the mistake of thinking Lord Wraybourne idle because he made life appear effortless. As if anyone could manage such vast estates profitably in idleness, even with the best of staff.

A few had even made the error of thinking him an easy mark when he had been a young man. There had been two duels that he knew about. Both swords, of course. They had ended with a neat, healable pinking and another man taught new respect for Lord Wraybourne.

Trust David to snap up the richest heiress in the country. Mr. Moulton-Scrope would give a deal to know how he'd managed it. It might be amusing to see what the little bride would make of the enigma that would be her husband. Unless she was a total fool she would have a pleasant, ever-courteous partner in life, but there was another man behind the surface. It would be a shame if she was never to discover him, a shame for her and for David both.

It was all his father's doing. The old Lord Wraybourne had been something of a *grand seigneur,* a favorite of the king and great on dignity and duty. He had left his four other children to his wife to rear and concentrated on his heir. Couldn't say he'd done a bad job. David was popular, pleasant, and an excellent landholder, but there was something . . . It was exactly like him to pick a bride by the book.

It was as well it wasn't a love match, however. He had no wish for David to be distracted in the next few weeks. Perhaps he'd have a word with Maria too, for all the good it would do. If she could keep Sophie in line, then maybe Lord Wraybourne would apply his mind to the problem. Overall, Mr. Moulton-Scrope was in an optimistic frame of mind as he entered the lofty halls of the Home Office that day.

2

IT WAS A day later that the crucial issue of the *Post* arrived in Gloucestershire and Jane Sandiford read the announcement of her betrothal.

As she was preparing to change for dinner, an early meal, of course, for they kept country hours, she was summoned to her mother's *boudoir.* Jane was past childhood and her height and shapely figure made her look very much a woman but visits to her mother's room were still associated with punishment and she had to suppress her nervousness as she approached the heavy paneled door. Lady Sandiford was in a rare state of geniality, however, and her thin lips even curled in a smile as she proffered the paper to her daughter.

"You will wish to see this, Jane. It contains your announcement."

Jane took it but realized after a moment that she was supposed to read it then and there. Suddenly daring, she asked, "May I keep this, Mama—as a memento?"

Lady Sandiford rarely expressed her feelings in movement. Perhaps she felt it might jeopardize the precision of her posture and demeanor, but this request caused an eyebrow to twitch infinitesimally.

"You have been most carefully reared, Jane. Where did you acquire so trite a notion? I am forced to wonder whether Mrs. Hawley has followed my directions for your upbringing as I would wish."

Her mother's slightest displeasure still had the ability to throw Jane into a panic, for it had so often meant the removal of a treasured object or occupation. Soon she would have to lose her companion and friend but not yet, she hoped. Carefully, she formed phrases which would be acceptable and yet still achieve her end.

"I am sure Mrs. Hawley has always done exactly as she ought, Mama, and I am grateful to you for your care of me. Surely a little sentiment is permissible at such a time as this. I would wish to treasure this sign of my future dignity."

It seemed her expressions were acceptable for once. Apart from saying acidly, "The sign of your future dignity is the ring you wear, Jane," her mother raised no further cavil and Jane was free to escape with her prize.

In truth it was the paper itself, and not the betrothal announcement, which was the prize. The newssheets were not allowed in the schoolroom. The idea of having one in her possession—to read every article without censor—was both novel and exciting; but first there was her announcement.

Safe in the quiet upper corridor, Jane looked for the words which predicted her future. How happy those words might once have made her. Now they seemed only to promise a further extension of her misery.

When Jane first realized that her mother was thinking of a marriage for her, she had been astonished and thrilled. Though she knew it was the usual lot of women to marry, especially when they were heiresses and the sole continuance of a proud bloodline, it had never seemed possible that something so momentous would happen to herself. Nothing ever happened at Carne.

Though her mother never discussed the subject, Jane had nonetheless gleaned scraps of information pertaining to her future. She discovered that her mother had queried her acquaintances, seeking an eligible bachelor of high position and impeccable morals. What Jane never heard was the results of the inquiries. She had a vague notion that she would end up as the wife of a bishop and was a little disappointed that he would doubtless be old. She had managed, despite her stringently regulated upbringing, to gather the raw materials for very typical romantic dreams, and she would have preferred a young, handsome knight-errant for her husband.

On the other hand, she had learned to take such pleasures as were presented and consoled herself with the fact that any marriage would take her away from Carne and give her a position in Society, perhaps even afford the opportunity to travel a little. A bishop would surely be good and gentle, and Jane was rather frightened of men.

She had become so attached to the notion of her kindly

old bishop that she had been taken aback when her mother baldly announced that they were to receive a visit from the Earl of Wraybourne, who would doubtless make Jane an offer of marriage if he found her acceptable. Jane knew there was no purpose in questioning Lady Sandiford, who would only decry the vulgar curiosity. It would, of course, be demeaning to go to the servants for gossip. Fortunately, Jane had one valid source of information—her governess, Beth Hawley.

Mrs. Hawley had come to be Jane's companion nearly ten years before. She had been the wife of a young naval officer less than a year when the Battle of Copenhagen made her a widow. At first Jane had seen the tiny, pale-faced woman as yet another extension of her mother, but as Beth's grief faded and the two became acquainted, friendship had flowered. It was this friendship that was largely responsible for the young woman Jane had become.

Without offending the strict rules laid down for Jane's upbringing, Mrs. Hawley had enriched the girl's education. If only textbooks and sermons were allowed, Mrs. Hawley sought the best-written and most sensitively considered ones. With the introduction of music lessons came ballads and lullabies. The rudiments of history and geography could be expanded to cover a great deal of human knowledge. Thus, the governess had most scrupulously adhered to the directions of the girl's parents while still managing to encourage her spirit and sense of humor.

If anyone in the house could tell her more of Lord Wraybourne, it would be Beth. Unfortunately, even that lady could be little help since she had never moved in Society. She rather thought that the gentleman occasionally spoke in the House, and she had never heard any scandal of him—that was the sum of Beth's knowledge. Jane had been forced to fall back again upon imagination, from which she had constructed a revised picture of a stern, but kindly man her parents' age, elegantly yet soberly dressed, much given to reading weighty tomes on statesmanship. Jane convinced herself that marriage to this paragon would be even better than life as a bishop's wife. She would be the wife of a government man, hearing all the great issues of the day discussed around her dinner table.

The reality, when Lord Wraybourne finally arrived, had, therefore, been stunning. He was not precisely young, but he was nowhere near her parents' age. He was well-informed and intelligent, but she was sure he did not spend all his time with his books. His dress might be sober, but it spoke clearly of expensive elegance even to her unsophisticated eye and did not disguise a quality about him for which she did not even have a word. In all her dreams of a husband, even in the dreams of her own Sir Galahad, the shape of the man's body had played no part. Yet it was this—the fluidity of movement, the bones of his face, the fine strength of his hands—which overwhelmed her. At times, despite his kindness, she would find her tongue stumbling over commonplaces or chattering inanities, something she was sure she would never have done with her bishop. Jane was at a loss to determine whether she was delighted . . . or terrified out of her wits.

For the first time in her life, she had given consideration to her appearance and been dismayed. She was forbidden to have a mirror in her rooms for fear she be vain, but there were mirrors around the house. She examined her plain, rather ill-fitting dresses and her hair in a thick plait down her back with dismay, and wished passionately for something more—something about her that would be capable of attracting this man. She was sure he would find her wanting and go on his way; and, though she feared him, she feared his absence more.

Then, one day she had found herself, without warning, alone with him for the first time. When she understood she was about to receive his offer, she had been panic-stricken. He was a being from another world. She was sure she could not live up to his expectations. She could never stand to live with the disturbance of the nerves that his mere presence caused her, nor the trembling which was the unsettling result of the slightest contact between them.

Yet, when he had finished speaking to her and patiently awaited her reply, she had known that she could not bear to have him leave the house, never to return. Whatever the cost, marriage to him was preferable to that. She had accepted his proposal. His strong hand over hers as he slipped the Kyle sapphire upon her finger set her nerves atremble once more, and, when she felt his lips against her cheek in a kiss, she had begun to shake in earnest.

"You must not be afraid of me, Jane," he said. "I promise there is no need."

Jane was not afraid of him exactly. It was only that, having once accepted the reality of a future with such a godlike figure, she was terrified she would in some way fail and lose this glimpse of heaven. She had confessed that she was sure she would disappoint him and he had coolly reassured her.

"I am not such a fool as that, Jane. I know you have all the qualities I look for in a wife."

Those were precisely the words that had come back to haunt her so often since. For not long after the earl's departure, Lady Sandiford had summoned Jane to her *boudoir*.

"I am most disappointed in you, Jane," she said most sternly. "You are neglecting both your lessons and your duties, choosing instead to moon about the place like an ill-bred widgeon. Is this the behavior you intend to visit upon your husband? He will not thank you, Miss, I assure you. He was assured by me that you are strictly reared and of high moral principles, quite without missish imaginings or romantical inclinations. Will you make a liar of me, Miss? *I will not have it.* You are not yet too old for a whipping. Lord Wraybourne has chosen you for your pedigree, your dowry, and your impeccable upbringing. Do not shame me. Do not disappoint him."

There was no question of doubting her mother's word. Lady Sandiford was resolutely honest. Jane had then realized what Lord Wraybourne's words had meant. How could she disappoint him when he looked only for money, bloodlines, and high principles? Her money and ancestry were fixed qualities. Doubtless his visit had been to assure himself that her principles were all they were claimed to be. Though it had been painful, she was now grateful for her mother's rebuke which had saved Jane from embarrassing both herself and her betrothed with uncalled-for warmth, perhaps even driving him away with her girlish enthusiasms.

Thinking back, with the newssheet still in her hand, Jane sighed. She slipped into a bedroom where there was a cheval glass and looked at herself again. How silly she had been to think for a moment that he could have any interest in her with her schoolgirl dresses and hair pulled so severely back off her face. Nor could she flatter herself that he had been overwhelmed by the brilliance of her mind and the sharpness of her wit. Shyness had kept her tongue-tied most of the time she was with him.

Ah well, she thought as she went on her way to her sitting room, perhaps in time she could gain his true regard. And even if her marriage should prove to be lacking in warmth she would still get away from Carne. She would meet Society, entertain, perhaps even travel. . . . It was strange how these enticements no longer thrilled her.

However, Mrs. Hawley *was* thrilled to have an up-to-date copy of the newspaper to read at leisure. The schoolroom ban on the paper theoretically extended to herself. Though copies usually passed through the servants' hall once the family had done with them, by the time she had leisure to skim one, it was tattered and often weeks behind the times. Now, she studied the *Post* intently, reading out pieces of interest, until Jane interrupted.

"That is such dull stuff. I know none of the people. And Papa will doubtless instruct me as to the importance of the Prussian invasion of Dresden."

The Sandifords' desire to protect their daughter from the newspapers did not mean they wished her to be ignorant. Each evening Jane received a tedious lecture from her father about the most important happenings.

Mrs. Hawley sighed. Jane had been in a withdrawn mood ever since Lord Wraybourne's visit and offer for her hand.

"You will doubtless follow all the business of Society with great interest in a few months when you are married," she said cheerfully.

"Yes, of course," responded Jane calmly, which dismayed Mrs. Hawley even more.

For a little while she had thought that Jane was truly happy with the husband chosen for her, and yet that seemed not to be the case. She had expected Jane to want to discuss her future husband, make plans, weave dreams; but, having accepted the ring upon her finger, the girl seemed to have put the whole matter out of her head. And yet, there was something . . . Mrs. Hawley wished she knew what was going on beneath her charge's calm demeanor.

"Lord Wraybourne moves in the highest levels of Society," she said, trying again. "The house parties at Stenby are famous. You will like to be hostess there."

"Will I?" Jane's mouth curved in a smile that did not reach her eyes. "You must know, Beth, that I am quite unprepared for that kind of life."

Mrs. Hawley saw a glimmer of trepidation in Jane's eyes and thought, with relief, that she understood her friend's problem at last. Jane knew little of the ways of Lord Wraybourne's set and was equally aware of the limitations of her upbringing. Luckily, with Beth to assist her, that was a matter which would be easily corrected.

"You will learn, my dear. And Lord Wraybourne will not expect you to manage your household immediately."

"Oh, *that* doesn't bother me," Jane said. "After all, I have been taught household management. Though I'm sure there will be many differences. I hope so at least. It would be pleasant to have a good fire on a cold day. I am confident of my abilities in that direction. Still, I don't know anybody in Society. I don't know anybody anywhere. Lord Wraybourne will not want me hanging upon his sleeve," she said firmly. "He will expect me to live my own life, I am sure, but how I am to do so I have no idea."

With this admission of fear, about which she seemed to be very much ashamed, Jane left immediately to prepare for the meal which she always ate with her parents. Mrs. Hawley gathered her warm shawl around herself and settled close to the small fire to read the *Post* but could not concentrate. Instead, she considered Jane's problem.

She had worried that the girl had taken a dislike to the earl but felt pressured into accepting his offer. It was difficult to imagine what fault Jane could find in Lord Wraybourne, though tastes varied, it was true. If the girl was nervous because of her ignorance of Society, however, that was a relatively simple problem to solve, or would be if Lady Sandiford did not have such antipathy towards any purely social occasion.

Jane really should have had a Season. With her marriage fixed only months away it was too late for that. . . . Or was it? Lady Sandiford detested the Season. She called it a circus for those of low class or low morals. The only part of it she acknowledged was the presentation at court, and she intended that Jane attend a Drawing Room after her marriage. Mrs. Hawley had been surprised by the Sandifords' choice of husband for Jane and detected in it the workings of pride. If Lady Sandiford would bend her haughty ideals to achieve a brilliant match for her daughter, perhaps she would bend them further to ensure the marriage was not a fiasco.

Mrs. Hawley was interrupted in her thoughts by the arrival of her dinner tray but continued to worry at the problem as she ate, without coming to any solution. When she was summoned to the drawing room to accompany Jane's singing she still had no line of attack planned. Luck, however, was to play straight into her hands.

Jane had a lovely contralto voice. Sir Jeffrey also sang well and joined his daughter in a duet, complimenting her afterwards.

"It is a pity," said Lady Sandiford coldly, "that one cannot converse in song. Perhaps then, Jane, we might hear more from you at the dinner table."

"I'm sorry, Mama," Jane said quietly. "I cannot think of anything to say."

"Polite conversation does not require thought, Jane. It is a habit, as are good manners. Mrs. Hawley, have you not taught Jane the Art of Conversation?"

Amazed, Beth saw her opening. "The Art of Conversation cannot adequately be learned in the schoolroom, Lady Sandiford. It needs practice in real situations."

After a few moments of silence, Lady Sandiford asked, "What would you recommend, Mrs. Hawley?"

"I would recommend that Jane spend some time in polite Society before she assumes the dignity of the Countess of Wraybourne, Your Ladyship."

This time the silence seemed to stretch forever. Nonetheless, Lady Sandiford, despite her many limitations, was a shrewd woman and worked through the arguments without assistance. There was no point in spending the interval in nearby Cheltenham. Who of importance would Jane meet there? If it were to be done it must be done thoroughly.

"A few weeks in London might be wise," she announced at last. "I will write to Lord Wraybourne. Jane, you may enclose a note if you wish."

Lady Sandiford turned to her husband. "You agree, Sir Jeffrey?" This was rhetorical, of course. "I dislike the necessity, but I would not wish Lord Wraybourne to find Jane wanting in social accomplishments. He has a sister making her curtsy this year. Jane will accompany her. Sophia. Yes, Lady Sophia. I am sure that a sister of Lord Wraybourne is a decorous and modest young lady. The old Lord Wraybourne was a most admirable man of the highest principles. There can be no impediment to the matter."

Mrs. Hawley wondered what would happen if this arbitrary rearrangement of everyone's plans was *not* agreeable but was not about to raise any objection to such a desirable outcome of her interference.

Back in the schoolroom, Jane, who had not shown any apparent interest in the discussion, looked at her governess wide-eyed. "Oh, Beth, what am I to do?"

"What do you mean, Jane?"

"I cannot go to London! I know no one. I am ignorant

of dancing and all the social conventions. I will appear a veritable bumpkin!"

Mrs. Hawley was amazed to see that her charge was almost in tears. "But this is your chance to learn, my dear. You would have to join Society eventually."

Jane sat and stared at the meager fire, with the pallor of one condemned to death. "I had thought it would be after I had been married for some time."

Mrs. Hawley took her charge's cold hands. "Your marriage will be a Society affair. Even during your honeymoon there will be coming and going. The Earl and Countess of Wraybourne will not live in seclusion. It will be much better to practice your social arts on strangers than upon your husband and his friends."

Jane swallowed tears. Her governess had confirmed her fears. "You are saying he will be ashamed of me."

"No, dear, of course not. There is nothing wrong with your behavior. It is just that you will find things strange. All young girls do," she lied. "Those doing their first Season are expected to be a bit ignorant and wide-eyed. A countess is not. Better to be shocked and surprised now than later."

Jane looked at the Kyle sapphire on her finger and sighed. Though it seemed Lord Wraybourne had chosen her as his bride for practical reasons, she was haunted by the fear that he would realize her many shortcomings and change his mind. When the wedding had been planned to occur before Jane's presentation, she had believed her married future to be *a fait accompli*. Now it appeared she would have to prove herself. He probably *would* wish her to be sophisticated as well as rich, moral, and unromantical, though how he could realistically expect such a thing she could not imagine.

"I suppose I can try to fit into that world," she said at last. "As long as I still have my dowry and my virtue, I do not suppose Lord Wraybourne will lightly break the engagement."

Mrs. Hawley was confused by this speech, but she could reassure her charge. "He cannot possibly back out of the marriage, Jane. That would be unthinkable for a gentleman. Only the lady may do so, and then only at risk of being labelled a jilt."

"Is that truly so?" Jane asked, seeing reprieve.

Mrs. Hawley took the girl's wide eyes as indicative of distress, not relief, and was concerned. "Of course, my dear. I thought you knew that. I should have told you earlier. Now your betrothal is announced it would cause a great deal of talk if you were to draw back."

"But how terrible to be forced to go through with a marriage when all desire for it has left."

"Indeed it would be," said Mrs. Hawley, now positively alarmed. "In such a case, to end the engagement might be the only honorable course. But Jane, do I understand you no longer wish to marry the earl?"

Jane's eyes opened even wider, but this time the expression was unmistakable—surprise. "I? Of course I wish to marry the earl, Beth. But what if he no longer wishes to marry me when he sees how little I know of the ways of the ton? Then would I not be honorably bound to release him?"

Mrs. Hawley shook her head. "Jane, what maggot has got into you? Lord Wraybourne made his choice after becoming acquainted with you. You have not deceived him as to your nature. Why should he suddenly decide you are unsuitable, merely because you are unaccustomed to Society?"

That, thought Jane, was depressingly true. She supposed it did not matter how tongue-tied she was, how many *faux pas* she committed. If she still had her money and her pedigree, the marriage would go forward.

She desperately wanted to marry the Earl of Wraybourne on any terms, but she really did not think she could bear it if he did not want as desperately to marry her.

3

THREE WEEKS LATER a carriage deposited Jane, her father, and a newly trained maid, Prudence Hawkins, at the pillared coach entrance of The Middlehouse, the country seat of Lord and Lady Harroving. Being close to Great Missenden, this was a convenient place to break the two-day journey to London. As Lord Wraybourne had agreed to meet his betrothed there, Sir Jeffrey did not need to escort his daughter all the way to Town. It was also suitable because Lady Harroving was to introduce Jane and Lady Sophie to Society in the coming weeks.

As Jane and her father entered the impressive Italianate entrance hall of The Middlehouse, she was very aware of the danger of showing her naivety and worked hard not to gape at the lightly clad deities who played in the clouds of the *trompe l'oeil* ceiling. As their hostess approached across the vast tiled hall, Jane could not help feeling Lady Harroving would have been at home if she had suddenly found herself transported to those painted Olympian heavens.

Lusciously plump and blond, she was obviously fighting the fact that she was in her thirties and a wife of many years. Her weapons were a daring style of dress and skillful, but not undetectable, use of cosmetics. There was marked contrast between her delightful expensive day dress of dusky pink muslin and her guests' dark and serviceable travelling clothes.

Some unpleasant emotion seemed to flicker across her face when she set eyes on Jane. This reinforced Jane's unhappy belief that she must present the very picture of dowdiness, but Lady Harroving's manner was bright and welcoming as she arranged for their comfort.

"I am sure you must be exhausted! I dislike travelling above all things. Our other guests are out at the moment, but I'm sure that is a relief to you, my dear," she said sweetly to Jane. "You do not want to be meeting Lord Wraybourne again in all your dirt. I will have tea sent to your rooms and you may rest before dinner tonight."

Jane recognized the false tone of this welcome. In fact, her hostess scarcely bothered to hide it. The lady was doubtless put out by the arbitrary increasing of her responsibilities.

Still, any ungraciousness was not reflected in the room Jane was given. She sighed with contentment at the feel of a velvety carpet beneath her feet and breathed deeply the delicate aroma of the *potpourri* in a china bowl on the dressing table. She had no need to be politic as she admired the yellow sprigged wallpaper and the matching hangings on the bed.

Once Lady Harroving had left, Jane continued her exploration. Lavender sachets in the drawers, rose-scented soap in the dish and, in the grate, an enormous fire despite the fact that it was May and seasonably warm. Such luxury seemed a sign of better things to come. Jane surveyed her new domain with satisfaction, trying desperately to ignore the shadowy fears which troubled her mind. Lady Harroving's reaction had made it very clear that Jane's betrothed would think her an unfashionable, tongue-tied bumpkin. It was intolerable rather than reassuring that he would accept her because of her money, bloodlines, and upbringing even while he despised her appearance.

How she wished Mrs. Hawley was here with her. That lady would have shared Jane's delight in the unaccustomed luxury, but she would also have been able to advise and support. Alas, Beth was to stay on at Carne to help with preparations for the wedding and then would leave to take up another position. Jane missed her dreadfully already. Tomorrow her father would leave to return home and she would be alone with strangers. For a moment she was afraid she would cry, but she never cried. She had prayed for years to be allowed to escape from her home, to learn something of the world beyond Carne. Now that the opportunity was granted her, tears were uncalled for.

Resolutely, she drank the tea and ate the delicious cake sent up for her refreshment, then let Prudence remove her outer clothes so that she might lie down upon the soft bed. Heaven, a feather mattress! In moments she was asleep.

Some hours later, when Jane was awakened by her maid, she felt disorientated but she recovered to realize that she was, in fact, well rested and able to face what could be a trying evening. She had longed for new experiences. Now she would enjoy them. If anyone looked down on her, she thought wryly, she would remember her fortune, her bloodlines, and her moral superiority. As for her betrothed, she could only try her hardest not to make him ashamed of her. Above all, she must not moon over him or cling to him. Her mother had given her another lecture before departure, warning expressly against such ill-bred behavior.

Jane knew she would have faced her first contact with fashionable Society with more composure if she had clothes with some pretense to *à-la-modality*. Her measurements had been sent weeks ago to a fashionable *modiste* who was to make her *trousseau*, but the garments were to be collected on arrival in London. This had not seemed to matter when they were merely to stay with Lord Wraybourne's cousin in the country; but now, having seen the cousin, Jane knew she would be a figure of fun. She gazed at her only evening gown, a plain white silk with a neckline neither high nor low and no ornamentation whatsoever.

"Oh, how I wish I had my London wardrobe," Jane sighed. "I will look like a pauper cousin in this dress."

"There's the pearls, Miss Jane," offered Prudence Hawkins in consolation.

Jane took out the long, perfectly matched string and let it trickle through her fingers. She nodded thoughtfully.

"And I'll try your hair in a new style, Miss. You can't

keep wearing it down your back or in braids round your head."

"Very well." Jane looked up at the maid. "Have you become acquainted with any of the servants here, Prudence?"

"Lady Sophie's maid was quite kind to me, Miss Jane. Above me, of course, but she showed me a few things."

"Could you go and ask whether she knows of any white silk flowers I could borrow?" Jane was a little pink. "I dislike having to ask, but better that than to appear so . . . plain."

Enthusiastically, Prudence hurried off and returned in a little while with a box of trimmings and flowers.

"There's any amount of folderols in the sewing room here!" she exclaimed. "Stuff is worn once and thrown aside. Tomorrow, if you wish, Miss Jane, I'll see about trimming your other gowns a little."

They worked together, and soon Jane decided that she presented a tolerable enough appearance. She made no attempt to be fashionable, for she had little idea what the fashion was. She suspected neither the frilly gowns worn by Squire Masham's wife nor the heavily trimmed style favored by the wife of the vicar of Carne represented the latest style. Still, she was confident that the discreet use of trimming had disguised the poor cut of the dress. Small white rosebuds decorated the neckline of her gown and larger open blossoms were fixed in her hair, which was now gathered in a knot on the top of her head. With the pearls wrapped round her neck four times, she believed she could hold her head high.

Nonetheless, she felt the need of moral support when

she received a message saying that her father had one of his sick headaches and would not be down that evening. On shaking legs and feeling very alone, Jane followed the footman to the drawing room, where her name was announced to what seemed to her a large and glittering company. She froze for a moment, but the dreaded first meeting with Lord Wraybourne passed easily. He appeared to her not so much a critical judge as a gallant rescuer and refuge. He might only see her as a fortune on well-bred legs, but at least he was a familiar face and inclined to be kind.

"You are looking very well, Jane."

He was not so familiar after all. After so many weeks of absence, he was a stranger too.

Jane studied him as if for the first time. He was handsome, she supposed, and very elegant. She did not remember his clothes being quite so fine at Carne. Doubtless he chose them to suit the company. There, in the evening, he had worn knee breeches and dark colors like her father. Here he was dressed in a deep blue coat and buff pantaloons molded to his body. His cravat formed crisp, white folds around his face to emphasize his well-shaped features. She stiffened as she became aware of the direction of her thoughts. She *mustn't* start mooning over him, even if he was extremely handsome.

"I will look even better," she replied prosaically, "when the London *modiste* has done her work."

Lord Wraybourne's finely shaped lips twitched slightly. "I am sure of it. As with the hairdressers and perhaps even the cosmeticians. But they will be gilding the lily."

Despite her determination to be cool and sophisticated, Jane was shocked. "Face paint is totally improper!" Then she saw the gleam in his eyes. "Are you teasing me, my lord?"

"One of my privileges, I believe," he said with a smile, tucking her arm in his. "Come along and allow me to present you to your host and the rest of the company."

Lord Harroving was a solid man with red face and a leering eye. Jane did not like the way he looked at her and was relieved when he did not seem to find her worthy of continuing interest. He was considerably older than his wife and spent most of the evening with the *Sporting Pink*, ignoring the company.

A very tall, muscular man in his thirties was introduced as Sir Marius Fletcher, a particular friend. Be that as it may, his greeting to her was less than warm, Jane felt, but perhaps such a chiselled face could not help being stony. Unlike Lord Wraybourne, Sir Marius's evening clothes were almost casual. He was most certainly not a dandy. When she became more familiar with Society, she would realize he belonged to the sporting Corinthian set.

After two such daunting introductions Jane was relieved to be presented to a young woman of her own age. Lady Sophia Kyle, Lord Wraybourne's sister, seemed reserved at first, then she suddenly smiled and embraced Jane warmly.

"I *am* pleased to meet you after all. I am going to like you very much, I think, and we will be the best of friends as we are to make our curtsy together. And soon, of course, we will be the best of sisters!"

While relieved at the offer of friendship, Jane couldn't

help but think that Lord Wraybourne's sister was not quite as her mother had expected. Her blue silk dress with its foot of embroidered fringing round the hem and startlingly low—at least in Jane's experience—neckline could only be called dashing. Jane was hard put not to stare at Lady Sophie's hair, which was cropped short and bounced in auburn curls very like her brother's. Blue ribbons were threaded through it, their ends hanging down one side to her shoulder.

"I admire your hair style very much, Lady Sophia," Jane said warmly and was rewarded by a squeak of delight.

"How wonderful of you. It is quite the thing! I have just had it cropped. My stuffy brother does not like it, but he cannot stick the hair back on." Her stuffy brother merely grinned and tweaked one of her short curls as Jane tried to come to terms with this offhand approach to authority.

"It's nothing to do with me, pest," Lord Wraybourne remarked, apparently unalarmed. "Doubtless you'll soon capture some poor unsuspecting male to run your rigs with."

He directed Jane's attention to his sister's partner. "This, Jane, is Lord Randal Ashby. He cannot resist the urge to flirt with a beautiful woman, so be on your guard. As you see, he has been unfairly equipped by nature."

Jane was cast into great confusion by both the casual compliment and the sight of the most handsome man imaginable. Only a poet could describe Lord Randal. Sadly, the few poets who had attempted the feat had given up under threats of violence from the young man, who found his spectacular good looks a trial. To say that he was tall, slim, and blond was insufficient. Every feature was perfect, and each enhanced the next. Even without striking a pose, his stance was elegant. Jane was to discover that it was, in fact, impossible for his body to arrange itself in unpleasing lines.

In response to his greeting, uttered, of course, in a mellow and musical voice, she could only murmur polite nothings for fear she would blurt out that he was the most beautiful thing she'd ever seen and she wished she could look at him forever.

Lord Wraybourne dragged her away, commenting good-humoredly, "I see I will have to keep you out of Lord Randal's orbit. Meanwhile, I would like you to meet the final member of our party, Mrs. Phoebe Danvers."

This lady possessed a chilly kind of beauty, being tall and slender with pale skin and even paler blond hair.

"The Sandiford heiress!" she said with a slight smile. "How pleased I am to meet you. We have all been so anxious to know what qualities could capture our elusive David."

Jane stiffened. Mrs. Danvers was surely implying what all the world knew, that Jane had been chosen for her ancestry and money. Her rare temper began to stir as she decided she did not like this woman at all.

"I was not aware Lord Wraybourne had been the victim of a hunt, Mrs. Danvers," said Jane with an air of innocence. "Who was in the pack?"

The lady seemed to catch her breath. Her eyes narrowed, but she said calmly, "Every unwed lady in town, Miss Sandiford, and quite a few of the married ones."

Jane would have dearly liked to ask whether the lady included herself in the latter group. An instinct as old as time told her it was so. Nonetheless, she was alarmed by her own impulsively sharp comment. This was no way to impress her betrothed with her *sangfroid*. Jane was further bewildered by the notion that Lord Wraybourne might have an interest in married women. She had assumed that, even if he was marrying her for her money, a husband chosen by her mother would be upright and faithful. Was that yet another instance of naivety? Had her mother been grossly deceived?

Such considerations were for later on, however. For the moment Jane must content herself with adding that she was pleased Lord Wraybourne would no longer have the uncomfortable role of quarry. Even so, Mrs. Danvers had the last word.

"I have always contended the hunt may not be so bad. The capture is the unpleasant part. I am speaking of the fox, of course."

Lord Wraybourne led Jane quickly away, his lips twitching with amusement. "Why on earth have you got your claws into Phoebe Danvers? She has a sharp tongue."

Jane looked up at him, intending to reply, but found herself suddenly arrested by his face so close to hers. When he became her husband he would expect more than a kiss on the cheek. Those finely shaped lips would be pressed to hers. Just as at Carne, she was unnervingly aware of her body's reaction to his proximity.

This would never do. She glanced aside to hide her consternation. The pause had been too long, however, and he asked, with concern, if she was unwell or overtired. At least, he had not guessed the direction of her thoughts. She reassured him hastily, hoping that, as usual, her creamy skin would hide rather than reveal her embarrassment.

Meanwhile, Lord Wraybourne misunderstood the cause of her discomfort and said with a smile, "You would be wise not to cross swords with such as Mrs. Danvers until you have developed your guard."

"You are probably correct," Jane replied, recovering her wits. "And thank you for raising my status from peevish kitten to swordswoman."

He raised her hand and touched it lightly with a kiss. Her second kiss ever, she thought, fighting to control her reaction. She would *not* become a tongue-tied ninny again.

"I see you perhaps as a little of each," he murmured.

"A kitten with a sword between its teeth?" she replied breathlessly.

"A tiger cub more like. You have tiger eyes."

Jane could feel her heart thudding in a most alarming way, which must surely be visible.

"I am not sure I would wish to be such a ferocious beast. Especially when I have just been accused of hunting you down."

His smile teased. She could hardly see his blue eyes beneath the heavy lids. "Ah, but you are only a baby tiger and what am I? I assure you I am no lamb."

Feeling quite dizzy from this exchange of *repartée* Jane agreed. "Of that I am quite sure, Lord Wraybourne!"

What was she to do? He seemed to think it his duty to

pay these intimate attentions to her. Perhaps it *was* proper behavior in this circumstance; but, in that case, what was the appropriate response? Her mother had given her no guidance in this.

Jane's very acute mind was also making other observations and deductions. The company at The Middlehouse was completely different from anything she had known in her life. The color and laughter, the looks which flitted between ladies and gentlemen—all exuded an aura which Jane could only think of as licentious. She knew she was naive and supposed these people could not possibly be as wicked as they appeared to her. Some of them were quite old, after all. Yet, such behavior would definitely not have been permitted at Carne. Still, her betrothed seemed at his ease and undisturbed.

He had obviously not chosen his bride from Carne out of insistence on elevated principles. If Mrs. Danvers was to be believed—and, despite the fact that she could not take to the lady, Jane had no reason to doubt her veracity—there were dozens of well-bred, young debutantes desperate for the chance to wear his ring. So it could only be her money which had attracted him. She knew she was one of the greatest heiresses in the land. If Lord Wraybourne *needed* her money then it explained his desire to please her and lessened any chance that he would lightly break the engagement.

For the first time in her life Jane felt herself to be in a position of power. She still had no desire to be a figure of fun but she also no longer felt excessive fear of failure. In fact, from this new position of confidence, she regarded

Lord Wraybourne's attention with some skepticism. He was charming and skilled in social pleasantries, but she would be foolish to take him too seriously as yet. She did not intend to become doting-fond of a man who wanted only her fortune. In time, she hoped, a true regard would grow between them. Until then, she must keep a tight rein on her feelings.

Her worst fear put to rest, Jane began gradually to find her feet in this strange new world. As the dinner party was informal, the conversation proved general, and Jane needed only commonplace pleasantries to supply her part. She concentrated on listening to the others. The talk was mainly of people and events of which she was in ignorance; but being attentive and clever, she learned a great deal.

Mrs. Danvers, she decided, *did* have a particular manner when addressing Lord Wraybourne and she was a special friend of Lady Harroving. Did the woman have tender feelings for the earl? Were they returned? Would they have married if the lady had been free? And where was Mr. Danvers?

Jane also noticed that an intimate manner seemed *de rigueur* between ladies and gentlemen. Lady Harroving had a similar demeanor when she spoke to Sir Marius and Lord Randal but not when she spoke to her husband. She seemed to despise her husband, who did appear to be unpleasant, eating greedily and noisily and paying no attention to his wife or his guests. Jane wondered if the marriage had been arranged. Perhaps, like herself, Lady Harroving had been given no choice. If so, honesty forced

Jane to admit, despite Lord Wraybourne's pragmatic approach to matrimony, her own parents had made a much better arrangement in her case.

Uncomfortable with the manners of the older ladies, Jane turned to Sophie in search of a model. She and Lord Randal chattered away like precocious children, seeming to be of an age even though he must be ten years the elder. Jane decided that, though she would give a great deal to be able to exchange witticisms with the younger couple's air and *joie de vivre,* their behavior was as yet beyond her range. What was she to do?

"A penny for your thoughts, Jane," said Lord Wraybourne, "or perhaps, more tempting, an apricot tart?" He held the plate towards her, and she took one.

"The food is delicious," she remarked. "And so many courses."

"Oh, this is informal. Maria would not consider this anything special. Was that what you were thinking? About food? You did take a tart so you owe me your thoughts."

With effort, she met his eyes directly. Lacking a model, she must be herself. "But they are not your tarts to bargain with, Lord Wraybourne."

His eyes glinted appreciation of her wit. "Then perhaps I should offer you a penny, or a bracelet of tigereye quartz. Would that tempt you to reveal yourself?" His voice was soft and light. Yet there was a particularity in his manner which enveloped her in a disquieting way.

She laughed to break the mood. "Perhaps. If I could remember what I was thinking. Thoughts are like dreams. Soon forgotten."

"Dreams can come true, Jane. Have you ever had a dream come true?"

She dropped her eyes. This party was a dream come true, but she must not tell him that. He would take the credit. She wished he would turn his attention elsewhere. She could not think when he had his eyes fixed upon her.

"I don't remember dreams," she said. "I just told you so."

"Merely because you don't talk about them soon enough," he responded in a much more casual tone, turning to cut some grapes from the bunch hanging on a grape stand nearby. "That is what we decided, was it not?" he asked, placing purple grapes on her plate. "In a few weeks I will be in a position to inquire about your dreams when you awake. Then we shall see."

His nonchalant tone was deceptive. Jane stared up at him with enormous eyes, forgetting her determination to be a sophisticate. She didn't know what to say. The vision of intimacy he had so casually laid before her was shocking and yet beguiling. She was flattered that he spoke easily to her of such things, as if she were a woman of the world, and yet she was terrified that he might expect some appropriate response of which she was quite in ignorance. Perhaps her pretense of worldly wisdom was *too* convincing.

She had not been aware that her mouth was hanging open until he put out a finger and gently closed it.

Lady Harroving's sharp voice broke in.

"David, I will not have you billing and cooing at my dinner table! Save that for when you are married. Besides, it is my job to keep your little bride safe till then, even from you."

Sir Arthur gave a snort of laughter at this, which was ignored by his wife as she led the ladies from the room. As soon as they were settled in the drawing room she came to sit by Jane.

"You must be careful, Jane, how you behave with the gentlemen. Even with your affianced husband you can be deemed fast, and that will do you no good in Society."

"Oh, Maria, don't be so stuffy," exclaimed Lady Sophie. "I don't know what has come over you since you became a chaperone. If David and Jane wish to play love games let them be. They've had little enough chance so far and will be married in a matter of weeks."

Lady Harroving turned sharply on her cousin. "You had better guard yourself too, Sophie. *Love games* indeed. Your fine status and your large dower won't help you if you are seen as flighty."

"Do you think not?" asked Sophie saucily. "Not even combined with my *beaux yeux* and my *belle taille*?"

"Heaven preserve me. I doubt I'll survive this Season!" declared the older lady and flounced off to sit near her friend Mrs. Danvers.

"There, that removed her," said Sophie with satisfaction as she sat down. "Why, Jane, you look quite upset."

Jane was struggling with the desire to weep, convinced that in her ignorance she had shamed herself in some way.

"Why did she say such things? I cannot help it if Lord Wraybourne behaves so."

"Oh, she's in one of her pets. Of course you can't. But if he bothers you, just tell him. He's the kindest soul really. He is probably not accustomed to someone so gently reared as yourself. I'm sure he would not go beyond the line."

Jane wished she could bring herself to tell Sophie that her beloved brother had been talking of *bed*. Then she would see what he was capable of. Instead, Jane turned the conversation to matters of fashion. Shortly afterwards, she used her journey as an excuse to retire before the gentlemen appeared and so avoided another encounter with her bothersome fiancé. He would not be banished from her thoughts, however, and she found it surprisingly difficult to sleep despite the fluffy cloud of the feather mattress after a lifetime of horsehair.

Lord Wraybourne obviously felt obliged to woo her at every opportunity. Perhaps it was *de rigueur* for a betrothed couple to behave so, but it made Jane most uncomfortable. She tried to tell herself she found his attentions embarrassing, but she knew that the real problem was their effectiveness. He would soon have her eating out of the palm of his hand. She could imagine how everyone would laugh to see the country miss making sheep's eyes at the man who was marrying her money. It was an exciting game all the same, for one so new to it. If only she could believe she had a chance to attach his true interest. . . .

With these thoughts jostling in her head, she fell asleep at last to dream of a man's voice calling, "Come to bed, Jane." But, try as she might, she was unable to decide whose voice it might be.

Later that night, after the rest of the party had retired, Lord Randal and Sir Marius lounged in chairs in the billiard room, taking time between games to share some of their host's excellent brandy and discuss their friend's forthcoming marriage.

"I agree," said Lord Randal, "that it's a strange start for David to pick a bride from nowhere when all the beauties of a decade have been his for the asking, but the girl will do when she has a little bronze and the family wealth is fabulous. I wish I'd known she was hanging there like a plum in the wilds of Gloucestershire, waiting to be picked along with her thousands of pounds."

"Is that why you were doing the pretty?" asked Sir Marius sardonically. "If you think anything will prevent the marriage, you're about in the head. David can't cry off and still call himself a gentleman, and the Sandifords would never permit anything so notorious."

Lord Randal's smile was angelic. "But if they felt the marriage was likely to be even more scandalous . . ."

Sir Marius used his toe to tip his friend's chair so that he was in danger of falling on his back.

"Hey, damn you!" Lord Randal exclaimed. "Stop it, Marius. I was only funning. It would be criminal to spill this cognac, especially on my beautiful coat."

"I'll spill your blood on your beautiful coat if you start trouble. Besides, even your ingenuity couldn't paint David as more scandalous than yourself. Lady Sandiford would have palpitations at seeing you in company with her little nun."

"Don't you think we should rescue David from such a connection? I hear she's a gorgon."

"I am sure the gold will be some compensation. Forget

it. Just because I count the girl a dowdy bore, don't think I'll support you in mischief."

"A dowdy bore?" Lord Randal said quizzically. "Hardly. She's quite beautiful, and the Sandiford fortune will ensure she's soon dressed to equal the finest. I doubt I would find her boring."

"A bore," asserted his friend.

"You think all women are bores. Ah, David," he exclaimed as the door opened. "Come and sample this cognac. Really fine. Do you not agree that Marius simply dislikes women and cannot be trusted in any statement he makes about them?"

Lord Wraybourne raised an eyebrow. "I don't think 'dislike' would describe his attitude to Julia Devine last time I saw them together."

Lord Randal shouted with laughter. "True indeed. Perhaps I should say he dislikes *ladies*."

"Not at all," responded Sir Marius equably. "I have an aunt of whom I am tolerably fond, and I have enjoyed the company of a number of other *married* ladies. Most *unmarried* ladies, however, desire only to rectify that state."

"Ah," said Lord Wraybourne as he inhaled the aroma of the brandy. "Now I see the topic. You are talking of Jane Sandiford." His tone was perfectly amiable, but there was something in his lazy eyes which warned them not to overstep the bounds.

"You know my views," said Sir Marius, undeterred. "Marriage is for fools. You have two brothers. Let them be the victims."

"Frederick could be carried away at any moment by

a Frenchman's bullet, and Mortimer is currently adhering to an extreme form of High Anglicanism which urges celibacy."

"Good God!"

"And actually," continued his lordship, "I have no particular objection to the married state."

"Tell me," said Lord Randal eagerly. "How did you find her, and did you encounter any other similar specimens in your search?"

Lord Wraybourne delayed his reply to savour a mouthful of the cognac. "Her parents found me, or rather her mother did," he said at last. "Sir Jeffrey is a cipher. She sent the word out among her friends and asked for suggestions of eligible men. Goodness knows what qualities she specified, but my godmother, Lady Peebles, was most insistent that I visit and look the girl over."

He shrugged. "I had decided to choose a bride rather than wait for Cupid's arrow which seems slow to find a target in my breast so I took the bait. I didn't seriously think I would offer for her," he reminisced. "I think she brought out the gallantry in me, like a princess in a tower awaiting a rescuer."

Sir Marius stared gloomily into his glass, but Lord Randal responded with laughter, "Indeed. And the fact that she's rich and beautiful had nothing to do with it?"

"Princesses are always rich and beautiful," replied Lord Wraybourne dryly.

"I suspect she's rather clever too. I suppose that didn't weigh with you either?"

"A bonus, I admit. She has a fine wit, and as she begins

to be more comfortable with strangers I anticipate much pleasure in her company."

Lord Randal quirked an eyebrow at this and looked to make a comment but thought better of it. Instead he said, "But her clothes! Her mother dresses her like an impoverished puritan, David. It's a sad waste. You should do something about it."

"I hardly think my interference would be welcome at this point," remarked Lord Wraybourne. "Time enough to arrange her clothing when we're wed."

"Or disarrange it," chortled Lord Randal irrepressibly, drawing groans from both his friends. "At any rate try to persuade her not to cut her hair. You saw how impressed she was by Sophie's crop."

"Yes," said Lord Wraybourne, much struck. "And hair takes so long to grow."

Lord Randal sighed, a beatific smile on his beautiful face. "Imagine her naked with that mass of ebony hair swirling around her."

"I would really rather you didn't," said Lord Wraybourne gently.

"What? Oh . . . I suppose not. But it will be deuced hard." He smiled sensuously. "To a connoisseur, such thoughts are inescapable."

"You may enjoy your *thoughts* all you wish," was the amiable response. "In fact, to show how much I trust you, I will ask you to spend a little time introducing my bride to the art of flirtation. I must be losing my touch. She obviously regards me with trepidation. I find this marriage business not as simple as I expected." He ignored a snort from Sir

Marius. "She liked the look of you though, Randal, so do the pretty, and then maybe she won't swoon every time I try to kiss her hand."

Lord Randal agreed enthusiastically to this proposal, but Lord Wraybourne was to endure a fair amount of good-natured teasing before the gentlemen retired that night.

4

J ANE SUFFERED A moment of confusion at waking the
next morning in a strange bed. This was followed by a
surge of excitement, however. With the sunshine of a new
day and adventure before her, her fears faded. The idea
of seeing Lord Wraybourne again—exchanging teasing
words, feeling his lips upon her fingers—was a large part
of that excitement, with its strange mingling of wariness
and anticipation.

She tugged on the bellpull, impatient to begin the day.
Prudence, full of news from the servants' hall, arrived with
her washing water. Though Jane knew her mother would
not approve of encouraging servants to gossip, she did not
stop the prattle. After all, this was as much an adventure
for Prudence as it was for herself.

"... ten garden staff and that doesn't include those at

the Home Farm, Miss Jane. There's a sewing woman comes in but there won't be time for her to do much for you so I trimmed your fawn cambric last night."

She produced the gown, which Jane admired with genuine pleasure.

"Prudence, you are a marvel!"

The plain high-necked gown was greatly improved by rows of ruched lace around the collar and hem. Prudence had also added false buttons and braid to give the bodice the look of a jacket.

"I had help from some of the other maids, Miss. They were quite challenged, and I gather Lord Wraybourne is a great favorite here so they were very pleased to help you."

"Prudence, I am truly grateful. When we are in Town and I have my new clothes, you shall have all these for yourself and so benefit from your work."

The maid turned bright pink with excitement. "Lordy, Miss. I'll be as fine as you like! Thank you."

"Thank *you*, Prudence." Jane added with a grin, "After all, I am only ensuring that you will continue your wonderful work. We are here for two more days and so I will require a number of other gowns."

Jane felt pleasantly comfortable with her appearance as she entered the light and sunny breakfast room. She couldn't help being disappointed to find only Mrs. Danvers and Lady Sophie at the table. The young men had apparently eaten earlier and gone off on some sporting enterprise. The Harrovings and her father had chosen to break their fast in their chambers.

"Good morning, Jane," declared Lady Sophie gaily as

Jane allowed the maid behind the chafing dishes to give her eggs and ham. "I do hope I am permitted to call you Jane for I consider us sisters, and I must be Sophie to you. It is a glorious day. I am pondering the relative charms of fishing, archery, and sketching. What activity would please you best?"

"I have never attempted fishing or archery," said Jane as she seated herself, "so I think I must content myself with my easel."

"But that will mean sitting still for so long, something I am quite unable to do! Besides, I am sure David would be delighted to instruct you in the art of angling and even more charmed to teach you how to draw a bow." This was said with a wicked glance at Phoebe Danvers, who was apparently enthralled by the kidneys on her plate.

"How do you intend to pass your day, Mrs. Danvers?" the girl pursued, forcing the older woman to pay her some attention.

"I have not considered, Lady Sophie. I will wait, I think, until Maria rises and consult with her. I may attempt a watercolor sketch of the Chinese bridge."

"What is a Chinese bridge?" asked Jane.

Sophie bounced. "Of course! You haven't seen the grounds. The first thing we must do is to explore. The landscaping here is famous. There is a Chinese garden with a pagoda and an Italian garden with statues which will make you stare."

She continued to chatter as Jane finished her breakfast, then dragged her away, pulling a naughty face at Phoebe Danvers' back as they left.

"I cannot abide that woman," she declared as soon as the door was closed. "She has such a high opinion of herself and is forever sneering at people. I thought at one time that David might marry her and was quite cast down."

"She is a widow, then. She cannot be very old."

Jane felt a momentary alarm that Mrs. Danvers was free, but that was swiftly followed by satisfaction. The older lady had been available for marriage had Lord Wraybourne wished it. Then Jane realized that the widow was doubtless not rich enough, and despondency settled upon her once more. She forced herself to pay attention to her companion.

"Oh yes," Lady Sophie was saying. "Quite thirty, I assure you. She has been a widow for three or four years. Her husband was ancient, I believe, but he left her money so perhaps it was worth it."

How much money, Jane wanted to ask.

"But let us not talk of her," Sophie went on. "Shall we send for shawls? There is a breeze."

Jane put aside questions about the widow to consider a new problem. She was not quite sure what was expected of her during this visit. She knew she must first see her father off on his return journey but beyond that she had no guide. Lady Sophie seemed to enjoy more license than Jane had ever imagined possible, and she did not yet have the nerve to emulate her.

Who was she to ask for advice? Lady Harroving? She did not feel at ease with her. Lord Wraybourne? She had no wish to appear the fool before him. Jane explained a little of her quandary.

"Of course you must attend your father," agreed Sophie and dispatched the footman to find out Sir Jeffrey's plans. "Beyond that you must please yourself. Maria will expect us to find our own entertainment and here in the country there are few rules. It is what makes ruralizing supportable."

The footman returned to say that Sir Jeffrey's carriage was called for and he expected to leave very soon. Jane went to the coach entrance to bid him farewell and found her father in a bleak mood. Travelling did not agree with him.

"This is a frivolous household," he said sternly. "The indulgence, the waste! Take care not to be corrupted by this style of life, Jane." He fixed stern eyes on her gown. "Where had you that gown, Jane?"

She caught her breath in horror. She suddenly realized there was a very real danger of being pushed in the coach and dragged back to Carne.

"It is just an old one, Father," she said hurriedly. "My maid put a little braid on it so I wouldn't look out of the ordinary. You wouldn't wish me to look *peculiar* would you, Father?"

He shook his head, obviously unsure of what to do. "It is all most strange," he sighed at last. "This whole business is strange. A simple, upright man of our parts would have done as well, I think."

He gave her a brief kiss and entered his coach, still frowning but happy at least to be headed back to his orderly and predictable life.

It was unfortunate that all Jane could wear for her walk with Sophie was a plain snuff-brown spencer and matching close-bonnet with no trimmings. However, given the recent close escape, Jane was grateful to be still present in The Middlehouse at all. Her father's words had taken effect, nonetheless, and she determined not to give herself totally to vanity. This resolve soon weakened at the sight of Sophie by the sundial, pacing up and down, causing the golden tassels visible at the ankles of her boots to swirl. She had draped an enormous paisley shawl about her shoulders and wore a dashing high-poke bonnet upon her head.

"What an age you have been, Jane! I am sure it is very rude of me," she continued, "but I must say that your clothes are the most dismal I have ever seen."

Jane was unoffended. "Are they not. But I have a whole new wardrobe waiting for me in London."

"Chosen by whom?" asked Sophie dubiously, creating horrible visions in Jane's head. She had been anticipating clothes like Sophie's but that would not be so. What *had* her mother ordered for her?

"Don't worry about it," said Sophie sympathetically. "Maria and I will fix it, even if we have to order a whole new wardrobe. Your parents must have given Maria *carte blanche*."

"We couldn't do that," Jane protested.

"Of course we can. Maria will never allow you to come out under her aegis looking a dowd." She linked arms with Jane and led her down to the French knot garden below.

As they passed through the formal gardens and the wilderness Jane learned a great deal about the life of a rich aristocrat at The Bath School for Young Ladies and was amazed. Sophie, in turn, was horrified to learn something of the life of a rich aristocrat who had been educated in a rigidly formal country house.

"It will all be different now," she assured Jane. "To be *out*! It will be delightful not to have people looking askance at me if I dance or converse with a gentleman. And, of course, the gentlemen will be forced to take me seriously at last. There is nothing worse than to be a schoolgirl."

Jane could not quite agree with that but she did share her new friend's enthusiasm. "It will be pleasant to dance at all, and I am already finding the company of gentlemen agreeable."

"Well, it is quite different for you, of course. Because you are engaged to David you can mix with men with a great deal more freedom than a poor, unspoken-for female such as I." Sophie's manner made it clear she did not take her restrictions very seriously.

"So I would be in no danger of encouraging the interest of a young man, even if I were to spend time with him?" Jane asked.

This was a question which had concerned her. She had no desire to hang on Lord Wraybourne's sleeve, and yet she feared to be seen as a flirt if she spent time in the company of other gentlemen.

"No *honorable* man. And the other sort would be wary of meddling with Lord Wraybourne's betrothed, I assure you. David is known to be a dangerous man."

"He is?" Jane queried in amazement.

"He has fought dozens of duels," Sophie said with airy

exaggeration. "Of course he always fights with swords and causes only minor wounds so there is never any fuss."

"Good gracious," said Jane, wondering how this information had escaped her mother, who deplored the practice of duelling.

"Oh yes," said Sophie happily. "You will find him well able to take care of his own, but you will be quite safe to indulge in discreet flirtation. Almost as if you were already married. I cannot wait to be married myself."

Jane was silent, considering this new information, seeing it merely as a new hazard. She would die of shame to be the cause of a duel. But for some reason the vision of Lord Wraybourne, sword in hand, defending her honor, was strangely exciting.

Sophie was speaking again. "If I were not his sister, I would marry David myself, Jane. He is the dearest man, and you are the most fortunate of women."

"We are not very well acquainted," Jane said, feeling obliged to make some cavil.

"I always did think that it was a mistake for you to marry with so little knowledge of each other, but now all is right. You will soon learn how to please him."

This echoed too closely Jane's determination to learn to be the woman Lord Wraybourne would most admire, and so she countered with, "And he learn to please me, I suppose."

Sophie's laugh rang out. "Heavens, are you a rare species?" she asked. "I haven't known a woman not pleased by David in his life."

Jane was devastated. Not only was she affected by the

man, she was one of hundreds. Perhaps he was not even, as she flattered herself, making a special effort to fix her interest, but acting merely out of habit.

"If it weren't for his morals," Sophie continued, blithely ignorant of the effect of her words, "he would be the worst rake there ever was, and even so . . ."

At that she did become conscious of what she was saying and of the uncomfortable expression on Jane's face.

"Oh look," said Sophie in a hasty change of subject. "There is Mrs. Danvers' Chinese bridge."

Their admiration of this feature, and Jane's consideration of the horrifying fact that she was engaged to marry a *rake*, was interrupted by the arrival of the young gentlemen of the party. Lord Randal let out a hunting cry and raced up the hill.

"Run you down!" he declared. "Devilish unfair of you to disappear. What are we poor souls to do when the beauties go to ground?"

"But Randal," said Sophie sweetly, "we were told you had gone off to kill something."

"There were supposed to be hawks in the Oakhill Coppice but we couldn't find a sight of them."

"So you returned to pursue other prey?"

"Much more rewarding," he replied with a grin. "To catch two beautiful birds without firing a shot."

Lord Wraybourne, ascending at a more leisurely pace, smiled upon Jane in a familiar way that made her heart catch despite what she now knew him to be.

"You must excuse Lord Randal. He is over-familiar, but it's permitted because he's so very decorative."

Lord Randal howled his protest at this description. "I won't have it, David. Pistols at dawn!"

"Nonsense. You are far too good a shot. But I'll give you foils this evening before dinner. Marius can judge."

"Done. It must be an age since I've tried my skill against you. I've been learning a few tricks."

"You'll need 'em," retorted Lord Wraybourne and ignored his friend's further attempts to argue.

He offered an arm to Jane, and the stroll continued. Sophie walked behind, in the happy position of having a gentleman on each arm.

"And what is your opinion of The Middlehouse grounds, Jane?" his lordship asked.

Jane was feeling a bit confused—by Sophie's revelations, by his presence, and by the thought that this very evening two young men were going to fight with swords and nobody appeared concerned.

"Th-they are very . . . elegant," she stammered.

"A word chosen with care," he said with a smile. "Do I gather you do not favor this type of landscape?"

She glanced up at him and gathered her wits. She had no desire to offend. "Are the grounds of Stenby in this style?"

"Very diplomatic," he approved with a grin, "but do not choose your words to please me. As it happens, the park at Stenby has not been 'improved' since Tudor times. The few prospects there are have been provided by nature. My father, however, established a herd of deer which you may like."

"Oh *yes*," she responded, meeting his amused blue eyes

only for a moment before looking away in more confusion. One of hundreds, she reminded herself, and concentrated on a pagoda which had appeared from behind some trees. "A pagoda is some kind of temple, is it not? I wonder why it is built in such an extraordinary style."

"I do not know, but I do know that they are not, strictly speaking, temples. They are more a monument than a place of worship. There is a fine one at Kew Gardens in London if you wish to continue your study."

"I'm sorry," Jane said, embarrassed. "I am forever asking why and how."

"I think that is excellent," he said amiably. "I suffer from a greedy and insatiable curiosity myself. At the moment, for example, I am curious about lavender water. Can you tell me anything of that?"

"Lavender water? Do you wish to make some, My Lord?"

"I do not think so, though I may wish to know how it is made. I would like to know how many people use it. How many men and how many women? Where it is used, on the linen or on the person? Whether people bathe in it. Anything, in fact, about lavender water."

Jane eyed him consideringly. "My mother thinks it effective against headaches. But I believe you are funning, Sir, to excuse me for my excessive curiosity."

"Not at all," he protested. "To prove it I will report back to you with the results of my researches. Now, we are nearly back at the house, you see. All that is left to view is the Italian garden."

Jane was amazed to turn a corner in the path and confront a marble faun. She knew what it was, for she had

received a smattering of classical knowledge in her education; but the illustration in her book had not been quite
like this. It was unashamedly and totally naked with a most
particular look in its eyes.

"My goodness," she said. Then remembering that she
was *not* a country bumpkin, she rallied. "Are the statues
here originals, My Lord?"

"Copies of originals. Do you like them?"

He was aware that he was teasing, and yet he couldn't
help himself. Jane looked so delicious in her confusion
and he enjoyed seeing the way she responded so gallantly
to challenges. In lieu of his primary desire, which was to
make love to her, he found this game amusing.

"I suppose they are educational," she said with a tolerable degree of composure.

She carefully studied each group, and he was proud
to see that no blush betrayed embarrassment. He was still
ignorant of the masking effect of her creamy skin. Jane, by
contrast, felt as if her face was burning as she maintained
her insouciance.

"If clothed," she remarked of one goddess, "that woman
would appear fat."

"Indeed," he responded. "Imagine her in very high-
waisted silk. She would rival the Princess of Wales."

Jane was betrayed into a giggle. "Is she truly so large?
But it only goes to show that in former times the princess
would have been elevated to goddess."

"In fact, she would have fitted in excellently on Mount
Olympus. The ancient gods had just such an earthy lust for
life as Caroline shows."

The more erotic groupings received no comment from her, only a pensive scrutiny. Lord Wraybourne thought she showed admirable composure. Actually, Jane was bewildered and could not imagine what the statues were supposed to be doing. Whatever it was, it looked most uncomfortable. Meanwhile, an urchin playing with a fish met with her condemnation.

"I cannot like that at all. He is not catching the fish to eat but to torment it. The head gardener's boy at the Abbey is just such a one."

He wondered what she would say of the fountain made by two little boys urinating.

After a moment's consideration, she merely remarked, "I suppose we should be grateful it is not a drinking fountain." Jane was, after all, country bred and had not been totally shielded from all the realities of life.

Lord Wraybourne laughed softly, well pleased with his betrothed. He had not regretted his impulsive offer for Jane. He was sure she was adequate to be his bride, but he had wondered occasionally, in the weeks between the betrothal and this visit, whether he might ultimately find her boring. Now, he did not think that likely. For her part, Jane was delighted to find she could speak her mind without fear of censure for the first time in her life.

"I'm grateful my father did not see this garden before he left," she said. "He would doubtless have wanted to take me straight back to Carne."

Lord Wraybourne looked down at her. "It is in my power to prevent that, I believe. You needn't concern yourself over such matters again, Jane."

"But they are my parents," she protested.

"And must be obeyed? But you will shortly promise to obey me. I think I will claim precedence, and I command you to enjoy yourself."

"In any way I please?" she asked, astonished.

"Yes."

Jane looked away. He became more strange and unpredictable with each passing moment. Was this perhaps a test of her high principles?

"That is rather foolhardy, My Lord," she said. "Who knows what I might be about."

"Ah, but I didn't say the command was infinite. If you go too far, I will stop you."

Jane had been obedient all her life but the idea that she would be completely subject to this man's will roused a flash of rebellion. She faced him. "Will you, indeed!"

He smiled. He had wondered just how docile she really was. He was pleased to find the answer to be—not very.

"Of course. Do you doubt it?"

"Until we are married," Jane said boldly, "I will do as I please, under the guidance of Lady Harroving, of course."

She watched him warily. Her first protest had been instinctive. Now she was having to struggle to maintain a posture which went so strongly against her training.

He did not seem concerned. "Very well. But be guided by Sophie also. Of the two of them she probably has more sense of decorum. Randal and Marius will stand as your friends too. Randal is a rattle and not always to be depended on, but Marius is a rock. If you need help when I am not by, apply to him."

Jane was amazed that her rebellion had been taken so calmly, and, on consideration, this worried her more than it reassured. If what she considered outrageous was perceived as normal, she obviously had *no* idea of how to go on. His last comment also concerned her. Sir Marius frightened her even more than her betrothed did.

"I think, My Lord, that merely encourages me to stay by your side whenever possible."

"Excellent," he said in a teasing tone as he placed his arm around her waist and drew her close.

She tensed by reflex but realized, at the same instant, that she liked it. Jane had not been held like this since she was a child, and the comfort she felt was amazing. To be able to go to another person and be held close whenever she felt the need would be a wonder almost beyond imagining. She relaxed tentatively against him, then drew back slightly. This was obviously another of his skillful, rakish tricks, and he was doubtless amused to see her so easily beguiled. Why did she have to be so vulnerable to this man?

She looked up and found him staring at her with a slight smile. For some reason, she knew he was thinking of kissing her properly and, unconsciously, she licked her lips. His smile broadened, and at the sight of his amusement she pulled away from him farther still. Dropping his heavy lids, he released her. The kiss she had expected was planted gently on her gloved hand.

Jane suppressed a twinge of disappointment and congratulated herself on once again avoiding too early a commitment.

5

A HEARTY NUNCHEON was served at The Middlehouse, as dinner would be fashionably late. The whole party was gathered for the meal, and there was a lively discussion of the activities for the afternoon. Lord Harroving wanted all the men to go with him in search of pike in the river and was disgruntled at the lack of interest. The other gentlemen seemed much more interested in staying with the ladies, so eventually he took himself off to his favourite pastime alone. His wife and Mrs. Danvers decided to attempt some watercolours. The rest of the party settled on archery and went to find the equipment.

Amid much laughter, the butts and bows were discovered in a shed near the stables, and a number of servants were sent to set them up. Sophie, Lord Randal, and Sir Marius hurried after, but Jane found herself behind with Lord Wraybourne, who seemed disinclined to hurry.

For a moment she was panicked at being alone with a man for the first time in her life, if one did not count the brief interlude in which he made his offer, but his easy manner and the beautiful day composed her. Even with her arm in his, feeling the firmness of muscle beneath cloth, she experienced no alarm in his company. In fact, she was very much at ease, as if he were an old friend. The air had a special clarity, and the sweet, earthy smells of spring were like a perfume.

"I am reminded of when I mounted my first pony," she said dreamily, half to herself.

"Was that a special day?"

"Oh yes," she replied with a shining smile. "She was just a tubby little thing called Jenny, but she was mine. I was six, I think."

"And now you have Serenade," he said, referring to her current mount.

"Yes," she replied, some of the glow leaving her face. "She's a slug. Mama does not think fast horses suitable for young ladies."

She thought he might say something, but he did not so they walked on in silence.

"Are the archery butts in this direction?" she asked after a moment. "I would think we are going down to the lake."

"Excellent geography," he admitted. "The butts are close to the house near the tennis court. I thought it would be pleasant to walk for a little. Do you realize we have never really been alone?"

"I do not think it is proper," she said, wondering if she had been wise to relax with him.

"But we are betrothed," he responded, steering her to a convenient bench. "Being alone in such safe circumstances as these is one of the privileges of our situation, Jane. Another is that I am permitted to give you handsome presents. What shall the first one be?"

Oh no, My Lord, thought Jane. Having failed with your blandishments, do not think you can buy my affections.

"I do not need anything, thank you, Lord Wraybourne. I think we should join the others, or they will look for us." Her attempt to rise was thwarted by the fact that he had a gentle but firm hold on her hand.

"Nonsense. Sophie is an excellent archer and will be delighted to steal the attention all afternoon, if needs be. I wish you were a little more comfortable in my presence," he added plaintively.

She met his eyes and was touched, despite herself, by the honest note in his voice. Perhaps he was only behaving as he thought proper. Perhaps his attentions were honest.

"So do I," she admitted, feeling some explanation was called for. "I am unaccustomed to the company of men, especially ones I am to marry. All this is so different for me. I feel . . . unsure. I am afraid of behaving incorrectly."

He pressed her fingers reassuringly. "Your behavior is impeccable, Jane. As for men, you have nothing to fear. Being betrothed gives you a certain immunity."

"Except from you," she said abruptly.

"But what can you possibly imagine I would do?" he asked in surprise and added, "Be assured that I will never do anything to hurt you. If I distress you in any way, you have merely to say."

She turned away from his distracting blue eyes. Was this a declaration of warmer feelings or a practical admission that he could not afford to offend her? Whichever, he was making it impossible for her to be rational. She wished she could have a little time to sort out her confusion in peace.

"What if I were to request that you stay away from me?" she asked, turning to catch his expression. He looked merely thoughtful.

"Stenby Castle is a huge barracks of a place," he remarked. "I suppose it would be possible for us both to live there without meeting. In fact, I have two great-aunts in the north wing at the moment and haven't seen them in an age. But the town house is a trifle small for separate establishments."

Her eyes flashed with annoyance. "You are being absurd to tease me, Sir!"

Suddenly serious, he managed to possess her other hand and forced her to face him directly. "I am trying to understand you, Jane. Do you wish to draw back from our betrothal?"

"No!" she exclaimed.

That was not what she intended at all. Tears formed in her eyes, and he quickly released her and proffered a linen handkerchief.

"I did not mean to disturb you so, Jane," he said quietly. "When you are recovered we will go on our way without me teasing you any more."

"You disturb me all the time," she said with a sniff. "If you did not do so, we would get along a great deal better."

If she had looked she would have seen a triumphant gleam in his eye, but his tone was serious. "I will have to study the things I do that disturb you so." He retrieved his handkerchief and drew her to her feet. "Now when I hold your hand like this. Does that disturb you?"

"No-o," she said hesitantly and distrustfully.

"But if I were to kiss it . . . ," he said with a wicked smile, suiting action to words.

"Yes!" she declared, attempting to snatch her hand away.

He placed it instead in the crook of his arm. "Surely you do not find this excessively disturbing?" he inquired with concern.

"No," she said, unwillingly beginning to enjoy the game he was playing. She glanced up at him in a way which was instinctively flirtatious.

His eyes gleamed with appreciation, and he placed a chaste kiss upon her cheek. "Am I permitted that?" he asked.

She turned her head to answer and found his lips ready to claim hers. It was the gentlest of kisses, although he lingered a little. She pulled away as an aching shudder stirred within her.

"Oh no, please!" she gasped.

"Pity," he said amiably as they resumed their stroll. "I found it very pleasant. However, I promise not to disturb you again—at least not for a while. Perhaps you will become accustomed to me. But remember," he added seriously, "if I should do anything else which—er—disturbs you, please tell me immediately. I will keep a mental list."

She looked up at him suspiciously and was sure she could see a twinkle in his eyes, but he met her gaze so frankly that she was thwarted. She should have won a victory and persuaded him to cease his blandishments for the time being. Instead, she felt as if he had marked her and the disturbance of which she had complained would be with her always.

At least, he kept to the spirit of their agreement when they reached the archery butts by happily handing her tuition in the sport over to Lord Randal and challenging his sister to a duel. Both the Kyles were excellent archers, and at short range Lord Wraybourne's extra strength was little advantage. Sophie was jubilant when she won.

"How do you go on, Jane?" she asked, coming over to them. "David should be teaching you. He is a much better archer than Randal." Her teasing eyes suggested other reasons for a change in tutor.

Lord Randal, his arms around Jane as he corrected the angle of her bow, protested at any thought of depriving him of his task. Jane refused to make any comment. She was surprised to find that Lord Randal's body close to hers had none of the power to disturb her that she complained of in her fiancé. It must be her awareness of their special relationship which made her so very sensitive to Lord Wraybourne's every touch. How then was she to resist his influence?

Glancing at Lord Wraybourne, she saw one elegant eyebrow raised in teasing query and blushed as she realized he was living up to their agreement. She had to admit that the mere thought of standing with his body pressed close to hers caused an uncomfortable warmth. She released the arrow prematurely, and it sailed over the target to land in the earth.

"I'm sorry, Lord Randal," she said firmly. "I am clumsy at this sport. Please, let us watch the contests."

She was happy to be a spectator as the others played one against the other, and, by carefully avoiding looking at the earl, she found his presence no bother at all. She congratulated herself that he had taken her words to heart and given her the interlude she needed to come to terms with her new life and their relationship.

During the rest of her stay at The Middlehouse, however, Jane became less and less comfortable with Lord Wraybourne's lack of attendance. It was pleasant, of course, to talk with Lord Randal and to partner him as she learned simple card games or to follow his steps as he taught her the cotillion and the intricate quadrille. It was strange to dance the *risqué* waltz with him, however. She thought her betrothed might object to her being whirled about so by another man, but Lord Wraybourne merely glanced up benignly and returned to his conversation with the beautiful Mrs. Danvers. Jane couldn't seem to help how often her eyes were on them as they smiled and talked. Desperately, she would drag her gaze away only to have it drawn back irresistibly a moment later.

And this was not the only time he commanded her thoughts. Even when he was absent, she found the memory of the fencing match etched in her mind. The two men had fought in the armament room, well lit by dozens of candles. The rest of the party sat to one side except for Sir Marius, who stood opposite to referee.

Jane was relieved to discover that the fencers used foils with buttons on the ends for safety and thus was able to relax and enjoy the event, but she was disconcerted when both men stripped down to shirts and breeches and removed their boots. They also removed their cravats and high starched collars, leaving their shirts open at the neck. Jane was seeing more man than she had ever done in her life. As swords had hissed and stockinged feet padded back, then forwards, she found her eyes drawn to the column of Lord Wraybourne's throat and the muscles which stretched and tightened there and gradually became glossed with sweat.

She knew nothing of the finer points of the sport. The applause of the others for a skillful pass was meaningless, but she saw beauty and grace in the lithely stretching and twisting bodies. As the bout progressed, the men's fine lawn shirts began to cling to their bodies, outlining them for her admiration. The memory returned to disturb her time and time again, and she was infuriated that, try as she would, she could not recall Lord Randal's body as vividly as she could that of her betrothed.

On the final evening of her stay, Jane's lessons were the excuse for a small dancing session in the music room. The Harrovings' governess was brought down from the west wing to play the piano, and even Sir Arthur consented to stand up in the fourth couple necessary for most of the dances. As the partners rotated, Jane found Sir Arthur was a clumsy dancer and Sir Marius, too tall to be the most graceful, but she could not decide whether *that* title should go to Lord Randal or Lord Wraybourne. The former had the edge in beauty of movement, but the latter was more elegant.

She stood with Lord Wraybourne ready for the first cotillion. "Now I will find out whether my dancing is really adequate or my teacher has just been kind," she said to him with a nervous smile.

"Good heavens, how am I to take that? Do I appear to be a critical sort?"

Jane stared at him, distressed. "Oh, Lord Wraybourne, I never meant . . ."

"And I am a swine to tease you when you are on edge. Forgive me, and do not worry. I have been watching your lessons, and you are a natural dancer."

Jane's faint color was due to gratification and not embarrassment. "I *do* love dancing," she confessed. "I hope I am invited to dance every dance all through the Season."

He laughed. "You will be worn to a frazzle, my dear. But whenever I am present you will not lack a partner."

"Surely, that would be very unfashionable?"

He raised his brows. "But I, and therefore you, are fashionsetters, Jane. We will start a new style for marital fondness."

It was such an attractive notion that Jane felt obliged to protest. "We are not, however, married yet, Lord Wraybourne."

"I am very aware of that, Jane," he said as the music started and they began the steps.

Jane was glad the conversation had gone no further. During the lively dances there was no opportunity for more than the lightest conversation. Then, Lord Wraybourne claimed her for the waltz for the first time. Even though they danced at arm's length as was proper, Jane felt ill at ease and kept her eyes down in the pretense that she was watching her steps.

"You'll find it easier if you look up, you know," he said after a while. "You'll just become light-headed doing that."

In fact she was feeling a little dizzy. "I am anxious not to make a mistake."

He smiled. "Then look up at me and tell me what a dreadful crush this ball is and how absolutely exhausted you are from all the invitations you simply *have* to accept."

"Oh yes," she agreed. "I must practice my social conversation." And with a slight and artificial smile she said, "It would be *so* much more enjoyable to spend a quiet evening at home for once, would it not, My Lord?"

"Absolutely," he agreed. "But then we poor gentlemen would miss the company of beautiful and charming women such as you. . . . Now Jane, you mustn't gape at a compliment or they'll put you down as the merest country bumpkin."

"But I am not *accustomed* to compliments."

"Tush. Randal must be losing his touch! I shall have to work at it. You will soon come to accept them as your due, and quite unworthy of the slightest consternation."

"Please, I wish you would not," said Jane, lowering her head once again.

"But the top of your head is quite delightful. If you do not wish me to rhapsodize it, then you should not present it to view."

Jane raised her head hastily.

"And, of course, your eyes are superb."

Jane promptly closed them.

"With long, long lashes like thick, dark silk against ivory velvet skin."

Jane's eyes flew open once more, and she stared up at him, completely forgetting even to think about her steps. "Lord Wraybourne, *please.*"

"More?" he queried wickedly. "What a shame your dress is so concealing. I am sure your shoulders are smooth and milky white. Of course, there is your harmonious speaking voice, the elegant column of your neck, and the supple curve of your waist beneath my hand."

Overcome, Jane astonished both herself and him by hiding her burning face in the shoulder of his jacket. Though the music went on for a while, all movement and conversation stopped. Lord Wraybourne was himself frozen, for the moment, with surprise at finding Jane in his arms. Nonetheless, he recovered quickly.

"I think Jane is overheated. We will walk in the gallery for a little while."

He then took her swiftly from the room, discouraging any attempt to accompany them and ignoring the knowing laughter behind.

"Lord Wraybourne," Jane protested, trying to escape from his side. "What will people think?"

"That you are hot and wish to cool down a little. Truly, it was too warm in there. There is no need of a fire in the grate on such a mild night."

With her new sophistication, Jane retorted, "They will think you are out here making love to me."

He smiled. "I will if you want me to."

"Of course I don't!"

She was quite unaware of how magnificent she looked, with her cheeks tinted rose and her eyes flashing.

"Why not?" he said lightly but with a glow in his eyes. "We have already seen how disastrous it is to be unprepared for compliments. Imagine if that had happened at a grand ball or Almack's." Jane shuddered. Still, she knew that the problem was not the flattery, but the flatterer.

"Now what," he said softly, "if you are the recipient of a little lovemaking and cause a scandal by screaming or fainting?"

"But that would never happen," Jane declared triumphantly. "Sophie tells me all the men will be terrified to tamper with Lord Wraybourne's betrothed."

He laughed. "Sisterly exaggeration, I assure you. I'm willing to lay odds some poor rash fellow will be carried beyond discretion by *you*, Tiger Eyes."

Jane could feel the pounding of her heart and no longer had any idea of how to handle the situation.

He placed a gentle finger beneath her chin. "What if you found yourself in a secluded corner during a ball," he said softly, "and a gentleman said you have the softest and sweetest lips in the world."

"I would leave," she answered breathlessly and, after a delay which made him smile, turned to do so, but he caught her hand and swung her back, hard against him.

Held tight against his body, she stared up at him, her eyes enormous and lips softly parted.

"At this point," he went on gently, "you really should scream. But then, everyone would come running, and I would have to call the rascal out. The scandal would be dreadful. Would it not be better to endure one little kiss?"

Jane scrambled for control of her wits. "I fear you are a practiced seducer, Lord Wraybourne," she whispered, with a gallant attempt at lightness.

"Oh, I haven't even *tried* to seduce you yet, Tiger Eyes."

His head began to lower, but at that moment they heard the music room door open. He unhurriedly released her and moved away.

"You see," he said smoothly, "this would probably happen at a ball as well. Someone always interrupts. Ah, Maria, you've recalled your chaperone duties? How kind of you. I think Jane is quite recovered."

Jane was not at all sure that described her condition. She had a powerful wish Lady Harroving had delayed just a few moments longer in finding them.

Later that night, Lady Harroving and Mrs. Danvers were lounging in comfortable undress in the former's *boudoir*, sipping at chocolate.

"Well, she's a dull miss," Lady Harroving remarked with a sly smile. "David is already tiring of her. He's hardly spent a moment with her, and I found them standing out in the gallery, feet apart, looking very uncomfortable.

"When I first heard I was supposed to bring the chit out," she continued, "I didn't see the advantages. But it should be easy to allow her to commit any number of *faux pas,* whilst appearing, of course, to take every kind of care. She has only to follow Sophie's example, without having my cousin's worldly wisdom, to be quite undone."

Phoebe contemplated her friend and patron. "Nothing would please me more than to see her derided, but do you think that would cause David to cry off? He could not. To make his marriage unhappy helps me not at all. I do not wish to merely return to being his mistress."

"It was a great mistake to take him to your bed at all," said Lady Harroving severely. "I'm sure he would have offered for you had you but held him off."

Mrs. Danvers merely shrugged.

"My point is," said her ladyship, "that there will be no question of crying off if she runs off with a fortune-hunting officer or some other scoundrel."

"She wouldn't!" declared her friend, aghast.

"She's just the kind of sulky miss capable of any wildness. I've seen these quiet ones before. Do you remember Lady Liza Yelland? Such a little nun until she went to Town, and then, after two major scandals, her father had to double her dowry to get Lanchester to marry her. You know David. If the girl can be encouraged to behave with a lack of decorum, he will cut up stiff. If he attempts to correct her it will put her back up, and she'll soon be well on the way to hating him. She doesn't want to marry him. That's obvious. And I cannot see that he can possibly want to marry her now he's had a chance to see her in Society. In fact, we will be doing them both a charity. All we need is a clever seducer, and I know a few of those. I did think of Ashby, but I know he wouldn't do it with David being his friend. Speaking of our Adonis, my dear. Do I gather you have been playing Aphrodite?"

Mrs. Danvers smiled and licked chocolate from her shapely upper lip. "I have to amuse myself, Maria. Randal and I are old friends. He knows he can always depend on me if he has a really interesting idea. Speaking of which, how was Sir Marius? I have not yet managed to be seduced by him."

"He never seduces anyone. I had to seduce *him!*" snorted her ladyship and then stretched sensually. "He's such an interesting man!"

"Tell me all about it," invited Mrs. Danvers, avidly.

6

THE JOURNEY NEXT day from The Middlehouse to London was a far less decorous business than the journey from Carne. Jane and Sophie travelled in one luxurious coach, accompanied by their maids. Lady Harroving, Mrs. Danvers, and their maids travelled in another. Two simpler carriages had started out earlier in the day containing those other servants essential to their employers' comfort in Town.

The gentlemen with their attendants journeyed in their own curricles, and a race was made of it from one stop to the next. The coaches, though each drawn by four fine horses, could not keep up with the lighter sporting vehicles. However, engaged as they were in chewing over the previous stage and their good or ill luck, while enjoying flagons of home brew, the gentlemen didn't seem to mind waiting for the ladies. As the high-spirited party sat to luncheon at the Bull in Gerrards Cross the gentlemen were still arguing about the previous stretch.

"I would have beaten you if it hadn't been for those damned sheep, Randal," said Sir Marius with grim certainty.

"You're a poor loser," was the jaunty reply. "*I* had the presence of mind to go across country and bypass them."

Sir Marius grunted. "Which only proves you've the devil's own luck. You could have broken an axle!"

Mrs. Danvers favored Lord Wraybourne with an intimate look. "And where were you, David? I was used to think you a formidable whip."

He shrugged with a smile. "It was my turn for the bad luck. I began to feel a wobble from the wheels and found one of the pins working loose. I had to take it easy till I found a wheelwright to fix the rig. Now I'll show my mettle."

"Do you think you can beat me?" asked Lord Randal with shining eyes.

Lord Wraybourne laughed. "I know I can, for I have before. Today I may."

"So clever with words," taunted the younger man. "Let's have a bet on it, David."

"Certainly."

"Count me in," said Sir Marius firmly. "I'm a better whip than either of you fribbles. Will you join us, Lord Harroving?" But the older man declined, to his wife's disgust.

"What stake, gentlemen?" she asked eagerly.

After a moment's hesitation Lord Wraybourne said, "Fifty pounds. The two losers to pay a pony each."

"Saving your blunt now you're to be a married man?" teased Lord Randal, confirming Jane's suspicion that Lord Wraybourne might be purse-pinched. "Fifty it is." He paused a moment and looked round at the company. "To be used for a gift for the winner's lady."

Eyes bright with mischief he stretched a hand to Lady Sophie. "My lady, may I wear your colors?"

Sophie pulled out a delicate white lace handkerchief and passed it to him, saying dramatically, "Strive well, my champion!"

Lord Wraybourne turned to Jane. "Are you willing to condone this insanity and honor me with your colors, my dear?"

Jane hesitated a moment, sure she would be condemned for joining in with such behavior. But as there appeared to be no protest, she shyly tendered her handkerchief, which was plain, edged with pink embroidery.

Sir Marius smiled ruefully at his predicament. "Maria," he said at last. "I can hardly champion a married lady. Mrs. Danvers, will you honor me with your handkerchief?"

"With pleasure, Sir Marius. And by great good fortune it is trimmed with green." She graced him with her intimate smile. "I wish you all good fortune and freedom from livestock. You may buy me an aquamarine with the purse. It is my good-luck stone."

The three gentlemen tucked their colors in the buttonholes of their driving coats and called for their vehicles. Within minutes they had swept out of sight.

Sophie passed the journey in a fever of excitement to see whether Lord Randal had won. "He will buy me a gold bracelet," she declared. "What will you choose if David should win, Jane?"

Jane was miserably sure that the heavens were going to fall in long before she benefited from such ill-acquired monies. Gambling was above all things abhorrent to Lady Sandiford.

She managed to say, however, "I think I would leave the choice of gift to Lord Wraybourne."

Sophie considered that. "You are cleverer than I, Jane. That is much more subtle and dignified and will ensure that the gentleman must spend some time thinking of your tastes and wishes."

Jane blushed and stammered a disclaimer. She had made her reply from fear, having no idea what fifty pounds would buy or what would be a suitable gift from a man to his betrothed. Sophie, however, was thinking for the first time that there were things she could learn from her new friend.

When the carriages drew to a halt before the Harrowings' mansion on Marlborough Square, Sophie could hardly wait for the steps to be let down before dashing into the house. Following more slowly, the other ladies found the four gentlemen at their ease, enjoying a fine claret.

"Well?" demanded Sophie. "Who won?"

Lord Wraybourne shook his head. "No patience, Sophie. Just like Randal. He tried to pass the stage too soon and ended in the ditch. Lost twenty minutes."

Lord Randal smiled apologetically and returned her handkerchief, but she cheerfully let him keep it, "as a reward for a bold attempt."

"Sir Marius?" queried Mrs. Danvers.

"Now Sir Marius is not a hasty man," said Lord Wraybourne weightily. "Like you, Phoebe, he is clever and cool-headed. He waited till just the right time to pass the stage."

"You won, Sir Marius!" she exclaimed.

"I am afraid not, Mrs. Danvers. David is right. I waited till just the right moment, when I had a clear view of the road and a good breadth to pass in, but he had already gone through on an idiot's chance. There was no way, David, that you could have known you could pass there."

He turned to Mrs. Danvers. "May I keep my insignia, Ma'am, as a memory of the one time David Kyle took a risk I was not willing to take?"

Laughing, she agreed.

Lord Wraybourne came over to Jane with his colors. "I hope you will allow me to keep this, Jane. In truth, I am not likely to take such a risk again, but it will be pleasant to remember in my old age."

She murmured her assent, and when he asked what gift she wanted, she made the same reply that she had given Sophie and earned a smile.

"I shall afford it careful thought. I hope you will forgive me, Jane, if I am not always in attendance for the next few days. I have a number of matters to attend to after being out of town. I am sure you will be busy with new gowns and new friends, but if you have need of me for any reason, you have only to send round a note to Alton Street."

Jane was happy with this arrangement. It would certainly take her time to find her equilibrium among her new companions, and she would manage a great deal better without the turmoil her handsome husband-to-be seemed to stir within her. Jane's resolution only lasted until the next afternoon, however, when she'd donned her first fashionable outfit and was delighted to discover that Lord Wraybourne would be with them for their introduction to the fashionable parade in Hyde Park. She wanted him, above all men, to see her looking so fine.

The gown was made of cream-colored muslin, flounced around the bottom. The gathered bodice was hidden beneath a rust-colored velvet spencer, and the high frilled collar framed her face. Her cream straw bonnet was trimmed with velvet ribbons to match the spencer, and cream slippers completed the outfit which had been awaiting her at the *modiste*'s. Upon surveying herself in the mirrors, she saw a young woman of fashion with some claim to beauty. Perhaps she did, after all, have a chance to gain her husband's true affections.

Lord Wraybourne was gratifyingly quick to comment on her elegance.

"But I have few other clothes," she told him with a grimace as he settled her on the seat of Lady Harroving's smart barouche and then took his place beside her. "Madame Danielle, the *modiste*, said that most of the colors chosen for me by my mother were unsuitable."

"Then what are you to do now?"

"Oh, she will make more," Jane said airily, unaware of the task the seamstress had undertaken, "and sell those my mother ordered to some other young lady whom they would suit. I am to wear mostly cream and yellow, some green, and reds with an orange tint."

Lord Wraybourne was observing her excitement indulgently. "Did Sophie accompany you?"

"Oh yes. And you ordered some outfits, did you not, Sophie?" she asked of the young lady opposite.

Sophie made a face at her brother. "Just two new gowns, David. Madame Danielle is very skillful."

"Did I say a word?" he protested.

"You were doing accounts in your head. You will have to take care, Jane, or he will have you in the same gown for years."

So they *were* in financial difficulties. Jane made haste to reassure him. "I am really very frugal, My Lord."

He took her hand. "Sophie is teasing, my dear. I will always be delighted to have my wife be a leader of fashion."

"Oh, I don't think I could be that."

"Do you not? You are beautiful, and you have the height for fine dressing. Your carriage is extremely graceful. I am sure your mother is a great advocate of the backboard. I see no reason you should not become a standard for the rest to follow."

Jane was quite overset. She had hoped for some appreciation, yet again he had turned to outright flattery, and she did not wish to be paid in hollow coin. She wished she could tell him it was unnecessary, that there was no doubt she would marry him and endow him with her fortune.

Instead, she had to resort to a light tone. "Lord Wraybourne, are you paying me compliments to upset me? Be assured, you will not succeed again."

By the gleam in his eye, Jane guessed he was about

to take up this rash challenge. She was grateful that they were entering the park, as Lady Harroving began to bow and wave and point out people of importance. Lord Wraybourne was happy also to be a guide.

"That lady in the gray landau is Lady Foley. She is acknowledged a beauty. Her husband is standing over there with some other men. He is commonly called Number Eleven because he is so thin, you see."

"Does he not mind?"

"Good heavens, no. It is the aim of everyone to be distinguished for *something* even if only for lack of flesh."

"Oh. For what are *you* distinguished, My Lord?"

The gleam in his eye warned her before he spoke. "Why for capturing the richest and most beautiful heiress in England, what else?"

She took refuge in severity. "If you continue to lay the butter on so thick, My Lord, I will refuse to speak to you entirely."

"Many a husband would consider that a blessing," he said mischievously and then added, "But I could be persuaded to stop for a little while by a lady who would address me as David, rather than My Lord."

Jane smiled triumphantly. "Sophie," she called to attract that damsel's attention away from a group of friends too far away to actually hear her greetings. "Your brother says that he will cease pestering me with high-flown compliments if *you* will ask him."

Sophie was bewildered. "Why ever would you wish him to stop? David, what are you about?"

Lord Wraybourne was laughing. "Merely being outmaneuvered in a masterly fashion. Very well, Jane. I give you victory, for now."

Sophie regarded them in indulgent perplexity for a moment, then returned to the fascinating business of greeting old friends.

Jane relished the warmth of her victory, not acknowledging that a great part of the pleasure was generated by the admiration Lord Wraybourne obviously felt for her quick wits. She used those wits to observe and remember as her companions threw names and tidbits of gossip at her, and she only spoke when introductions were made. Despite her concentration, her head was soon spinning, and she knew that she was as likely to call Gentleman Jackson the Duke of Rutland as to get any of the names right.

"I have forgotten every one of them," she whispered in dismay to Lord Wraybourne as the carriage turned for home. "What am I to do?"

"Good heavens, don't even try to remember names yet. You'll soon get to know all the important people. Maria, Sophie, and I will be around to prompt you."

Jane cast a doubtful glance at the older lady. It had become obvious that she had no intention of putting herself to any effort for her charges. Still, Jane made no comment. She knew her brain to be keen and had no doubt she could learn about the bewilderments of the ton with only a minimum of help. She had noticed how popular Lord Wraybourne was and how knowledgeable about Society. It would be to her advantage if he was to devote himself to her in the next few days, even if he insisted on his flattering ways. But how was she to reverse her previous order to him to cease his attentions, without losing face? There was only one way. For the first time in her life, Jane set out to flirt with a man, and believed she was being quite subtle until he handed her down at Marlborough Square.

He held her hand and said, with a slight smile, "Whatever it is you want, Jane, it would doubtless be easier if you just asked me."

This had the effect of rendering her speechless, and she hurried into the house so fast she appeared to be in flight.

"Whatever are you about, David?" asked his sister in surprise. "I would have thought you a little more skillful. You appear to be constantly casting poor Jane into a panic."

"Dear Sophie, you know nothing of the matter," replied her brother amiably.

"You look odiously self-satisfied. If you are mean to Jane you will have me to deal with. She is my friend."

He gave her a very warm smile. "Excellent. I hope you will look out for her. Everything here is new and since Jane won a victory and I am no longer allowed to tease her with compliments, you have no need to worry about me. I am a toothless lion."

Sophie shook her head. "You are an idiot. If I didn't know better, I'd say you were in love." With that she swept into the house and went to seek out Jane.

She found her friend had forgotten any distress over her betrothed and was staring helplessly at a huge mound of packages on her bed. After visiting the *modiste* earlier in the day the three ladies had stopped in at Layton and Shears for some trimmings and at Mills Haberdashers for other necessities such as silk stockings and gloves. Jane knew she had bought a number of items and remembered the attendant footman had had to make many trips back to the carriage with their purchases, but surely not as many as this.

"What am I to do with all this, Sophie?"

"Open them." Sophie poked at the pile. "Some of these are mine, I think." Decisively she rang the bell and when Prudence arrived she was given the task of opening the parcels while the young ladies made their judgment.

"Those silk stockings were mine, Jane. I remember the clocks. Are they not delightful? Bronze flowers! Are those yours?"

"Yes, Madame Danielle said I should wear bronze but I'm not sure I like them anymore."

"Positively gothic," was Sophie's comment. "I cannot imagine why anyone would wear metal flowers except gold or silver. Give them to Prudence."

Jane was pleased with her purchase of plain silk stockings, the first she had ever had, and some artificial cherries, which were all the rage, but found six pairs of plain cotton stockings for everyday wear to be too coarse, so Prudence was given those too. When the maid left, she was piled high with items: string mittens that were too short in the fingers, ivy leaves that Sophie declared would make her look like an ancient monument, braid that was quite hideous, lace that did not, after all, match Sophie's green Pyrenean mantle, and a reticule which had probably been purchased by Lady Harroving. Sophie gave it to the maid anyway, saying it was ugly and Maria needed to be protected from herself.

At this rate, thought the maid as she staggered away under her load, she would be able to retire and open a haberdashery shop of her own.

Jane, meanwhile, was full of guilt. "How terrible. All that money wasted."

"Nonsense. Prudence will make good use of those things."

"But my parents did not provide money for the ornamentation of Prudence Hawkins. My mother would have an apoplexy if she knew. I cannot imagine how I came to buy so much. It is as if a madness overtook me."

"Yes," said Sophie happily. "It is always the same when shopping. And what else is money for?"

No wonder Lord Wraybourne needed to marry a fortune. Jane's upbringing warred with her new delight in frivolity and, by a mere margin, upbringing won.

"I will not behave so again," she resolved. "If I have money to spare, I will give it to a worthy cause."

"Good Lord, Jane, if you are to turn Methodish on me I shall cut your acquaintance. Think of poor Prudence. She will have no status at all in the servants' hall if you are not generous with your castoffs." With that Sophie took herself away and left Jane to struggle with her conscience.

She started to read the sermons of Dean Bagnold, a parting gift from her mother, but when she came upon the words, "Clothing as ornament is an abomination. Simple garments of sturdy stuff, suitable for modest covering and protection from the elements, are all that is needed by all ranks of men and women . . ." she slapped the book shut in irritation.

Even her mother did not believe that. Otherwise, why had she ordered such fashionable clothes for Jane and why were her own gowns always of the finest cloth? Happily, Jane gave the victory to Sophie's side. It was a young woman's duty to uphold her family's dignity in Society. Had not Jane's husband-to-be specifically said that he wished her to be fashionable? And since it would be her own money which would purchase the necessary finery, she need feel no qualms at all.

Her conscience thus appeased, Jane could be happy once more, and this gave her leisure to reflect on Lord Wraybourne. Would he really cease his flattery, and did she wish it after all? Even if she knew he had chosen her for cold-blooded reasons, she could still find pleasure in his skillful attentions. She found herself eager for the next opportunity to match wits with her betrothed. She held a wreath of yellow roses against her dusky hair and regarded herself in the mirror with great satisfaction.

7

THAT PARTICULAR EVENING, the party did not go out or entertain at home, and Jane was glad of it. She would soon discover that to be in her bed before two or three in the morning was rare. Eventually, her body would learn to accommodate by allowing her to sleep until nearly noon, but on her second morning in London, her constitution was still keeping country hours. She was up unfashionably early. To pass the time she decided to explore the library, a small and carelessly stocked room, used more for card-playing than reading. It held a number of popular works, however, and Jane was suddenly aware of another aspect of her newly gained freedom. She could read whatever she wished.

She retreated to her room with a Minerva Novel called *The Castle of Modena,* of which her mother would totally disapprove, and was soon entranced by the world of the heroine, Virginia, who was being compelled by her heartless parents to marry the evil but rich Count Malficio when she really loved the honorable knight Sir Tristram. In some respects, the story seemed to address Jane's own situation, and she began to suspect that she had been unfairly persuaded into her betrothal. Moreover, though Lord Wraybourne was inclined to flattery, he showed none of the respectful adoration with which Sir Tristram addressed his lady.

Jane sighed as she read of the faithful golden-haired knight, kneeling before Virginia. "You are a gossamer angel, tranquil and ethereal in this elysian bower. It cannot be, it will never be fitting for a mere crude man to touch even the hem of your mantle!"

It was only with reluctance that Jane laid down the book at this touching moment in order to go to breakfast, where her inclination to linger in Modena was disturbed by the reminder that Lord Randal and his twin sisters were due to call so that they might all ride together.

"But Sophie, I do not have a habit. My old one was left at Carne, and Madame Danielle refused to allow me to have the gray one which had been commissioned."

Sophie was dismayed. "My old one would not fit you, Jane. What are we to do?"

Jane smiled nobly. "You must go, of course. In a few days I will have my new habit, and then we can ride together."

"Are you sure? I will keep you company if you wish."

"Of course, I'm sure, you goose," said Jane, truly moved by this offer. "I have any number of things to do. For example, I really should write home." And I have the entrancing world of Modena waiting upstairs, she thought guiltily.

As soon as she had waved the riding party on their way, she fled to her room to resume her reading. She was soon interrupted, however, by the news that Lord Wraybourne was below. Caught in the middle of the passage in which Count Malficio was suavely assuring the trembling Virginia that she was in his power and could not help but become his bride, Jane felt a stab of fear much greater than her irritation at having her reading interrupted.

She'd forgotten Lord Wraybourne's gentle humor and remembered only that he was a man of the world, a dueller. Heaven knows what he might do if crossed. Thinking herself very much the persecuted damsel, Jane sent for Lady Harroving to accompany her before going down to the salon.

Confronted with reality, however, Jane had to admit that though Lord Wraybourne might fall short of the standards set by Sir Tristram, he did not fit her notion of Count Malficio. His face was clear and honest, and even if those tantalizing lids tended to droop at times and conceal their meaning, the eyes they concealed could never be described as deep and fiery. The smile with which he greeted her was genuine, not sneering.

"I have come with your gift," he said, holding out a package, "bought with the purse from the curricle race."

Assailed by guilt at having allowed her mind to be so distorted by fiction, Jane opened the wrapping to find an embroidered girdle worked in golden thread and seed pearls with a large flower cameo for the clasp. What coals of fire were heaped upon her head then! Lord Wray-bourne was not her enemy at all, and she was a wretch for her misjudgment.

"Oh, it is beautiful," Jane sighed. "My first true gift and exactly what I wanted."

"It is more in the nature of a trophy," he said. "From the fact that Sophie has been pleading for one for weeks, I suspected it might find favor. Still, I cannot have you over-whelmed by every little trumpery. I shall have to give you so many gifts you will sigh and scarcely bother to open them."

She laughed at this absurdity.

"I met Sophie and her party," he continued. "They ex-plained you are not yet able to ride. Do you know when your habit will be ready?"

"A few days at least."

"May I beg the privilege of being your first riding es-cort in London?" he asked warmly. Jane could not stop her heart giving a little flip at the expression on his face. Could it be false? "I will provide the mount. Merely send a note when your riding gear is ready."

She supposed it was his role to provide her a mount and escort her. Nonetheless, it was heartening that he was seek-ing her company a little, and the gift had been thought-fully chosen. Jane did not try to fight the glow within her. Even if he had originally made his offer for cold-blooded reasons, there was no reason true feeling could not grow eventually.

She remained aware of how easily her mind had been distorted by the novel and thought that perhaps her mother's ban on such books had been wise. Jane resolved to travel no more in the land of Modena and, as penance for her error, ceased avoiding Lady Harroving. Instead, much to that lady's astonishment, Jane sought her out, to ask which tasks she would wish to assign.

"Such as what, my dear?" she asked, looking around her deliriously flounced *boudoir,* as if a task might be lying on the ground somewhere, previously undetected.

"At home I wash the fine china and mend linen. I also help to prepare and preserve food, though I know there will be none of that in Town. I am not accustomed to being idle."

"Nor will you be idle in Town once we get under way!" said Lady Harroving with a titter. "Good heavens, Jane, no matter what your life at home, here we leave such tasks to the servants. Soon we will be busy with engagements all day. For the moment, take a turn around the square with your maid or do an acrostic or something."

With this irritated pronouncement the lady waved her away, but Jane still felt the need of penance. Remembering her earlier words to Sophie, she went to make that falsehood into truth by writing to her parents and was surprised at how tediously proper it was possible to make the past exciting week sound.

The stay at The Middlehouse had been pleasant, she related, with long walks and music in the evenings. The journey to Town had been a little enlivened because it was a large party, and her time since then had been taken up with her wardrobe and making new friends. Among her new acquaintances she mentioned Lord Randal's sisters, the Ladies Caroline and Cecilia Ashby, as Jane was sure her mother would approve of their pedigree.

In fact, she reflected, the Ashby sisters, with their quiet, beautiful manners, were among the few she had met in these last days of whom her mother *would* approve. Yes, Jane might well put a great deal in her letters about the Ladies Caroline and Cecilia.

Jane then wrote a more informal and honest letter to Mrs. Hawley but was dissatisfied to discover that it seemed to be entirely about Lord Wraybourne. Anyone would think Jane had met no one else at all. She hastily threw in so many names she then began to fear that her governess would put her down as a toad-eating name-dropper. It would be so much easier if one could just be honest. But what was honest? Jane attempted to compose an honest letter in her head.

> *Dear Beth,*
>
> *I am a mishmash of feelings—excitement, fear, delight, and insecurity. I am never sure from one moment to the next what I or anyone about me will do. I love having beautiful clothes though the expense troubles my conscience. It is strange and a little frightening to have such freedom and so many idle hours. I foolishly began to read a novel and found myself quickly led into all manner of errors, even to thinking Lord Wraybourne a monstrous villain.*
>
> *Quite the contrary, Lord Wraybourne is both kind and charming and does not seem to begrudge the time he spends in my company. I no longer feel chagrin at having been chosen for my fortune. There are many other heiresses, and*

he is considered eligible. So there must be something about me which he finds pleasing. Even if his present attentions are dictated more by courtesy than warmth, I harbor hopes that in time he will come to be sincerely attached to me, which will be a relief, for then I can relax my guard and become attached in turn to him. It will be difficult, however, for one so inexperienced as I to judge when that time comes.

Jane smiled a little to think of the bewilderment with which Mrs. Hawley would receive such a maundering. But the last question was, nonetheless, a valid one. She had no comparisons upon which to base the answer. Her parents were too old to be guides for young love. In fact, she found it impossible to imagine that they had ever been young or in love at all. Lord and Lady Harroving were obviously no models either. Of course, if Sophie were to form an attachment, there would be much to learn, but she was, as yet, heart-free.

Jane did indeed need more time to learn about people and her betrothed. In a few weeks she would be better able to judge his behavior and respond appropriately. Until then, she must be careful to be moderate in her manners so as not to embarrass herself or him.

She folded the letters and sealed them, ready for a frank. Unfortunately, this left her without occupation. She succumbed to temptation and returned to her novel. After all, she assured herself, she was now aware of its dangers and absurdities and could guard against their influence on her mind.

An hour later, Virginia was locked in the cellar while

Count Malficio made dastardly plans with her venal parents. Then, Jane was forced by Sophie's return to lay down the book.

"I am sorry you missed such a delightful morning, Jane. I encountered any number of old friends and a group of dashing hussars on furlough from the war. A Major Heckleton is a friend of Randal's and so we were soon one party." Sophie's bright blue eyes twinkled mischievously. "I do *adore* a uniform, and it is, after all, our duty to make our soldiers' brief respite from war a pleasant one, is it not?"

These same soldiers in their brilliant regimentals were predominant in Sophie's court that evening when they attended a performance of *Twelfth Night* at Drury Lane. At every intermission the Harroving box was crowded with visitors, many of them male. The official escorts of the party—Lord Randal, Sir Arthur, and a young man named Crossley Carruthers—found themselves pushed to the wall.

Sir Arthur promptly went to sleep. Lord Randal watched Sophie with an amused smile, but Jane noticed Mr. Carruthers looking rather cross. She felt sorry for him. He was a fine-looking man with bright gold curls, cunningly dressed, and a magnificent cravat which held his collar so high he was forced to move only with slow dignity. She was sure that ordinarily, he would have received warm attention, but, competing with the charisma of the uniform and the effortless elegance of Lord Randal, he was, for the moment, a mere cipher.

Lady Harroving had introduced him as a distant connection brought in to substitute for Lord Wraybourne, who had received a last-minute summons to dine at Carlton House. Connection or not, she paid no attention to him, being much too busy enjoying the company of so many more handsome men. Jane smiled warmly at him across the crowd of bodies and was pleased to see his expression lighten. She was quite unable to do more for him at the moment. Besides being entranced by her first visit to a theater, she had to do her duty and entertain those of Sophie's court who were not yet able to attract that lady's attention.

Surrounded by gallantry and light flirtation, Jane should have been delighted by such an opportunity to learn the way of the world but, quite simply, she missed her betrothed. If there was a joke, she wished to share it with him. If there was a question, it was he she would have turned to for the answer. Jane acknowledged she was more under Lord Wraybourne's spell than she had wished to be, but there was little she could do except disguise her feelings and hope they would soon be returned in equal measure.

For now, the easy interplay within the party was pleasant, and Jane found it increasingly effortless. In only one case did she find socializing arduous. An unlikely young man had attached himself to Sophie, having gained introduction because his widowed mother was the sister of Sophie's godmother. Sir Edwin Hever was thin, pale, and prematurely balding. His clothes were barely tolerable and of drab color. Among the bucks of fashion and the military uniforms, he stood out like a thistle in a flower bed.

He was up from Essex to find himself a wife. Being his doting mother's only child, he was arrogantly sure that he had only to make his choice. He had apparently scrutinized Society during the Little Season without finding a bride to fulfill his exacting requirements. Now he was back, and his choice was obviously Sophie. The fixed, almost fanatical gaze he kept upon her and his tendency to hold her hand a little longer than was correct both spoke of an attachment. There was no chance that she would have him, but in the same way that the infantas of Spain had delighted in dwarves, she found him amusing.

"Is he not a grotesque?" she murmured discreetly to Jane. "I will keep him by to see to what insufferable lengths his self-importance will drive him!"

Jane noticed that, despite this tolerance, after the first few moments Sophie took care not to be the recipient of Sir Edwin's conversation, which was tedious beyond belief. He did not listen to others but merely lectured. To make matters worse, he had only the most superficial, ill-understood knowledge of any subject. Having endured his dissertation on silk production, Jane gladly relinquished Sir Edwin so that he might give a colonel of the dragoons the benefit of his views on the war. She hoped the officer would slice him to ribbons in return.

Fortunately, entertaining the other gentlemen who surrounded Sophie was a pleasure and they showed no reluctance when forced to make do with Jane. In fact, they appeared only too pleased to indulge in a little light flirtation with the safely spoken-for Miss Sandiford. Jane blossomed under their admiration, confirmed in her belief that she looked very well indeed in her first real evening gown, of ecru levantine woven with bronze stripes, and the latest Marie sleeves decorated with knots of matching bronze ribbons. She only wished Lord Wraybourne were present to appreciate the effect.

There were others, however, to give praise if she sought it. She accepted light flattery from witty Major Heckleton with just the right degree of modesty, in imitation of Sophie. Lord Wraybourne would be pleased, Jane thought, by her lack of alarm at being told her eyes were like the midnight sky sprinkled with stars. Her lips twitched into a smile as she thought how pleased her mother would be that her daughter was having so much practice in the Art of Conversation . . . as long as Lady Sandiford remained in ignorance of Jane's conversational partners and their flirtatious tone!

After the theater they all attended a *soirée*. Jane took the opportunity to be kind to Mr. Carruthers, since he was her partner, and found it most rewarding. Here was a man who approached the knight-errant she had once dreamed of, the one so close in many respects to Sir Tristram. Mr. Carruthers' gray eyes were large and sensitive, his lips full and sweetly curved. In the most respectful manner he managed to slip delicate compliments into their conversation, always stressing, of course, how very far above him she was. Jane was embarrassed when she mistakenly called the young man Sir Tristram but that revealed to her where her thoughts were leading. She felt a little thrill of guilty excitement, even as she realized this feeling was a phantasm and had nothing to do with the emotion she harbored for Lord Wraybourne. Still, it had a charm all its own. To have a secret admirer would be very dashing and, with Sir Tristram, very safe.

"Tell me, Mr. Carruthers," she said. "Is this your first visit to Town? Are you perhaps, like Sir Edwin, in search of a wife?"

"My first visit, Miss Sandiford? Indeed no. I've practically lived here for years." With a self-deprecating smile and endearing honesty he added, "I have only a small estate which takes little time to manage, and the country is devilish dull when one has no work to do there and no loved ones around."

Was it her imagination that his eyes spoke of a particular loved one, herself?

"Then you *are* looking for a wife, Sir," she said.

His silvery eyes, framed by long lashes, rested soulfully on hers. "Alas, but the fairest maids are quickly taken."

Her nerves aflutter at the game, Jane turned away to show she had understood his reference but glanced back to say, "Perhaps you must learn to be more speedy, Mr. Carruthers, or more daring."

Appalled at the gleam in his eye, she decided she had overplayed her hand and rose hastily, saying she must find Lady Sophie. Sophie, however, was surrounded as usual. Lord Randal was supporting a nearby pillar as Jane approached him.

"Got rid of Carruthers, have you?" was his casual greeting. "Good thing too. He's a mushroom. I don't know why Maria would invite him along."

"I find him charming," she protested. "It is a pleasant change to find a man able to talk sensitively on a subject."

Lord Randal looked disbelieving, but he merely grinned and said, "You probably mean that you haven't yet received a surfeit of compliments tonight. Only a thousand or so."

She laughed. "I am not so greedy, Lord Randal."

"Are you not? Then, alas, you must be sickened by now, so I won't tell you how magnificent you look."

"Won't you?" she asked with a smile. She knew Lord Randal was a safe partner in this kind of conversation.

"No."

Disconcertingly, he did indeed stop then and lapsed into silence. She burst out laughing.

"You are an original, Lord Randal." Struck by a sudden thought she asked, "Tell me, why exactly do you hover about us? Surely Sophie does not have such a claim on you?"

He looked sharply at Jane, as if surprised by the question. "I've known Sophie all her life. It amuses me to see her success."

Hardly thinking of her words, Jane said, "And I suppose you wish to vet her choice of husband?"

The planes of his face seemed to tighten. "Of course," he admitted bleakly. "After all, I know all the cads, intimately. Which reminds me, stay away from Carruthers."

"That is absurd," she protested. "He could never be described as a *cad*!"

His smile was grim. "I was trying to keep within the language fitting for a lady. The music is about to begin. Let me find you a seat, Miss Sandiford."

It was only as she sat listening to a young lady playing the piano that she realized his ridiculous attack on an innocent man had been to deflect her from their previous conversation. It occurred to her that Lord Randal might in fact be harboring deep feelings for Sophie. But why hide them? He held a high rank in Society, even if he was a younger son, and was an intimate of Sophie's family. Jane could see no reason for him not to press his suit if he were so inclined. Perhaps, she thought, he had asked and been refused. Sophie seemed to treat him as a brother. Jane sighed for an unhappy lover.

The amateur concert continued, with performances ranging from dreadful to superb. Jane was pleased to hear Sophie acquit herself tolerably upon the harp, making up in verve for a lack of practice. Jane glanced at Lord Randal to see what his face might reveal, but at that moment it told her nothing.

All such matters were driven from her mind when Lady Harroving said, "Jane, will you not sing for us?"

Finding herself the focus of so many eyes, Jane wished the earth would swallow her. Even though she had been told she had a fine voice, she had never sung before strangers. She was amazed that Lady Harroving would put her in this position without asking whether she wished to perform, but Jane quickly perceived that refusal was impossible.

Thankful for the creamy skin which did not show her blushes and for her long training in self-control and composure, she went to the piano. Playing from memory, she sang "The Aspen Tree" and a lullaby. Though she was not aware of it, the room became quiet and attentive in response to her rich voice. She finished to enthusiastic applause and calls for an encore, which she prettily refused.

However, as she looked about her in glowing pleasure at this acceptance, she was disconcerted to note what looked like anger upon the face of Lady Harroving, but quickly forgot that when she saw Lord Wraybourne standing behind the lady. An irrepressible joy swelled in Jane's breast, not lessened by the fact that he had witnessed her little triumph. This would show him she had some qualities other than her pedigree and upbringing.

He came to meet her, his eyes glowing. "You were magnificent. What a treasure you are, Jane."

Jane's spirits descended. Treasure immediately made her think of her enormous dowry.

"Rich and entertaining too?" she said.

The warmth in his eyes did not diminish. In fact, he seemed less reserved than usual. "And very beautiful and, I believe you said, frugal?"

He was holding her hand and smiling in a way which would have been embarrassing, if it hadn't given her hope that his feelings might already be strongly engaged. Jane could feel that tingle of excitement building in her again, flowing from his touch on her hand. Unable to deal directly with that right now, she took refuge in frivolity.

"Those were compliments," she accused, "and so against the rules." Then she made a shocking discovery. "Lord Wraybourne, are you *inebriated?*"

He chuckled. "Just a bit on the go. I usually go straight home after the third bottle at Carlton House, but I found myself passing here and remembered you were to attend. I thought you might have missed me."

Jane wasn't quite sure what to do with this mellow version of her betrothed. She had never in her life been associated with anyone affected by drink, and she wondered in dismay if that meant she should disregard his doting behavior. Her mother had always said that those who were inebriated were totally untrustworthy. Jane was relieved when Sophie came up to them.

"Did you hear Jane, David? What a wonderful voice. Why did you not perform at The Middlehouse, Jane?"

"I was not asked, and I have never before performed in public," Jane explained. "I would not have sung here if Lady Harroving had not suggested it."

"Yes," said Sophie, puzzled. "It was careless of her. You could have had a voice like a frog and put us all to shame. But no doubt your mother primed her as to your virtues." She looked at her brother, who was gazing at Jane with an anticipatory smile.

"Prinny's port," Sophie diagnosed with a grin. "I'd go home if I were you, David, before you make a cake of yourself."

"Yes," he said with a sigh.

Jane stiffened as she felt his fingers tickling the palm of her hand. Such a simple contact to have so alarming an effect.

"After all, you're not going to disappear, Jane. Are you?"

No reply was required, but as she watched him take his leave of the hostess, she caught sight of Crossley Carruthers watching her soulfully. She had mischievously encouraged the poor young man and had been, in a sense, false to her betrothed. Oh, the traps which surrounded the unwary in Society! Her mother had been right about that too. Guilt hung over Jane like a cloud. Fearing yet more indecorous behavior, she slipped for a moment into a quiet anteroom to collect herself. She was sitting quietly, making resolutions about her future conduct, when she heard a whisper so soft and hoarse that at first she thought her ears must be deceiving her.

"Poor little beauty all alone," the sibilance crept across the room. "Wishing for a man's hands, a man's lips? Wanton thoughts in a wanton's body. Woman's body, wanton's body, no difference . . ."

Jane leapt to her feet and peered into the shadows. The room was empty, but there was an open door in each wall. It was difficult to detect from which direction the voice had come. Though she longed to flee to safety, Jane had no desire to confront the whisperer and dared not exit through any of the doors when he might be waiting for her on the other side. Trembling, she turned first to one, then the other in indecision.

"Guilty conscience?" the whisper came once more. "Does the earl know how you cast lascivious looks at all the men, make promises with your eyes and your body?"

Her ears had fixed the direction now. He was in the small salon. Dry-mouthed, with eyes fixed by terror on the doorway through which the horrible words had sounded, Jane began slowly to retreat towards the safety of the corridor and nearby music room.

She heard a disgusting, spittly chuckle. "Will you have Carruthers to bed? Ashby? Or are you full of longings? Perhaps I'll fill your needs for you."

Gasping, Jane bolted for the music room. Only a lifetime of self-discipline kept her from hurling through the doorway into scandal. A hasty glance showed her that the corridor was deserted, and she took a moment to compose herself, again giving thanks for her creamy skin. All the time she kept a fearful gaze fixed on the corridor down which the whisperer would have to come if he had pursued her. As her heartbeat slowed, her mind began to clear once more. He would not come here. Two steps and she would be in the music room and safe. He obviously had no desire to be seen.

Was this some bizarre joke? If she told Sophie or Lord Randal, would they laugh, would it create a scandal? She was surely at fault in having gone off by herself. Once again, her impulsive disregard for correct behavior had led her astray.

Could he possibly have been one of the guests? Surely it must have been a demented intruder. . . . Yet, he had known all about her. With horror, she realized that the whisperer could already have gone from the small salon to the main hall and thus rejoined the company in the music room. The thought of returning to that company with him perhaps there, studying her, even touching her, made Jane feel faint. What was she to do?

Fortunately, rescue arrived in the form of Lady Harroving. "Why ever are you out here, Jane?" snapped the lady. "We have been looking for you this age. We are ready to go. Even if you are sometimes gauche, I had not thought you the sort to hide from the company. This will never do."

Jane let the tart comments wash over her as she gratefully allowed herself to be whisked away from danger.

During the carriage journey home, she decided to keep silent about the encounter, partly because it was so unreal that she doubted she would be believed and more so because she was very disinclined to repeat the words she had heard. Also, she felt at fault for having separated herself from her party. She would be sure never to do that again, when it could lay her open to such a fright.

Her sleep that night was troubled by distressing dreams of a whispering pursuer.

For his part, Lord Wraybourne walked the rest of the way to Alton Street, hoping to clear his head. He had a deal of thinking to do, mostly upon his uncle's business and the discussion which had been held at Carlton House. But his mind kept turning to Jane, so magnificent in the first neckline he had ever seen her wear which showed the roundness of her full breasts, with that rich and mellow voice swelling to fill the room, while the eyes of the other men upon her made him angry and proud and greedy.

With determination, he cut off that line of thought. The wedding was not far off, and she deserved the time she had requested to find her feet in Society without having to worry about his passion. It was as well he had plenty to occupy his mind in the next few weeks.

When he reached his house, he called for a jar of porter

to settle his head and went to his study. He laid out crisp, new paper before him and dipped his pen in the standish. Thus prepared for work, he spent the next few minutes deciding which of the fashionable miniaturists should be commissioned to execute a likeness of Jane. He liked the work of Andrew Robertson.

Lord Wraybourne shook his head to encourage clear thought and wrote the date clearly across the page: "May 19, 1813." On the line below he continued: "Dinner at Carlton House. Present HRH, Colonel Hanger, Lord Liverpool, the Home Secretary, Uncle M-L, Mr. Stokely, myself." Soon his pen was flying across the page as he recorded the discussion.

He had been surprised to receive an invitation to dine with the Regent. As an earl and eminent member of Society, Lord Wraybourne was a frequent visitor at Carlton House and Brighton, but he was not one of the Prince's intimates. Such invitations had usually been to events of the more public sort, especially as he was known to be a friend of Brummell, who was now totally out of favor with the Regent.

A brief note from Lord Wraybourne's uncle had advised him that the meeting was to be a business one—Mr. Moulton-Scrope's business. Lord Wraybourne had suspected that his uncle was under pressure about the assaults and reluctantly agreed to go. All in all, it had been an unpleasant experience.

The Prince was in a forceful and pettish mood. He insisted on action, obviously seeing himself as the defender of the weak. Though he had no ideas himself concerning how to proceed, he expected the solution to be easy and obvious. The most distasteful moment had come after the port circulated twice.

The Regent, his speech slightly slurred with drink, leaned back in his chair and muttered, "Shame we can't pin this on that damned Brummell, damned if it ain't."

As the protuberant royal eyes roved round the table and everyone smiled or laughed at his humor, Lord Wraybourne knew that the Prince hadn't really been joking at all.

Meanwhile, something must be done to catch the real miscreant. David had agreed again to make observations among the circle from which the victims had been selected. He had heard a rumor of another attack but had not yet managed to confirm it. He also agreed to read the various documents assembled on the cases. The politicians then joined in to wrap this lack of progress in words that made it sound as if new direction had come from the meeting. Finally, the Prince had been appeased and turned jovial, even remembering Lord Wraybourne's forthcoming marriage with congratulations.

With the meeting summarized on paper and proposed action noted, Lord Wraybourne threw down his pen and continued that last thought—his marriage. He saw a vision of his betrothed, waiting shyly in the marriage bed, her long, dark hair draped about her like a cloak.

He sat up with an oath, grabbed the mistreated pen, and blotchily wrote a further note. "Tell Jane she must NOT cut hair!"

8

L ORD WRAYBOURNE'S NOTE to himself was useless. The
coiffeur was at Marlborough Square before the earl had
time to review what he had written. Sophie had summoned
M. Charles to trim her own locks and consult with Jane. The
elegant Frenchman marveled at the length and thickness of
Jane's hair and then tried to persuade her to have it cut off.

"It is the style, Mademoiselle," he entreated. "The gamin
curls. See how well they suit Lady Sophie."

But Jane was not yet a creature of fashion. She could
not face the thought of losing her hair, even if it was difficult to manage.

"I am not Lady Sophie," she retorted, firmly, "and I will
set my own style. You may cut the front so that I may have
curls there. Then devise different ways of dressing the back
and instruct my maid."

Even the snipping around her face made her wince, as long snakes of hair fell to the carpet, but she had to admit that the effect was excellent. Relieved of its weight, the hair sprang back and needed only a little work with the irons to achieve glossy, fashionable lovelocks on her forehead. M. Charles then showed Prudence how to arrange the remainder in knots, twists, and braids for a number of different effects.

For Jane's first ball, which was to take place that evening, he considered her gown, then devised a Grecian style with the back hair concealed under a *bandeau* and only a few tresses peeping out at the crown. The style was severe for a debutante but perfectly suited the deceptively simple slip and tunic which Lady Harroving had ordered for Jane to wear. With only her new girdle and her pearls for ornament, Jane regarded herself in the mirror. Nothing could be further from the country miss she had so recently been.

"I wonder if it is not too sophisticated," she confessed to Sophie.

"It is wonderful," her friend protested. "Very daring. You will show them from the start that you are not a child. After all, you are not an ordinary debutante. You are betrothed."

"Why do I have to show *them* anything?" queried Jane in alarm.

"How naive you are. The whole town has been talking of your betrothal. Everyone is waiting to see what you are like, and the uncharitable expect you to be a bumpkin. Of course, jealous mamas are hoping to find you ugly and dull so they can console themselves that you caught David with your moneybags."

"Which is the truth."

"I doubt it," retorted Sophie in surprise. "To be sure, why marry poverty if money is available? But the Kyles have been blessed by three generations of thrifty spenders and clever investors. Not a gambler or wastrel among them. We are disgustingly rich and have no need to marry money."

Jane was astonished. "Then why did he choose me?"

"Well, you are wealth in a lovely package. Why would he not?" replied Sophie with a shrug. "Just remember you are the chosen one. Others as rich and beautiful have not been. They will scratch at you if you let them."

Jane felt a bud of hopeful joy begin to unfurl in her heart. It was a tender bloom, but full of promise. He had no need of money, there were others as wellborn as she, and, though his standards for his bride were doubtless high, they were not so very rigid that only a bride from Carne could match them. She had been *chosen*. Not, perhaps, for love, but for something personal.

Despite her new hopes, Jane found it difficult to keep her composure as she descended the wide staircase with Sophie. Lady Harroving was fussing with her train and hardly glanced at them. Her husband was, as usual, bored and half-asleep, but Lord Wraybourne watched their progress with great appreciation, as did Lord Trenholme, who was to partner Sophie. Sophie had been somewhat scathing about this gentleman who was her brother's favorite for her hand, but Jane thought him pleasing. He was a little taller and more strongly built than Lord Wraybourne and of about the same age. There was a composure about his face which was remarkable. Sophie called him stolid, but Jane thought that was too severe. He looked highly dependable, and she could see no particular reason for Sophie to be so against him.

Sophie, a vision in cerulean silk covered by an over-dress of silvery gauze which was caught into scallops at the hem by bunches of ribbons, accepted a warm kiss from her brother, then gave her hand formally to her escort. Lord Trenholme showed no emotion at this coolness.

Jane turned anxiously to her betrothed, watching for his reaction, hoping to see some answer to her questions about his feelings. She wished her dress were prettier. She felt Sophie's dress made her own gown look even more plain and wondered for the first time why such a style had been chosen. She had wanted to be glorious for her first ball and feared she was dowdy. He, of course, looked wonderful, his dark jacket and pantaloons, his white frilled shirt and black cravat seemed to highlight his lean good looks.

Though Jane could find no deep feeling in his expression, Lord Wraybourne was unequivocally pleased. "I can see you are eager to set your own style, Jane. You will be the most beautiful woman at the ball."

"I'm afraid that is flattery again, My Lord. This gown is so plain. Lady Harroving chose it, I think. I certainly did not and I doubt that my mother would have, but it is the only ball dress I have as yet."

"Don't confess that. Take the credit. With your hair in that style and just a few well-chosen jewels it is perfect." His eyes seemed caught by her hairstyle for the first time.

"I see the snipper man has been at you. How much has he left, I wonder?"

Jane had to confess her lack of fashion. "I just could not bear the thought of it all chopped off, My Lord. I hope you will not mind."

"Oh, I think I can endure it," he said with a little smile. "And bound up like that it is the height of *à-la-modality* and delightfully severe. My friend Brummell will love you. He is always preaching simplicity."

"My parents have always held him to be an unadmirable character, I'm afraid," said Jane as she accepted her white velvet cloak and they walked out to the carriages.

"He has his weaknesses and I'm very much afraid his gambling will be the ruin of him, but his taste is impeccable, I assure you, and he is still highly regarded. It will do you no harm to be approved by him."

Later on, it appeared the Beau *did* approve, for he smiled kindly at Jane and led her out for a country dance. She was surprised to find him not at all haughty but charming and humorous. They got along in great amiability. This, combined with Jane's natural dignity and poise, carried off her unusual gown very well and many of the more fussily dressed damsels were suddenly seen as slightly vulgar.

Mrs. Danvers watched Jane's success with her habitual cool smile, and turned to Lady Harroving. "I must assume you have decided to favor the match, Maria. First you urge the girl to cover herself with musical glory, and now you present her as the most elegant debutante the ton has seen in years."

Lady Harroving's eyes narrowed, and her mouth was tight. "How was I to know she could sing like an angel? And I never would have believed she could carry off such a gown. Cruder measures are called for."

Mrs. Danvers' smiling face neither approved nor disapproved, and a few moments later she pleasantly accepted an invitation from Lord Wraybourne to waltz.

At the beginning of the ball Jane had been suffering from nerves. The sheer number of people crowded into the ballroom, the glitter of the chandeliers, the beating wave of sound from music and voices and the fear that the whisperer might be somewhere among the guests all served to keep her off balance. She was perfectly content to stay by Lord Wraybourne's side and dance the first set with him.

By the end of the half hour and the promenade, however, she was more composed and had no desire to be thought peculiar in clinging to one man, even if she would have been delighted to spend the whole evening by his side. Her dance card was already well-filled, and she whirled off happily with partner after partner. Yet, when she saw Lord Wraybourne lead Mrs. Danvers out for the waltz, which Jane was not yet permitted to perform in public, she felt positively cross and turned warmly towards Mr. Crossley Carruthers, who was sitting out the dance with her. After her fright with the whisperer she had determined not to indulge in frivolous flirtation but now, suffering from pique, she forgot.

"The waltz is very graceful, is it not," she said, hoping her tone did not betray her thoughts as she watched the earl and the widow.

"Beautiful," he agreed, "but not perhaps quite proper."

He seemed to feel as he ought, she thought approvingly. But then her eyes strayed to the dancers, and she wished she were twirling with Lord Wraybourne.

"Do you not dance it then, Sir?"

He smiled a little guiltily. "Of course I do. I would happily dance it with you, Miss Sandiford. Whoever said that what was proper was most fun?"

Jane was taken aback. This was not Sir Tristram talking. She remembered then that flirtation could be dangerous and would have drawn back except that she saw Lord Wraybourne say something smilingly to his partner and deduced from the way the lady preened that she had been complimented—just as Jane had been at The Middlehouse.

One of hundreds, she remembered, for the first time in days.

"Do you recommend impropriety then?" she asked lightly.

Mr. Carruthers turned his soulful eyes on her. "I could never recommend it," he said. "But I am human enough to desire it from time to time."

This was definitely going too far. Jane retreated. "I fear you forget that my marriage day is set, Sir."

"How could I when it is the source of my greatest anguish, Miss Sandiford?"

"Mr. Carruthers, you must not!"

"Miss Sandiford, I cannot help it. Nor can you forbid me my feelings."

And what of Jane's feelings—the sudden mixture of panic and excitement—to be so loved that someone suffered! But, if she permitted this to continue, she could not reconcile it with her conscience. She might be expected to *do* something, and she had no wish to. Sir Tristram knew the rules, but did Mr. Carruthers? Then, the terrifying suspicion came upon her. Could Mr. Carruthers be the whispering intruder? She had no way of knowing for certain, but her behavior with this man could have caused her to receive such an insult in the first place. She must cease this foolishness at once.

She said firmly, "I *can* forbid you to express those feelings, Mr. Carruthers," and turned the conversation to more impersonal subjects.

Thus, Jane succeeded in controlling one admirer, but he was soon replaced by another. She now detected innuendo and insult in the most harmless gallantries, fuel for the whisperer in every admiring glance. The crowd of enthusiastic admirers which surrounded her and Sophie at every intermission had become not a joy but a torment. In her attempt to avoid any imprudence, her manner turned as cool as her mother's, earning Jane approval from the high-sticklers but strange looks from her contemporaries.

She greeted Lord Wraybourne with great relief when he came to take her in to supper and found him a comfortable and unalarming companion, compared with some of the others. An hour in his company along with Sophie, Lord Trenholme, and the Ashby party restored Jane's equanimity, and the rest of the evening went much more smoothly. She did not detect that Lord Wraybourne, seeing her distress, had carefully orchestrated these later dances so that her partners were only those who could be trusted to hold the line.

The next morning the Marlborough Square house was full of flowers. Of all those directed to Jane, Lord Wraybourne's were the most beautiful. He had sent her freesias in a silver holder, and the perfume filled the drawing room. Mr. Carruthers had sent her rather overblown pink roses. Sophie disregarded her masses of blooms, including a prim collection of red roses from Trenholme and some showy lilies from Sir Edwin, in favor of a small pot of primroses from Lord Randal.

"They remind me of the flowers at Stenby," she said simply.

From this, Jane deduced that there was still no impression on the beauty's heart. Flowers were forgotten, however, when she found that her riding dress had been delivered. Madame Danielle must have bullied the habit-maker unmercifully to have accomplished such a wonder in so short a time. It was made of a brown fabric so dark as to be almost black and dragoon-trimmed with gold braid. It was accompanied by a shako-style hat with a high plume and dark leather gloves fastened by gold tassels.

Jane immediately sent round a note to Lord Wraybourne to inform him of the delivery, and the footman returned with a reply which invited Jane and Sophie to ride with the earl that afternoon. Sophie was quite willing to fall in with this arrangement and full of praise for Madame Danielle.

"I must have a habit in the same style," she declared. "Mine is quite dowdy by comparison."

As hers was both new and very becoming, this was not entirely true, though it did lack the panache of Jane's. Still, Lady Harroving was not enthusiastic.

"I am not sure that it is proper, Jane," she said. "One would think you were in the military!"

"But the military is all the rage, Maria," protested Sophie. "With so many brave men fighting in the Peninsular we must show our admiration as best we can."

Lady Harroving pinched her lips. "You should ask David for his opinion, Jane," she said. "Be guided by him."

Jane felt slightly mutinous but said nothing, and her betrothed seemed only admiring when he saw her in her finery. Jane was, in turn, overcome when she saw the beautiful mare that Lord Wraybourne had provided for her use. The white-footed chestnut was a Thoroughbred with a dancing step and an elegantly curved neck.

"She is a darling," exclaimed Jane as she stroked the velvety nose and was gently butted in return. "What is her name?"

"That is for you to say," Lord Wraybourne replied. "She is yours."

Jane was almost speechless to be favored with such a gift—and such consideration for her needs. Had he remembered their conversation at The Middlehouse?

"Thank you," she murmured, swallowing her tears. "I cannot think of a name just now."

"I am sure she can survive without one for a little while," he replied as he tossed her into the saddle. "I believe her former owner called her Mitchin, for reasons known only to himself."

"How terrible to have had to part with her," said Jane, already in love with the sweet-natured beast.

"No tragedy, I can assure you. She was owned by a young man who simply grew too large. But she has been used to being a gentleman's darling and thrives on attention."

"She will have all she wants," promised Jane fervently. She guided the horse over to Sophie and Lord Randal for their admiration.

"Well, she is a handsome gift," approved Sophie. "I was beginning to think, brother, that you were a little lacking in gallantry."

"Jane had need of a horse," he said carelessly. "I would hardly wish to see her on a hired hack, and I would like to breed the mare to Abdullah. She is sired by Markham out of Negrina."

This immediately caused the two gentlemen to become involved in a complex analysis of equine bloodlines and dissipated some of the euphoria for Jane. So he had just been buying bloodstock, had he? No doubt it was an afterthought to allow her the privilege of riding the animal. Despite her hopes, she still had no evidence that he held her in anything more than regard. His kindness was, of course, appreciated, but it was not at all what Jane desired.

L ORD WRAYBOURNE RETURNED from the ride in a pensive mood. Who would have thought that Jane Sandiford would give him so much trouble? It was becoming
increasingly difficult to handle her with a light rein, particularly when she became cool as she had this morning.
At first, she had been warm and responsive. Yet, moments
later, he could have been a stranger. It was damned tempting to seduce her to the softness he knew was in her and
make her fall in love with him; but she was so new to Society, so innocent, that he feared he would alarm her. Look
how easily she had been overset by a few enthusiastic gallants last night. He must give her a little time, but he'd
also be grateful for a reason to be out of Town often in the
coming weeks. The excuse came later that day, when he
received a note from his uncle, asking the earl's presence

at his office. He found Mr. Moulton-Scrope in a state of agitation.

"There's been another one," he said. "Gel fought him off, which brought some passersby running, but not before he'd stunned her with his usual blow. Poor young thing came to to find herself the center of a crowd with her gown ripped and disarranged but her virtue intact. Of course, there was no keeping it quiet."

"Was he caught?"

Mr. Moulton-Scrope shook his head. "He was off in his carriage, and the description of that you wouldn't believe. It could be a brougham or a hackney, but it would seem he wasn't the driver. So there's an accomplice we might get at."

"What of the victim? Can she help us?"

"She was distraught. I'm hoping we can talk to her later. Now tell me if you've anything to add from your work."

Lord Wraybourne shrugged. "I am now an authority on the subject of lavender water. Yesterday I visited Steele and Meyer's, the largest manufacturer of the stuff in England."

"And?"

"The villain is either a randy septuagenarian or was given it by an aged aunt. The stuff is favored by the older set."

"Hardly useful. I have cupboards full of useless gifts from elderly relatives myself."

"So has everyone," agreed his nephew. He smiled. "I remember Randal's expression when his grandmother presented him with a flagon of the stuff."

His uncle's eyes narrowed. "Now he's a pretty wild one."

"Don't be absurd!"

"Just because he's a friend of yours don't mean Lord Randal is above suspicion."

"He is as much above suspicion as I am."

"Never heard that you went to Bar Street orgies. I've even heard talk of sodomy."

"You are misinformed," said Lord Wraybourne icily and then added with exasperation, "Randal is just a lodestone for ridiculous rumors. He could hardly be an *habitué* of the Bar Street Tavern and an unnatural!"

"Does seem unlikely," replied his uncle, unrepentant, "but he's been to Bar Street at least once. There was a raid. All the gentlemen slipped the jarveys a few golden boys and no more was said, but a list of the names was sent to us. You'd be amazed at some of our lists."

"The filth in your environment is no concern of mine."

Mr. Moulton-Scrope regarded his angry nephew ruefully. He had no wish to alienate him. "Are you going to wash your hands of me?"

"Damn you, no," said Lord Wraybourne with a reluctant grin. "But no more about Randal. The idea is ridiculous. He must find his normal amatory adventures sufficiently exhausting, without trailing unwilling women all over Town!"

"With his reputation, I'm surprised you let him run wild around Miss Sandiford and Sophie."

"Jane's in no danger from him. He's a true friend. As for Sophie, she regards him as another brother."

"He might be honorable but that don't mean Jane won't fall in love with him. I have to admit that he's an engaging rogue, and Sophie's growing up fast. What if one day she realizes that he's not her brother?"

Lord Wraybourne shrugged. "If Sophie ever looked to Randal as a husband she'd have a long wait, Uncle. He's not the marrying kind. All he wants is a set of colors and a quick passage to the Peninsular."

"Ashby wants a commission? Then why in tarnation doesn't he go instead of wasting his high spirits on us?"

"The duke is determined on a grandson. Randal's older brother Chelmly doesn't seem inclined to marry. Until he does and produces sons, Randal is refused permission to risk his neck in the war."

"If he had real spirit he'd go and be damned to the duke."

Lord Wraybourne smiled. "It's not like you, Uncle, to recommend such unfilial behavior. The duke is not a well man, and he suffers spasms whenever he's crossed. It is to Randal's credit that he doesn't relish having his father's death on his plate."

"Maybe so," muttered the older man, "but I'd still not want him around Sophie if I were you."

"If there was any suggestion of attraction, I would agree with you, Uncle. Randal is not what I would want for Sophie. Not because of his morals—he plays his games with women who know the rules—but because of his recklessness. Even if he never gets to the war, he's hey-go-mad for any crazy scheme. I probably shouldn't tell you this—you'll doubtless put it on one of your lists—but he was off with the free traders once last year, just to see what it was like. Now he's full of plans to go up in a Montgolfier balloon. No, he wouldn't do for Sophie. Thank God there's no question of it. They both need to be joined to a sober head. I have great hopes that Trenholme will come up to scratch. He would handle Sophie gently but firmly. As it is, Randal is an excellent escort, and his sisters are unexceptionable companions for Jane and Sophie."

"Quite so, quite so." Mr. Moulton-Scrope decided it was time to return to less heated topics. "So lavender water is a dead end?"

"Not necessarily. Remember, our villain *uses* his lavender water. Unfortunately, there are enough like him to make it impossible to arrest every young man who does so, though Brummell would approve. God, even that model of prosy rectitude, Edwin Hever, drenches himself with the stuff. It would almost be worth arresting him just to puncture his intolerable self-importance."

"It seems to me," said his uncle severely, "that you approach this with too much levity. Did the records of the previous assaults help you? I suppose you did read them?"

"Certainly I did, but a more pathetic set of documents it is hard to imagine. Place, time, name. That's about it. There must have been more information to find."

"Well, the young ladies would be upset, and their families wouldn't want them bothered. They could hardly be asked for details."

"How else are we to get those details?" asked Lord Wraybourne with asperity. "Everyone is too busy tiptoeing around. I suggest you ask the latest victim some real questions, such as how tall he was, how strong. She must have noticed something."

A little gleam came into Mr. Moulton-Scrope's eyes. "Well now, David. Who better than yourself? A peer of the realm. Miss Hamilton will doubtless be flattered—"

"Who?" Lord Wraybourne jerked to attention.

"A Miss Stella Hamilton. She lives in Clarke Street with a brother who is some kind of poet."

"I know," said Lord Wraybourne, wrathfully. "She is a friend. Damnation!"

Mr. Moulton-Scrope watched this transformation with interest. Now, perhaps, his lordship would apply himself to the problem.

"Of course I'll talk to her. I'll talk to all the others too. This has got to stop."

Mr. Moulton-Scrope put on a contented smile as his angry nephew strode out. There'd be action at last.

Lord Wraybourne went straight to Clarke Street, where he found his friend John Hamilton in an angry, frustrated state. They had been friends since their days in Trinity, and Lord Wraybourne knew that his stolid build hid a gentleness that would be bewildered by violence in his family. He suspected that Stella Hamilton would be better able to handle the attack upon her than her brother. But when he asked to see her and John's wife, Emily, went upstairs, she returned with the message that her sister-in-law thanked him for his visit but did not feel able to see anyone just yet.

However, as he left the house and walked down the

road, deep in thought, he was called from one of the ginnels which ran through to the rear of the terraced houses. It was Miss Hamilton. He went to her and expressed his concern.

"Thank you," she said with a wan smile. She was normally a pretty woman with a smooth complexion and soft brown hair. Now she was pale and strained, and her hair was partially covered with a bandage, inadequately concealed by a ribboned cap. "My sister-in-law refused to let me come down. She said that I was too weak, but it is really that she is ashamed of me. In some way she blames me for this."

"She cannot possibly," he protested.

"But she does," she said, eyes filling. "I am now a fallen woman in her eyes. She will not let the children near me."

As the tears poured from her eyes, he opened his arms. After a moment's hesitation, she fell into them and sobbed painfully. Apart from drawing her back into the shade of the passageway so that they would be unobserved, he let her be. Eventually, she drew away and accepted his handkerchief.

"I have drenched your coat," she said between blows of her nose. "I am sure it was dreadfully expensive."

"I am delighted to put it to your service. Do you need to leave your home for a while?" he asked directly. "I could find you a place to stay."

"Oh no," she said but with gratitude. "Emily is only suffering from shock in her own way. It is not every day that one of the family is found sprawled in the public street with her skirt up high and her bodice half off." She gave a gallant attempt at a laugh which sounded more like a gulp. "She will soon come about. And John has been nothing but kindness. It is just that he feels he has failed me in some way. Men are very foolish."

"This man too," he said, "and with more cause. I too feel that I have failed you, Stella."

"But why?"

"My uncle sought to interest me in the investigation, and I regarded it as an idle pastime, rather like an acrostic. Now I take it more seriously."

"You are investigating this, David?"

"Yes, forgive my arrogance. You are not the first lady to be attacked, Stella. The others did not escape so soon. I may be able to do nothing, but I will try. I need to talk to you about the attack as soon as possible. I warn you, I intend to squeeze out every bit of information you have."

"It all happened so fast," she said doubtfully. "All I really remember is the hoarse whispering before he struck." She shuddered at the memory, then continued gallantly, "But it would be better to try now, would it not? It is horrible to think of these attacks continuing, I will get my shawl and tell Emily. She cannot hold me prisoner, after all. Then, maybe we can walk in the park." In a few moments she exited by the front door and tucked her arm in his.

Jane watched this encounter from the opposite side of the street from the bow window of the rooms which housed Lady Sophie's old governess. Or her favorite of them, as she had confessed.

"I lost count of them. I was very good at dispatching the undesirables. I let Miss Randolf stay because she let me be. She is sweet, and I usually visit her when I am in Town."

Jane had been pleased to agree to accompany Sophie and see a little more of London than Mayfair. The governess's rooms were cozy and situated upon a new terrace of gray brick houses. The area had a comfortable feel. Children played in the street and cheerful servants went busily about their tasks.

Jane was watching the maids come out of the houses to get milk from the goat and cow being led down the street when she saw Lord Wraybourne walking along. He went into a house opposite. She thought that, if he left at the same time she and Sophie did, they might take him up. Such a simple notion to summon up the familiar excitement.

After a brief time, however, he exited. She saw him turn and go towards a passageway between the houses. A young woman fell into his arms, and he drew her back into the shadows. Jane felt a shock so great she had to clench her fingers to stop them trembling. She was grateful that Sophie was chattering away and paying no attention.

It was one thing to be willing to wait for his love to grow, quite another to see him with someone else. How dare he deceive her so? If he wanted to marry some other woman, there had been no one to stop him. But a woman from Clarke Street would have no money—at least, none to compare to the Sandiford fortune. The Kyles, according to Sophie, married money even if they had no need of it. How terribly Jane's mother had been deceived in her inquiries. Mrs. Danvers, this woman, who knew how many others there might be? Sophie had not exaggerated when she spoke of the hundreds of his victims. The man was nothing more than a mercenary rake, despite his rank and elegant exterior.

Hiding her pain, Jane did her best to take a composed farewell of Miss Randolf and listen calmly to Sophie's chatter all the way home. Jane also kept her eyes glued to the street, in watch for her perfidious betrothed and his secret love.

≈ 10 ≈

I T WAS FROM this date that the social career of Jane Sandiford and Lady Sophie Kyle began to turn outrageous.
Society watched with disapproval, envy, or admiration as
the pair enlivened every occasion, and talk was not lessened by the fact that Lord Wraybourne was conspicuous
by his absence. In fact, there were some who said that such
a high-stickler must be disgusted by the behavior of his
betrothed.

Jane was aware of this. Lady Harroving took delight in
telling her. Jane had not seen Lord Wraybourne since that
day in Clarke Street and had received only a note explain-
ing that he was called out of Town on business. That he
should go off casually with his lover, mistress, or whatever
she was and leave Jane to be the butt of such talk; that he
should not be nearby to see what a success she was, how

many admirers she had, what a beauty she was considered; that he should not be available to be spurned by her—all these were intolerable. She could not deny him her fortune and her pedigree, but she could deny him the rectitude he had supposedly valued.

She was unmoved by his attempt to court her at a distance. Every few days a package would arrive for her. Each contained a small gift and a note of further apology. She was at first tempted to smash each one. Instead, she brought them out before guests as evidence of his devotion and put on airs of being desolated by his absence. In fact, there was no acting involved, for her foolish heart did miss him. It had occurred to her, chillingly, that he might be sincerely attached to his latest love and regretting his betrothal. That thought was more intolerable than his absence.

She was bound to him far more than she wished and would be torn to shreds if he abandoned her. There had been some warmth between them. It could not all have been false. Surely, given a chance, she could fan the coals into a warmer flame. If he came back and asked to be released from the engagement, she determined to refuse. To strengthen her resolve she showed Society a devoted face. Her betrothal was not one in which the termination would be accepted with a shrug.

In the meantime, seeking to hurt the one who hurt her, she took great delight in causing talk, not by involvement with other men but by general misbehavior. She knew Lord Wraybourne would hate it, especially when she and Sophie almost caused a riot at Drury Lane during a particularly poor performance of *Hamlet* which someone had been inspired to sweeten by giving Hamlet and Ophelia a happy relationship.

"I really do not know why we are here," Sophie giggled as Hamlet danced a cotillion on stage with Ophelia. "This is ridiculous. Shakespeare would be affronted at what they are doing to his play."

Lord Trenholme smiled. "Certainly more like Beau Brummell than the Gloomy Dane. Do you think he will manage to kill anyone?"

"Oh, I doubt it," said Jane. "He will marry Ophelia, his uncle will abdicate, and they'll all live happily forever."

Lady Harroving hushed them. "People are staring!"

"Good," said Sophie. "I am sure we are more entertaining than the actors. Oh, look. There is Major Heckleton waving."

She waved back, and soon half the gentlemen in the pit were blowing kisses and shouting greetings to her.

"Sophie, stop that immediately," hissed her ladyship. "The actors look very cross. Jane, behave, please. What will David think?"

This was quite the wrong thing to say if Lady Harroving really intended to curb her charges. Jane, who had to this point been only a spectator to Sophie's mischief, now joined in. As she leaned forward to wave to a handsome captain, a rose worked loose from her posy and fell into the pit. Immediately, a number of gallants struggled for possession. Jane watched in horrified fascination as a fight broke out below. This was going too far. She drew back hastily. Sophie, on the other hand, appeared to have no qualms at all. Bright-eyed, she pulled a bloom from her own bouquet.

Lord Trenholme tried to stop her. "Lady Sophie, you must not."

"Must I not?" she said, chin very high. "Are you jealous, My Lord? Here, you may have this one."

She thrust it into his hand, then turned to toss the rest, but he firmly wrenched the flowers from her. Sophie glared at him, and he stared icily back. Jane waited for the explosion, but at that moment they all became aware of pandemonium in the theater.

The Cyprians who used the theater as a place to display their wares had not been pleased to have attention drawn from them by the well-bred part of the audience and could tell a good move when they saw one. Blooms were now showering the pit from all their boxes. Below, noncombatants were scrambling to safety while young bucks leaped from boxes to join in the fray. More sober people exited as quickly as they could, and the management had lowered the curtain.

In the Harroving box, Lady Harroving was trying to drag her party away, but her husband seemed to think he was at a mill and hung over the edge to cheer on his favorites. Jane and Sophie were watching too and laughed at the mayhem, while Lord Trenholme, sternly disapproving, incongruously clutched Sophie's bunch of violets. Mr. Carruthers, the third escort, seemed undecided. He joined Lord Trenholme in disapproval but found that gentleman taciturn and so commiserated with Lady Harroving, who commanded him to convince Sophie and Jane to leave.

But when he went to the front of the box, he became caught up in the sport and laid bets with Sir Arthur as to victors.

"I say, Miss Sandiford," he said. "If you are giving out your roses, you might give one to me."

Jane smiled without mirth. Her interest in Mr. Carruthers had evaporated when she had faced real problems. Though she permitted his occasional attendance at Lady Harroving's urging, she now found the young man tedious.

"There is a positive flower garden below, Sir. Go join in the melee." When he hesitated she laughed out loud. "Pudding heart! Sophie, I really think we have had all the amusement possible. Do let us go."

"Oh, very well. I'm sure Lord Trenholme longs to leave." She gave that gentleman a very saucy look as she swept past.

As is often the case with brawls, the origins never became clear to most people. Still, the rumor was put about that Jane and Sophie were in some way concerned, and that added to their reputations . . . as did the day they raced their horses in the park, allowing their court of hussars to place bets on the outcome. All the soldiers had been pledged to secrecy, but somehow the tale got out. Though most people discounted it, it was added to the tally by those inclined to be censorious. At one tedious musical evening, the young ladies organized an impromptu treasure hunt, though in truth Lord Randal had more to do with it than Jane or Sophie. He protested afterwards he had no idea that a number of guests had slipped away for clandestine amorous meetings, but at least one duel was fought as a result of that night's entertainment.

That was also the occasion upon which the whisperer chose to torment Jane again.

Despite the license she was allowing herself, Jane had been careful not to be alone. She did not desire any true scandal *or* a reencounter with the whisperer. On this occasion, however, searching with Sophie for a brass monkey supposedly to be found in one of the reception rooms, Jane had become separated from her friend. She gave the matter no thought until the noxiously familiar sibilance drew ragged through the air once more.

"Poor neglected one. Do you need consoling?"

Jane whirled around. Her situation was this time much worse. There was only one door, and the menace must be outside it. Where was Sophie?

"I caught your rose at the theater. Do I not deserve your bud? So sweet and moist . . ."

Jane thrust her hand over her mouth. His words made no sense. He was mad. Still, the touch of spittle in the whisper was disgusting. She could feel nausea beginning to rise and backed as far away from the door as possible.

"Snuff the candle, sweeting, and I'll come to you. You'll not be so wild when I have hold of you. But I'm afraid you've been naughty, my lovely. So a few strikes of the whip before the pleasure. You and Sophie both. The whip and then the pleasure . . ."

"Jane."

Sophie's voice calling cheerily broke into the macabre situation like sunlight into a tomb. Then Jane realized that her friend could be coming into danger and, forgetting her fear, ran forward to warn her. Jane emerged into an empty hall as Sophie walked out of a room opposite.

"I found the monkey. It was tiny. No wonder . . . Why Jane, whatever is the matter?"

Jane pressed fingers to her forehead to summon her thoughts. The violence in the whisperer this time had truly horrified her, and Sophie must be warned.

"Did you see anyone?"

"When? Randal is not far away and Crossley Carruthers searched my room before I did. He didn't find the monkey. And I just sent Hever off with a flea in his ear after he read me a lecture about my behavior."

Carruthers again. Had Jane so offended him by her flirtation that she had driven him to this insanity? She quickly told Sophie what had happened, both encounters with the whisperer, but mentioned nothing of her suspicions.

Sophie pulled a face. "Ugh. Nasty. But I don't see how anyone could hurt you here. You would only have to scream, though I can see why you did not."

"It must be my fault. My behavior is causing this."

"Don't be a goose. For all we know, this man is playing his tricks on dozens of women, each one too embarrassed to tell anyone. I shall tell Randal."

Jane relaxed under her friend's matter-of-fact tone. Of course. Lord Randal would know what to do; and he would doubtless tell Lord Wraybourne, a task Jane did not relish. The men would handle it, and she would be most careful never to be alone again.

However, she still could not quite convince herself that

her unruly behavior was not in some way responsible for the whisperer's unwanted attentions. She was already uncomfortable with the notoriety she and Sophie were achieving, and Jane's tender conscience had been afflicted when she learned that one young gallant at the theater had broken his arm in the *bataille des fleurs,* as the wags had termed it. Furthermore, she shuddered to think of the repercussions when her parents got wind of her doings. The whole point had been to strike back in some way at her betrothed, but in his continued absence that was futile. She resolved to put foolishness behind her and behave more properly in future.

Despite Jane's good intentions and her resolute adherence to them, real disaster almost struck at the Faverstowe Ball.

Lady Faverstowe's ball was a very ordinary social occasion. Neither Jane nor Sophie, who was out of spirits, intended mayhem. At supper Jane took care to sit down with the quieter military gentlemen and the Ashby sisters, whom she liked very well. They were known to have a restraining influence on the company they kept. But a dispute broke out among the officers in their escort.

As voices became heated, Jane leaned forward to intervene, anxious to avoid another scene. "Gentlemen! We cannot have this dispute. Explain your altercation to us, and we will attempt to resolve it."

Hotly, Major Heckleton spoke up. "Fallwell here will just not admit the truth. At Valladolid a few months ago we were given a choice of billets. From the outside the houses looked the same, but I found myself sharing quarters with a half-mad old couple who lived on gruel. He settled in with a family of pretty daughters who could cook like angels. I don't object to him taking the advantage," he continued angrily. "But I wish he would admit that he had prior information and not say it was just his good fortune."

"And I wish *you* would accept my word," replied the Irish captain in disgust. "I tell you I have the gift. If that is prior information, I admit it. But other than that I had none."

"Gammon! No one can be expected to believe such stuff," snapped the major. "Next you'll be telling fortunes at the fair."

The captain colored angrily and would have risen had Lady Caroline not pulled him back. "Perhaps you can show your skills here, Captain Fallwell," she said gently.

"I am not a fairground performer," he retorted bitterly. But after some persuasion he agreed to attempt his inspired guesswork if anyone could think of something not known to all.

"It must be something close by," he declared.

A number of suggestions were made—colors of handkerchiefs, coins in pockets, but these were rejected as being too easy to guess or possibly known. Then someone, it was never recalled who, said, "Tell us the color of Miss Sandiford's garters!"

Some were taken aback but others acclaimed the suggestion mightily. Rather pink, the young captain protested that Miss Sandiford would not agree and certainly the Ashby sisters looked horror-struck.

Jane had opened her mouth to refuse but she could

sense the explosive nature of the atmosphere around her. She glanced about for guidance.

Lord Randal would know how to handle this situation. He had been seated only a few tables away with Sophie and some others. Now she saw only Sophie watching the scene with amusement, and realized that soon other people would be drawn by the raised voices. She just wanted this scene over before it attracted more notice.

"I am perfectly willing for the test to go on," she said quietly, "as long as my word is taken as to who is the winner. I assure you no one has seen my garters this evening and no one is going to."

It was agreed that Captain Fallwell should write his guess on a card and then Miss Sandiford would give them the answer. As the captain sat and thought, Jane silently begged him to hurry. She did not notice Lady Caroline and Lady Cecilia slip away.

When he had finally written his prediction, Jane said, "Silver lace" and Captain Fallwell shouted in triumph. Picking up his card he showed the word "silver" upon it. In the midst of the exclamations and reconciliations Lady Harroving surged forward with the concerned Ashby sisters behind. With horrified exclamations and apologies she managed to convince everybody that she was covering up a scandal.

"Jane, Sophie, we must leave!" she whispered, amazingly loudly. They found themselves hurried along, Sophie protesting but Jane trying not to make the scene worse.

"Good evening." The three ladies looked up to see Lord Wraybourne at his most sartorially perfect, smiling at them with just a touch of amazement.

"David, thank heavens!" gasped Lady Harroving.

"Thank heavens, indeed," echoed Sophie angrily. "Maria has gone mad!"

Jane merely stared at him in mute horror. This was not how she had planned to face him when he finally deigned to return. He quickly assessed the situation and made a small gesture. A moment later, Sophie was being led off by Lord Randal, the two chattering amiably as usual, and Lady Harroving was dismissed to the card room, her favorite haunt. Lord Wraybourne held out his arm and Jane hesitantly placed hers upon it. Casually, they began to stroll around the room.

"Smile, Jane. Whatever has been happening will disappear under a smile. And you really should look pleased to see me, you know."

Jane was about to protest, but she realized that he was right on all points. It was essential that she appear pleased to see him if they were to avoid a scandal, and there was no need of pretense. Despite his behavior and her hurt, her unruly heart was humming to be with him again. He was even handsomer than she remembered. His lazy eyes held that touch of humor and hint of strength. Excitement was once again sizzling from the brief point of contact, her hand upon his sleeve.

Still, he did not deserve to know quite how she felt and so she merely said, through smiling lips, "Lady Harroving made a simple matter into a major scandal."

"Then we had better smile a lot, I suppose," he remarked dryly.

Jane detected a note of censure in his voice, and that

strengthened her resolve to remain cool. What right had he to censure her? She had not imagined that scene in Clarke Street. She raised her chin and looked at him, still smiling but tauntingly. Attack is the best form of defense, she reminded herself.

"It will take a great deal of good humor to wipe out your absence these past ten days."

His smile did not waver, but an arrested look came into his eyes to be quickly hidden by lowered lids. "Don't fight with me here, Jane. Tell me instead about Mrs. Cuthbert's musical *soirée*. From the gossip, I regret missing it. Was Admiral Finchley really found with Lady Storr?"

Jane giggled as he had intended. "So they say, but it was smoothed over. Of course, there can have been nothing to it. They are both so amazingly old. But Lord Randal says a duel between a Mr. Morgan and a Captain Youngman all came about because of that night. They both fired into the air."

"Very wise. As I remember, Mrs. Cuthbert's musical *soirées* deserve to be livened up in some way. If you are free tomorrow night, I would like to take you to hear some real music. A friend of mine holds impromptu musical evenings every Friday."

Jane remembered the other occurrence at the *soirée* and wondered nervously whether Lord Randal had told him of the whisperer yet and if Lord Wraybourne considered her at fault in laying herself open to such insult. Her stability was further undermined by his free hand, which he had placed over hers. He was gently teasing her fingers, to amazing effect, and Jane found herself staring up at him as if mesmerized. Clarke Street, she said to herself, like a defensive incantation, but it did no good.

She dragged her mind back to his invitation for a musical evening. "I would like that," she said softly.

"Good." He held her attention a moment longer, knowing the impression they were creating of a couple deeply bound up in each other. Then he broke the contact gently.

"A set is forming. Will you dance with me, Jane?"

She agreed. She knew she really should be very angry with him, and yet she could not manage that at the moment. She told herself that she was helping him to ease away the scandal but acknowledged that she had little control over her actions. All her confused feelings suddenly focused. She loved him. She could not possibly give him up to another woman. Jane would make him love her in return. These past weeks in Society had built her self-confidence and convinced her that she had attractions other than birth and money. Unconsciously, her hold upon his arm tightened and he looked down. As they moved into their places in the set he kissed her hand and gave her a warm and genuine smile. He could not possibly be indifferent, she told herself, and smile at her like that. Perhaps she would not have too much work to do.

At the end of the set, Lord Wraybourne was satisfied that the scandal had been stillborn. When Crossley Carruthers came up to claim Jane for the country dances, Lord Wraybourne gave her up with only the slightest hesitation. After a moment spent watching them thoughtfully, he moved through the room, exchanging pleasant words and letting drop in many ears how delighted he was with his bride-to-be. Then, he went towards the card room and came upon his cousin, conducting a meaningful flirtation with a military man.

"Good evening, Maria."

"David!" she exclaimed with an uneasy titter. "Allow me to present Colonel Sawyer."

Lord Wraybourne was perfectly polite, but for some reason the colonel decided it would be expedient to move elsewhere for a while.

"Well, really, David," said Lady Harroving, watching the desertion of the military. "That was just becoming promising."

"Does it occur to you that you are quite unsuited to the care of two debutantes?" he said in exasperation.

"All the time," she complained. "I said as much to Aunt Selina, but she begged me so."

"Let us promenade, dear cousin, so that we will be less conspicuous." As they began their leisurely perambulation he said calmly, "Having taken on the post, Maria, I suppose it was too much to expect that you might apply yourself to it?"

"I agreed to bring out Sophie," she said sharply. "She has been no trouble for she knows what she's about and, with her looks and fortune, Society will turn a blind eye to any number of pranks. Heavens, she can even be seen everywhere with Ashby without a brow being raised. Your dear Jane, however, was foisted upon me and has a wild and stubborn streak all of her own. I wish you well of her," she added waspishly.

"Thank you for your felicitations," he said with a dangerous smile. "Speaking of escorts, I would much rather you did not make so much use of Carruthers, Maria."

"But Crossley has such an air," she protested. "If you are tolerant of Ashby, I cannot see why you would balk at Crossley."

"I trust Randal implicitly. I wouldn't trust Carruthers with a bent farthing. I don't actually concern myself that Jane would be imprudent with him, I just do not think it adds to her consequence to be seen with him."

Lady Harroving was not misled into seeing his mild comments as anything less than a command and fury ate at her. "I am amazed you have such trust in the chit! She has no sense of decorum at all. The scandals I have had to avert—"

He cut her off quietly. "I am pleased you have been so assiduous in your duties." She heard the steel beneath the velvet tone. He was not yet ready for outright criticism of the baggage.

"It is all her mother's fault, of course," Lady Harroving said hurriedly. "She has kept her walled up in the country and then turns her loose. She's like a river in flood," she announced with unusual poetry. "There's no stopping her."

He seemed undeterred. "More exciting than a placid brook, don't you think?"

"I have always found a quiet stream most appealing," she persisted, casting a glance at Mrs. Danvers on the dance floor.

"You amaze me," he said with genuine amusement and

added wickedly, "Flood waters, suitably harnessed, can be a powerful benefit to man. Excuse me, Maria. I see the dance has ended. Perhaps I should go and—control the torrent again."

Lady Harroving glared after him in rage. How could men be so stupid?

Her original plan to wreck the betrothal had been idle mischief coupled with the desire to assist her friend to an advantageous match. She was spoiled, however, and the failure of her plans had led to a genuine dislike of Jane. The girl must be a witch to have managed to avoid the nastier traps laid for her.

Jane had happily allowed Lady Harroving to spend vast quantities of her parents' money on clothes but despite encouragement had chosen not a single unsuitable outfit. She had even managed to carry off that Grecian gown, which many a more sophisticated woman would have hesitated to wear, and thus started a minor classical revival.

Lady Harroving had in desperation ordered for her a silk evening gown so fine as to be transparent, with a bodice cut down to the nipples. It had been unworn. Finally she had persuaded the girl to wear it and the wretch had ruined the effect by wearing a heavy slip beneath and a great fichu of lace at the top. There was not even the consolation of her looking ridiculous, which she surely did. The style was taken up, and for days everyone was wearing old-fashioned fichus and calling them Sandiford shawls. It was all too much. Lady Harroving resolved to make a final push to puncture the girl's defenses in some way.

Lady Faverstowe, meanwhile, discovered that her ball

had suddenly soared from a mundane affair to one of the events of the Season. Those who had refused her invitations would be sorry. Delicious rumors of scandal were weaving through the guests. Lady Harroving would have been appalled to know that one version had her tying her garter before a bunch of officers, and Lord Wraybourne, normally the most perfect of gentlemen, was conspicuous by the fact that he refused to dance with anyone except his betrothed. He partnered her four times!

Mrs. Danvers maintained admirable composure in the face of all this, apparently enjoying the company of the ugly but witty Marquis of Dromree, but Lady Harroving was so cross she forgot to pursue the promising colonel and saw him snatched up by another matron. When she slyly attempted to discuss matters with her usual gossips, hoping to make them see the whole business as tawdry, she found them delighted by the romance of it all.

Lord Wraybourne completed his evening's work by sitting out a dance with his sister, to the dismay of her chosen partner for that set.

Deciding that attack was called for, Sophie said, "It is about time that you paid some special attention to Jane."

"It's about time I paid some special attention to you too, I think," he replied without rancor.

"Are you going to be stuffy?"

"Undoubtedly."

"I won't listen to you," she said with a toss of her head.

"Then I will send you back to Bath."

She flushed but retorted with cheek, "I can cut as many rigs in Bath as here, so it will serve no purpose."

"Thank you for warning me. Then you had better stay with Great-Aunt Clara in Yorkshire."

"You *wouldn't*," she declared, eyes wide.

"Do you care to try me?"

"I think you are the horridest brother in the world!"

"I have certainly been the most neglectful. Come now, you can't throw a scene here. I'm not expecting you to become a pattern card of perfection, just be a little more sensible."

She refused to reply, her mouth set.

"I am also hoping," he continued, intending to distract her, having made his point, "that you can make sure Jane does not do anything too outrageous in the next few days."

"Why in the next few days?" she asked, intrigued.

"Because I have to go out of Town again." He raised his hand in acknowledgement of her cry of exasperation.

"This will be my last journey, and it is not so long now before the wedding. I would rather not return to find her off to Gretna with Carruthers."

Sophie nodded with disconcerting maturity. "I'll guard against that," she agreed, "though I truly do not think there is any danger of it. Jane has lost the taste for his flowery compliments and for disorderly behavior. Did Randal tell you of her unpleasant encounters?"

He nodded. "I will handle it, but meanwhile they are not to be taken lightly. Behave correctly and you will both be safe."

"Do you know who it is?" she asked in amazement.

"I have a suspicion. As I said, he will take no risks so do

not be alone with any men and avoid isolation and you will be safe."

"It'll be dreadfully dull," said Sophie with a teasing smile and then added, "Do you truly care for Jane? She deserves to be loved."

"I do truly care," he said and added lightly, "Have you chosen your victim yet? Trenholme has spoken of you frequently."

She raised her chin. "He is far too old. I would drive him distracted."

"He is my age, and you are much of an age with Jane."

"That has nothing to do with it. Would I not drive *you* distracted?"

He was forced to agree, but added, "If you loved, you would mind such a husband, especially if he loved you."

"I do not see how any man can say he loves if he wishes to change his loved one. I will only marry someone who admires me as I am, which Lord Trenholme undoubtedly does not these days."

"Does it not occur to you that such an admirer would not be a reliable husband?"

She was genuinely hurt. "Am I so terrible?"

He reassured her that she was not. "But you cannot be wild forever, Sophie. One day you will wish for peaceful days and a husband you can trust and depend upon, particularly if you have children. If you marry someone who indulges your freakish starts now, you may not like him so well in a few years' time."

She smiled at him, her spirits restored. "Then I must marry someone who will grow sober at the same rate as myself, David. Do not discount my own ability to tame a beast. I have my counterpart in mind, but I shall not tell you his name yet. So do not tease me."

"Do you mean to say he's not yet enslaved?" he asked in astonishment. "I didn't think there was a man in Town who was not at your feet. I understand any number have been trying to catch me in Alton Street."

"Then kindly continue your wanderings. You will only have to tell them all there is no hope."

"What of the Chosen One?"

"He would not be so stuffy. He will sweep me off my feet."

"Is he suitable?" he asked. "I will not permit a misalliance, Sophie."

She burst into genuine laughter. "Do you not know me, brother? Of course he is suitable!"

"And not yet in your trap?"

"If he was to be so easily caught, I would probably not want him quite so much."

Lord Wraybourne escorted the Marlborough Square party home. Lady Harroving was disconcerted to find that he expected to be invited in.

"It is very late, David."

"It is not yet two. The night is young," he replied amiably. "I have a mind to speak with Jane."

Lady Harroving sent Sophie to her bed and then, her every step speaking annoyance, she led them to a small saloon. Lord Wraybourne surveyed the faded carpet, plain green walls, and sparse furnishings through his quizzing glass.

"Presumably your room for receiving the better sort of tradesmen, Maria," he remarked. "Never mind. It will suffice." He then gently turned her towards the door. "Now you can send the servants to their beds. When you are sure they are out of the way, I suggest you follow their example."

"You can't expect me to leave you two alone here at this hour!" she exclaimed, her color high.

"Goodness! So suddenly particular. You can't seriously believe that I intend Jane any harm, and if you handle the servants there will be no scandal."

"I would prefer," she said with icy determination, "that you call in the morning."

"I don't give a damn what you prefer," he replied without heat and took a pinch of snuff.

"Jane," the lady said sternly. "You will go to your room immediately."

Jane, whose eyes were bright with enjoyment of the scene and excited anticipation of what might be to come, lowered her lids demurely. "I do not think I ought, Lady Harroving."

Defeated on all fronts, the lady of the house swept out without a word. Lord Wraybourne turned to his betrothed with a smile that made her catch her breath and held out his hand.

"There's no guarantee she will arrange matters so that the servants will be unaware of this little tryst," he said. "We might cause a scandal."

She had placed her hand in his trustingly but now she drew back. "Are you being sarcastic?"

"Now why would you think that?" he asked, recapturing her and leading her to a sofa.

Jane's heart was thundering, and she felt as if she could scarcely breathe. Yet, it seemed important to attempt a casual manner.

"Because everyone is always telling me I'm going to create a scandal."

"How very bothersome of them."

"Yes, it is," she agreed as she sat down, studying him through her lowered lashes. Had he only brought her here to give her a scold? She could not bear it. "And if they weren't forever telling me not to do things, I would doubtless go on a lot better."

His lips twitched a little as he sat beside her. "I had no idea Maria could be so strict."

"Oh, not her. In fact I think her wits are lacking." Jane looked at him. "I'm sorry if you do not like it, but she is rather stupid. She seems to have no idea of the difference between her position and my own."

"What do you mean by that?" he asked, moving closer and making it difficult for her to marshal her thoughts.

Part of her mind was on the conversation but a large part was considering what she should do in order to capture his affection from the woman in Clarke Street.

"She expects me to wear gowns more suitable for her than for me," she babbled, eyes fixed on his wonderful face. "In fact, they are not really suitable for any lady. And she tried to . . . Oh!" she gasped and words escaped her as he dropped a number of kisses on her fingers. How could she possibly think?

"My goodness, am I disturbing you again?" he asked with smiling eyes.

"Very much," she breathed, his face inches from her own.

Was he going to kiss her? Please, he *must* kiss her. Was it perhaps like a handshake? Did the lady have to make the first move? Only half-consciously, she swayed closer. But he did not take her lips immediately. He merely brushed them lightly with his own.

"I wonder I can still have such an effect now that you know so many handsome men."

The aroma of his skin and the warmth of his breath seemed to melt her like wine. Why did he not kiss her? She was beyond *repartee* and gazed at him mutely. He lowered his lips and kissed her fully.

Her mouth opened to his, and her body pressed nearer. She felt wonderfully as if she had found home on a bleak and icy day. Her fingers tangled in his crisp curls, and their rough texture was exquisite. Her touch wandered downward to the smooth skin of his nape. The sensation sent tremors through her, causing her to clutch him to her. When he drew back she resisted, but he gently put her away.

"Though I hate to admit it," he said huskily, "Maria had the right of it. We are playing with fire."

"I like it," she replied, gazing at him, her hands still resting on his arms. "Now I am cold."

He rose and crossed the room. She followed him with her eyes, newly aware of his body in motion: his long, well-muscled legs, the taper from his shoulders to his hips, the clean line of his jaw. He fetched her Norwich shawl from a chair and draped it round her shoulders. His fingers moved for a moment at the back of her neck, causing shivers down her spine, then were gone.

He walked to the door and turned. "Randal told me of your unpleasant experiences. I believe I will be able to put a stop to them, but it would be wiser to avoid being unaccompanied, particularly if you leave the house."

"You think he might follow me?" asked Jane with a squeak of fright in her voice.

"It is a remote possibility only. Did anything about the voice suggest the speaker to you?"

Jane thought and then shook her head. "It is only an assumption that it was a man. A woman would never say such things, but it was someone who knew of my affairs to some extent."

"I think you can be sure it was a man so do not go apart with any gentleman, however safe he might seem to be."

Jane elevated her chin slightly. This cool discussion across the width of the room was rasping on her sensitized nerves, and she was remembering his less-than-perfect behavior.

"I have never done so, except with you, Lord Wraybourne."

A smile stirred his lips. "And see where it led us," he murmured, then continued in his normal manner. "Don't forget that we have an engagement for tomorrow evening, my dear. See if Sophie will come too. A little culture would do her good."

"Very well," she said.

"Then," he confessed, "I have one more journey to make. I should be away no more than a week."

"I have only two more weeks in Town," she protested. Two minutes out of his company was too much.

"We have the rest of our lives ahead of us," he said gently. Then, after a slight pause he added, "Those golden flowers in your hair are beautiful, but I did not give them to you. Will you tell me who did?"

Was he presuming to be jealous? Jane stiffened her resolve. "I will tell you that if you will tell me about your travels," she said stiffly. "You cannot say you are visiting estates because Sir Marius mentioned once that you were in Canterbury and you have no property near there."

Lord Wraybourne's manner turned suddenly distant. "I would not dream of lying to you. I am conducting some business for my uncle."

She knew she had been vulgar in her accusation, but she would not apologize, especially when he had obviously prevaricated in his reply.

"Then why so secret, My Lord?"

"How could I guess you would be interested, Jane?" he said more mildly and then smiled. "Let us not argue, Tiger Eyes. I will tell you every bit of my wanderings when I return, if you wish."

A desire to believe him and fling herself into his arms warred with the need to show him that she could not be manipulated by a kiss and a smile.

"Then that is when I will tell you who gave me these delightful flowers," she said haughtily. "Now go away!"

Lord Wraybourne obliged but did not seem to be cast

down by his dismissal, for he whistled cheerfully as he walked off down the street. Jane lingered for a moment to review the encounter.

She did not think she deceived herself. He did care for her. Could a man care for two women? Or had she perhaps been hasty in her judgement? If the incident in Clarke Street had been innocent—though how that could be was hard to imagine—and if he really was involved in business for his uncle, whom Jane knew to be an important government man, then, perhaps, she had been a ninny and risked disgusting him over nothing.

Jane did not like feeling so confused. She wiped away tears and retired to her virginal bed to suffer very unvirginal dreams.

Lord Wraybourne, meanwhile, felt strangely restless and, consequently, looked in at White's. There he found Sir Marius taking respite from Faro with a glass of brandy and was greeted with a grin.

"I hear you've been making yourself conspicuous by dancing attendance on your betrothed."

"The talk's started already. Excellent."

"I always thought you disliked being the subject of gossip."

Lord Wraybourne poured himself some cognac. "Let us say that I prefer the gossip to be of my choosing."

His friend laughed. "You've certainly handled this in masterly style. Tomorrow, the worst hatchet-wielder won't dare suggest that you want to cry off."

Lord Wraybourne nodded. "I have to thank you for

alerting me to the rumors about Town. I should have realized how it would be."

"Has Miss Sandiford let you off without a scold? How unlike a woman."

Lord Wraybourne smiled fondly into his cognac. "I wouldn't quite say that, but she's welcome to her pound of flesh. Especially as I have one more trip to make."

Sir Marius snorted. "I don't know which of you is more to the loose. She should realize that she'll be getting the best husband around, and you should stop running at your uncle's bidding."

"I run at my own bidding. This man has to be stopped. Did Randal tell you about Jane's experiences?" Lord Wraybourne's face tightened and his blue eyes were no longer lazy but threatened retribution. "It must be the same man. He's too much the coward, of course, to attack a lady but that he would dare speak to her that way is intolerable. He will be stopped."

"You have him?"

"I am so close I can smell him, but the trails cross. Once I talked to the victims scraps of information began to come together, but they lead as well to one man as the other. I have my preference, but proof is needed. I cannot give up now or the next victim will be on my conscience, and I cannot stand by while Jane is distressed. I suspect he knows I'm on his trail because the attacks have stopped, but now I am concerned that he might be impelled by spite to move against Sophie or Jane. If I could find the driver of the carriage, that would clinch things."

Their talk stopped as they were surrounded by friends

and acquaintances. Lord Wraybourne had to suffer a number of warm jokes about his coming nuptials but was at least satisfied that the world believed it to be a love match. When they were alone again he turned to Sir Marius.

"I understand I have to thank you and Randal for watching over Jane."

"Devil a bit," was the cheerful reply. "I think she's able to look after herself. She's trying her wings and not behaving perfectly, but there's sound enough bottom for her to keep straight. I think you're lucky to get a filly with spirit out of that stable. I have come to find her quite a tolerable example of womanhood. For one thing she can talk sensibly when she has a mind to."

"What of Carruthers?" asked Lord Wraybourne.

"She wouldn't choose him over you," scoffed Sir Marius.

Lord Wraybourne could think of a number of cases in which just such peculiar choices had been made.

"Women can be most unpredictable."

"Damnably so. I tried to tell you but you fell into parson's mousetrap anyway."

"It's time you did the same, my friend. I don't suppose I could interest you in Sophie," he teased. "She needs a strong hand."

For a moment he wondered if Sir Marius could be Sophie's target. What a thought. But Sir Marius nearly choked on his brandy.

"I'd sooner marry a viper!" he spluttered. "Nothing against Sophie, but she's not exactly restful."

"You've no need to tell me that. If she loves, however, she will settle down."

"Like a dormant volcano," was the disbelieving reply. "In fact, Randal and I will be well suited when you take up the petticoat escort for yourself, though poor Randal will be still shackled by his sisters. He's having a dull time of it this year. Anyone would think he was reforming. I met Verderan the other day. He said Randal had turned down an invitation to a special little party at his place, and rumor says he has some genuine Eastern houris in keeping these days."

"The less Randal has to do with him, the better. Anyway, I have one more journey to make, to see a victim who is presently in Essex, unfortunately awaiting the birth of a child. Two of the victims are pregnant, you know."

"If you could wait a few years," said Sir Marius with a grin, "you'd probably find one of the brats was the image of the father."

Lord Wraybourne shook his head at this levity.

Sir Marius nudged him. "More brandy, David?"

Lord Wraybourne sighed. "No, Marius. I'm for my bed. I've travelled a hundred miles today and danced half the night."

"You're looking a bit worn down, you know."

"I'm not surprised. I probably hold the record for most miles covered. I should enter it in the book here. I'm looking forward to sleeping in the same bed for more than one night."

"If you don't watch it, that'll be your marriage bed. Don't look for a repairing lease there," chortled his friend.

Lord Wraybourne threw up his hands in despair and headed for his home.

～ 11 ～

THE NEXT MORNING found the house in Marlborough Square in ferment. Jane refused to discuss
her midnight visit with Sophie and oscillated between
ill humor and dreaminess. Lady Harroving kept to
her bed, but her husband was so unwise as to visit her
to consult about their coming masquerade ball. He
beat a hasty retreat, a breath ahead of a hurled cup of
chocolate.

Maria Harroving could not stand to be crossed. She no
longer cared whether her friend should marry her cousin
or not, she was merely determined to destroy. The truth
was that, having made a brilliant match to a man she disliked and despised, she was made wretched by the sight
of others more fortunate. She could, perhaps, have come
to tolerate Jane if she had been subservient, but Jane had

been raised in a hard school. She did not openly oppose Lady Harroving's will, but somehow she never bowed to it. Her habit of studying a person with those solemn tawny eyes was enough to drive one mad.

For Jane Sandiford to be elevated to a countess, outranking Lady Harroving herself; for Jane Sandiford to enjoy the riches of Stenby Castle and the Kyle fortune and to enjoy the pleasures of Lord Wraybourne in her bed— these were intolerable to Lady Harroving. She denied all callers until Mrs. Danvers was announced.

"Not up yet, Maria?" queried that lady coolly, herself a picture of fashionable elegance.

"I have a megrim."

"Alas. Who has crossed you now?"

"You are unkind," wailed Lady Harroving. "You at least should feel for me. David was making love to that horrible chit in the green saloon at two this morning."

Mrs. Danvers seemed merely amused. "How precipitate. Forgive me, but is not that precisely the kind of behavior a chaperone is supposed to prevent?"

Lady Harroving raised a dainty handkerchief. The role of victim could be pleasant. "He ordered me out. Brutally. He used strong language!"

"Which you of course are quite unused to," said her unsympathetic friend. As the older lady was speechless, Mrs. Danvers continued, "I am surprised David should be so unconventional, but there is no harm done. The marriage is in a matter of weeks."

"Oh, I don't suppose he got carried away," Lady Harroving said, "but you saw how he was at the Faverstowes'.

They probably went on billing and cooing, and now it will be all April and May."

"I'm sure their friends must be delighted," said Mrs. Danvers lightly, admiring a tiny jade vase on the table beside her.

"Are you mad?" shrieked her ladyship. "You of all people should share my feelings."

Mrs. Danvers regarded her friend with cool cat's eyes. "In truth, I gave up on David weeks ago. I am not even sure we would have suited. He is not really exciting enough for me. He will probably want to spend most of his time at Stenby, you know. I never could abide Shropshire." After a moment, during which Lady Harroving regarded her dumbfounded, Mrs. Danvers went on, "I accepted an offer last night from the Marquis of Dromree."

Lady Harroving regained her voice in a screech. "Dromree! He's old and ugly and Irish to boot!"

"He's not yet fifty, and he's rich and amusing. He is also," she said with a sensual smile, "a most inventive lover."

Lady Harroving's eyes grew wide.

"Tell me more."

Mrs. Danvers obliged, and this pleasant interlude did much to calm Lady Harroving's rage, but when she finally rose and dressed she was still resolved to be observant for some way in which she might undermine her cousin's marriage—or at least sabotage the growing understanding between him and his betrothed.

Meanwhile, Sophie had abandoned her attempts to wheedle from Jane a description of the time spent in the green saloon. Sophie turned the topic to the coming masquerade ball.

"I have been looking forward to attending Maria's masque for years," she said. "It is supposed to be deliciously daring. It is to be hoped David does not suddenly recollect that and decide we should not attend."

"He must surely know. The invitations are out."

"Do you think he bothers to read the cards he receives? I doubt it. And he is grown monstrous stuffy."

"But if it is a social fixture, he must know it is to take place and would have made his feelings clear," Jane said with a frown. "And what of the whisperer? I have no wish to put myself in danger of another encounter with him."

"There is no danger of that. It will still be a public place. As for David, perhaps he thinks Maria will abstain this year. Men can be so stupid. David was all set last night to read me a lecture on decorum, but I distracted him with talk of the love of my life."

Before Jane could follow this tantalizing lead, Sophie turned mischievous eyes to her companion. "Maria hopes to ruin you at the masque, you know."

"I do not understand."

"Do you not realize she has been urging you towards the precipice ever since you came to Town?" Sophie asked with genuine interest. "I was not sure whether you were thwarting her with incredible subtlety or through innocence."

Jane leaned forward, eyes keen. "Do you mean that all those things she wanted me to do were malicious rather than stupid?"

Sophie laughed. "Poor Maria. You thought her stupid?

She is not exactly needle-witted, but not so gawkish as that. She has taken one of her dislikes to you. Fortunately, she underestimated your natural good sense. For a while it seemed I would have the unlikely task of teaching you good behavior."

"But why should she dislike me?" asked Jane in bewilderment.

Sophie shrugged. "Maria does not need a reason. She was cross as a crook when you said you wouldn't go to the masque as a nymph."

"How could she think I would?" asked Jane in amazement. "I thought her funning. To appear in public in a short tunic of transparent gauze, I would need be mad."

"And what of her suggestion that you rouge your nipples under your spangled sarcenet?"

"I thought she had merely forgotten my position. After all, she does rouge her own. I paid no attention. Anyway, that dress is far too flimsy so I always wear two shifts beneath it."

Sophie laughed and hugged her friend. "I do love you, Jane. No one else could have rolled up Maria so completely and with never a cross word."

Jane returned the hug warmly. "Do you think we ought not to attend the masque, Sophie?"

"Wild horses wouldn't keep me away!" cried the girl, executing a gay *pirouette.* "It will be tremendous fun. Your costume can cause no outrage. Nothing could be more decent than medieval garb. It is positively nunlike."

"And what of yours?" responded Jane with raised brows. "A page in knee breeches?"

"Deliciously wicked," admitted Sophie.

"Why is it," asked Jane, trying on Sophie's page's hat with the long, curling plume, "that I must be careful not to overstep the line while you run riot?"

Sophie grabbed back the hat. "It is like this hat. It simply does not become you, whereas it is devilish on me." She considered her friend a moment. "I suppose it is partly because you are so new to the ton, and we are disposed to be critical. Secondly, you yourself are not at ease being wicked. But thirdly, you appear so much more mature than I." She gave her gamin smile. "If you were to overstep the bounds you would be wicked. I would merely be naughty."

Jane ruefully acknowledged the accuracy of this assessment. She would, nonetheless, have protested the unfairness of it had they not been interrupted by Lady Harroving calling them to the drawing room for the receiving hour. It soon became obvious that they could expect even more callers than usual. Half the Town wished to find out more about the Wraybourne affair. Lord Randal arrived in the company of his two sisters and raised comical brows at the crowded room. After settling his sisters with Jane, he drifted to the corner where Sophie held court and managed to draw her apart.

"All the tabbies, I see. Tell me, Sophie, is a large black hat for afternoon receptions all the rage?"

Sophie raised a finger to flick the plume. "I am trying to get the feel of it for the masquerade. Do you think the plume should come forwards or go backwards?"

"Neither one. I think you should wear something more suitable. Besides, now everyone will recognize you."

She glanced up mischievously. "Goodness, are you grown stuffy too? That is the point, my friend. Or else how would I shock them? And, if I keep shocking people, perhaps boring suitors like Trenholme will cease bothering me."

He looked at her quite seriously for once. "The wilder you act, imp, the more determined David will be to shackle you to a stick-in-the-mud."

As quickly as it had come, the sober mood left him. He appropriated the hat, set it upon his golden locks, and considered his reflection in a large gilt mirror. The brim cast an unusually sinister shadow over his sensual eyes.

"I should have been a Cavalier, with long golden curls and a deadly rapier," he said.

She snatched the hat back. "You should be forced to wear sackcloth," she declared. "Then perhaps so many poor females would not be making cakes of themselves over you."

He glanced round in amazement, catching the eye of an innocent young miss who went immediately pink with confusion when he winked at her. His gaze returned to the table close by.

"Is that where all these cakes came from?" He picked up a pink confection. "My goodness. This must have been Miss Forbes. She always did look terrible in pink. And this meringue was Lady Stevenham. I recognize the shape—or lack of it."

Giggling, Sophie picked up a long, thin sponge finger dusted with fine sugar. "Why Mrs. Danvers. Fancy meeting you here." With relish, Sophie sank her teeth into the confection.

"Cat!"

"Well, she positively drooled over you at The Middle-house. Did you see the announcement? She's to marry Dromree. Beauty and the Beast."

"They will suit very well," he remarked with his secret smile.

Sophie turned startled, hurt eyes to him and was amazed to see a touch of color tinging his fine-grained skin.

"How do you always trap me into having such improper conversations?" he said sharply. "It is fortunate that virginity is a physical and not a mental state, or David would be after me with a pistol. Come and talk genteelly with my sisters."

Jane had been watching Sophie with concern. She was determined to bring some decorum into their affairs. Now, on the very day when the Town was agog for gossip, Sophie had to behave so strangely, wearing that hat and standing apart for so long with Lord Randal. As the couple moved to rejoin a group, Jane couldn't help remarking Sophie's eyes, as they rested a moment on her companion.

In Jane's own heightened state, she recognized the affliction immediately. Oh poor Sophie. No wonder Lord Trenholme, with all his attributes, was making no headway. How could he compete with the glittering brilliance of Lord Randal? Jane wondered again about his feelings. She knew by now how unsuitable Lord Randal was considered to be as a partner for a young innocent. What a coil this was likely to be.

She turned to Lady Caroline Ashby. "Your brother is a fascinating man, Caroline."

"Randal? He has the Ashby charm. The only one in our generation to be so gifted. Coupled with our mother's looks—she was a great beauty, you know—it is alarming. I feel so sorry for all the poor women who fall victim. He is careful, you know, only to entangle himself with a certain type of married lady. Still, the others hurtle after him like moths to a flame. At least you are safe, my dear Jane."

"Yes. I am fortunate, for he is a pleasant friend."

"And a wonderful brother. If only Father would let him join the hussars. Or rather, if only Chelmly would marry and get an heir."

Jane was bewildered until the twins gave her a quick and quiet-voiced briefing on their family troubles.

"But why does your elder brother not marry?" she asked at last.

"He used to come to Town on occasion, many years ago. He fell in love. Then he found that she was only interested in him for the dukedom. So now he stays home and grows turnips. He is quite impossible. Our poor father's wishes mean nothing to him."

"How sad for you all," said Jane, but she was thinking of Sophie.

If Lord Randal were permitted to go to the war, perhaps she would recover her wits. Jane wished Lord Wraybourne were here so she could lay the problem before him, but then she realized it would be impossible to betray her friend. Perhaps she could speak to Lord Randal? No. That she could not handle.

Jane wondered why she felt so disturbed. It was an unfortunate situation, but unrequited love was hardly novel.

Sophie would eventually recover and fix her affections elsewhere. Despite that rationalization, Jane felt a tremor of alarm and impending disaster. Sophie could never be depended on to do the predictable.

For the moment, however, Jane was forced to put the matter out of her mind and return to the business of convincing Society she was really a perfectly behaved young lady, soon to be married to an excellent young man. She could congratulate herself that most of the callers left convinced their recent speculation about the match had been unfounded. She had managed to drop into conversation mention of his many gifts to her and of the occasions upon which he had escorted her, so that many even began to doubt he had, in fact, been so much absent from Town. When all the callers were gone, Sophie picked up her feathered hat and placed it on her head. She tipped it to Jane in salute.

"Excellently done, my friend," she said. "Maintain your saintly rectitude for a few more days, and you will have the ton believing they have been subject to a fit of spring madness."

"What can you mean, Sophie?" asked Lady Harroving, who had, as usual, paid no attention to anything except herself.

"Did you not notice, Maria?" asked Sophie innocently. "Jane and David are busily convincing Society that she is a prettily behaved young lady and he is a man in love. Droll, is it not?" Since Lady Harroving appeared to be speechless, Sophie added, "Particularly as it is true."

This caused Jane to color slightly as she snatched at the hope Sophie so casually offered.

Meanwhile, Lady Harroving turned brick red. "I wish you would not be so ridiculous, Sophie," she snapped. "And take off that hat. It is quite unsuitable."

"I like it," said Sophie unrepentantly. "I think I will set a new style. It could go very well with a riding habit."

"Indeed it would," said Jane, hoping to turn the conversation.

"But would it attract Sir Edwin Hever?" asked Sophie. "If so I must forgo it. He is such a dreadful bore."

"If you play the honeypot you must expect the bees," said Jane.

"Wasps," corrected her friend. "Sir Edwin is a wasp. He is actually going to ask David for permission to address me. Conceited prig! I told him it was pointless, and he went pale with affront. And, speaking of nasty insects, what will Mr. Carruthers think of your exploits?"

Jane feigned ignorance. "Whatever can you mean?"

"I am sure the poor man believes he is going to sip your nectar," replied Sophie with a naughty twinkle.

"Sophie, you go too far!" exclaimed Lady Harroving.

Receiving neither acknowledgement nor repentance she swept out of the room.

"Poor Maria," said Sophie sweetly. "She must be between lovers."

"Sophie!" exclaimed Jane.

Sophie merely grinned. "I am not sure she has had a beau since The Middlehouse."

"Sophie, you really should not speak of such things. What is the matter? I have never known you so outrageous before."

"But then you do not know me very well," said Sophie rudely. "Maria goes from one lover to another. Sir Marius was her lover at The Middlehouse. My maid told me. I am sure she has had all the other men as well—Verderan, Lord Randal, probably even David."

"No." Jane's denial was emphatic.

Sophie glared at her. "What of Phoebe Danvers then?"

Jane made the effort to meet the other girl's eyes and could see beyond the shocking talk to the hurt beneath.

"It is not unusual for men to behave so, though in truth I scarcely know what such behavior involves."

"Shall I tell you?" said Sophie nastily.

"No," replied Jane. "I would rather you tell me what is bothering you. You act as if your heart were breaking."

Tell me, Sophie, she pleaded silently, and we can discuss this. But Sophie just stood there as tears rolled down her cheeks, then dashed them angrily away and summoned a smile.

"I apologize. I have been hateful. It is just that you are to be happy, and so many people are falling in love. What is for me?"

Jane hugged her. "You have more suitors than can be counted."

"But not the one I want."

Sophie broke away and wandered over to a plate of cakes to study them. Jane watched amazed. How could Sophie become suddenly so interested in food? She picked out two cakes and turned with them in her hands. One was covered in blue icing, the exact color of her own dress. The other was a yellow sponge very like the color of Jane's muslin with a topping of chocolate cream.

"Behold," said Sophie with a bitter smile, "how we all make cakes of ourselves!" She crumbled them both onto the carpet, then dusting off her hands, walked briskly from the room.

For the first time Jane was seriously concerned about her friend's sanity. She recalled all she had learned since coming to London of the affairs of Lord Byron and Lady Caroline Melbourne. They had entertained the ton the year before with a public and passionate entanglement which had left the lady, so it was said, mad when Lord Byron rejected her and turned to Miss Annabella Milbanke for consolation.

Was Jane wrong to detect some similarity between Sophie and the wild Lady Caroline? But then, Lord Randal was no Byron. Jane had met the poet, and, though his work was brilliant and he was very handsome, he seemed himself to be a most unstable character. Besides, Lord Randal was not encouraging Sophie's infatuation. Was he even aware of it? Jane pondered this thought and decided he couldn't be. He was too kind to torment Sophie by his teasing if he knew how she felt. Jane wished she had the courage to tell him. Marriage between Sophie and Lord Randal was so impossible, it would be better he left her to form other attachments.

The two maids came in just then to clear the room and exclaimed at the pile of crumbs in the middle of the carpet. Jane only sighed and left to follow Sophie upstairs.

☙ 12 ☙

As Jane anticipated her evening with her betrothed, her sense of disquiet disappeared. The mere thought of his company set her nerves tingling in a most delightful way. Despite her moment of jealousy the night before, she now realized she had nothing to fear. He was now hers alone, even if there had been another woman for a while. Sophie had spoken the truth, or close to it. He might not yet love his bride-to-be, but he was far from indifferent. Though inexperienced, Jane recognized a strong and genuine feeling in him.

Lady Harroving had been happy enough for them all to cancel their engagements that evening, for there was nothing special arranged. Sophie had been reluctant but eventually agreed to accompany her brother and Jane and was in good spirits as the coach rolled through the dusky streets into a quieter part of town, very like Clarke Street. Jane had a moment's alarm as she wondered what she would do if Lord Wraybourne introduced her to that woman, then told herself he would do nothing so ill-bred.

Lord Wraybourne explained they were to visit Peter Medcalf, a composer and musician, who held open house for his friends and patrons every Friday. When David saw Sophie pull a face, he laughed.

"You will enjoy yourself, Sophie. There are all kinds of people. The food is excellent, and there are cards for those who do not wish to attend to the music. It is time you met true artists instead of pretentious appreciators and boring teachers."

Certainly, the noisy, vibrant house they entered was very unlike the hushed reverence of some musical *soirées*. People were talking and laughing and calling across the room for comments. The trio which played in one corner could not be heard but obviously did not care, as they were stopping and starting and trying out something new. A tall, ruddy man surged forward to wring Lord Wraybourne's hand.

"David, my dear friend! It has been too long. And whom have you brought? One of these beauties must be your bride-to-be. At least, I hope so or you are a rogue, Sir!" His bright eyes scanned them both and then he said, "I can detect your sister. The resemblance is remarkable. Welcome Lady Sophie! So this must be Miss Sandiford. An honor to meet you, my dear."

With a broad smile, David introduced the young ladies to their host, who promptly appropriated them both, one on each arm.

"Go away, Wraybourne. You have these two beauties every day and must now share them for a few moments at least."

Lord Wraybourne obeyed and was quickly absorbed into a welcoming group.

The musician turned to Jane and Sophie. "Do you like music, my dears? No, that is a silly question. Everyone likes music. What kind of music do you like best?"

Sophie raised her chin. "I do not like music very much. It is all right in the background, but I can do without it well enough." She smiled up at him, but with a challenge in her eyes.

"Ha! Ruined by a bad teacher. I can detect the signs. You will see, young lady. I will convert you. And you, Miss Sandiford?"

"I like music very much, Mr. Medcalf, particularly symphonies with very large orchestras, for I have heard them so rarely."

"Ah, yes! The vibration seems to shake the bones. Now, I have someone I wish to introduce to you. I am sure you will be pleased."

With gentle pushes and a word here and there he eased them across the room to where a tubby little man was talking animatedly to a small group.

"Ah, Lane," exclaimed Mr. Medcalf. "Here I have some admirers, I am sure. Young ladies, may I present Mr. William Lane of the Minerva Press. Mr. Lane. Lady Sophie Kyle and Miss Jane Sandiford."

In a moment Medcalf was gone off to greet other newcomers, and Jane and Sophie were happy to be left in the company of the publisher of their favorite books. They were soon privy to a list of upcoming titles. Sophie was resolved to order *Subterranean Horrors* while Jane felt drawn to a novel entitled *Bewildered Affections*.

All too soon, Lord Wraybourne collected them and took them around to greet the other guests. The new poet laureate, Mr. Southey, was there and the famous scientist, Sir Humphrey Davy. Jane was enthralled by his talk of the strange effects of something called laughing gas, and Lord Wraybourne promised to take her to the Royal Institution to witness Sir Humphrey's next demonstration. She was not surprised to find the earl kept his own box there for the lectures.

He also introduced them to the famous miniaturist, Mr. Andrew Robertson, and Jane gathered he had been commissioned to paint her portrait soon after the wedding. However, she found the way he studied her alarming. He seemed to be looking beneath her skin, stripping off each layer of bone and tissue.

All too soon, for Sophie at least, it was time to sit for the music. She breathed an audible sigh, but Jane was amused to see that she was soon enthralled. Jane herself was delighted to experience such excellence. All the performers were professionals playing for their own and their friends' amusement. The pieces were short and lively. Some were new, and occasionally a member of the audience, caught by a particular passage, would rise up and take an instrument to join in.

Little musical jokes were played, and, though Jane and Sophie usually missed the allusion, Lord Wraybourne could often supply it. If not, the atmosphere of good humor was satisfying in itself. Jane and Sophie both laughed heartily at the last item, when a violinist and a cellist conducted a musical conversation. Even without words, one could hear the stern husband and flighty wife as they argued and then made up.

"That was fun," said Sophie in surprise.

"Perhaps we'll turn you into a connoisseur yet," remarked her brother.

Sophie was about to retort when she said instead, "Oh, good heavens! What is *he* doing here?"

They all turned and saw Edwin Hever at the back of the room. He gave a bow in their direction and started towards them.

"David, do let us move. I cannot abide one of his lectures. I am sure he is not a music lover. He has no soul."

Unfortunately, it was impossible to escape and soon they were being greeted by the young man.

"What a charming surprise! But I should have known such a patron of the arts as you, My Lord, would be present at these occasions. The very best of music, is it not; though I am not sure artists of quality should debase themselves by vulgar entertainment of that last sort. Suitable for the lower orders maybe, but not for such as we."

"I liked it," said Sophie bluntly.

Sir Edwin smiled beneficently at her. "Perhaps also it appeals to young ladies, dear Lady Sophie."

"Along with the lower orders?" she queried indignantly, but her brother broke in.

"I would have thought you would spend your time in Town at the more elevated social gatherings, Hever."

"Oh, goodness no, My Lord. What is the point of visiting the Great Metropolis if only to dance and engage in idle chatter? One must broaden one's mind. I will have so much to relate when I return home. My mother will be delighted to learn of the many matters I have touched on. Why only yesterday I visited—"

"Excuse us," said Lord Wraybourne ruthlessly. "We must speak to Mr. Lamb."

Once they were safely away, Sophie remarked, "I wish I knew how you did that. I have never seen anyone cut him off in full flow before."

"He recognizes determination. If you marry him, I'll cut *you* off."

She laughed. "As if I would!"

"Good. I am now going to ask Percy Wetherby to take you in to supper. He's a philosopher and took a first at Cambridge, but you'll like him anyway."

A few moments later Jane watched as Sophie, somewhat alarmed, was led off by a handsome, fashionable man. Before they had left the room, Sophie was laughing.

"At last. A moment alone with you, Jane," said Lord Wraybourne.

She glanced around at the twenty or so people still in the room and raised her brows.

"Well, to be really alone would be dangerous, don't you think?" he added. "Are you enjoying this?"

"Very much. I never realized when I was growing up how starved I was of good music. I think sometimes of the poor people who never have an opportunity to listen to such excellence."

He smiled. "That is kind of you. I hope we can always think of those less fortunate. But it is surprising how music exists for everyone. The simple folk have their whistles and their fiddles, and always their voices. I have heard beautiful music in poor surroundings."

This delightful moment of conversation was interrupted when Jane noted, from his change of expression, that someone unexpected had entered the room. She turned and saw Crossley Carruthers approaching, all smiles.

"Lord Wraybourne, Miss Sandiford, what a pleasure! I hardly expected to find such as you at this humble gathering."

"I could say the same, Carruthers. I was not aware that you were musically inclined."

The handsome young man made an airy gesture. "A bit of this. A bit of that. A man of the world has to get around."

Jane was aware, even though Lord Wraybourne's manner was impeccably polite, of a constraint in the conversation.

"This is my first visit here," she said hastily. "Is it the same for you, Mr. Carruthers?"

"My first, Miss Sandiford? Indeed no, not at all. I am quite a regular. And at the Lambs on Wednesday for a bit of literature and Peacocks now and then for scientific philosophy."

Lord Wraybourne obviously found this itinerary fascinating. "And do you participate in the arts, Mr. Carruthers?"

"Participate? Me? Well a little, maybe. Here and there, don't you know. But mostly I like to listen. Quite amazing to listen to, all of it. But must go through to supper now, don't you know. Jolly good food here. Your servant."

With an elegant, stiff-necked bow he was gone, and Jane had to stifle the desire to laugh. She had never thought him brilliant, but she had not realized before how silly he was. He performed well enough in his own *milieu* perhaps, but, once out of it, he lost his magic.

"I wonder why he *really* comes to these evenings?" she asked, half to herself.

"Just what I was wondering," said Lord Wraybourne. "But he has one right idea. The food is excellent. Let us go and enjoy it."

There was no further opportunity for private discussion as they took supper with a group and then listened to more music. Jane enjoyed herself thoroughly and felt pride at the universal popularity of her betrothed. She was not quite sure enough of him, however, not to be watching the other women present. None of them was the woman from Clarke Street, but quite a few greeted him as a friend.

The atmosphere was informal, so unlike that to which she was accustomed. One Italian singer actually kissed Lord Wraybourne on the cheek, and no one except Jane seemed even to notice! She did her best to suppress any jealousy, particularly when she saw him watching her. But she also noted one or two young ladies whose eyes, when he was turned away from them, reflected the same emotion as Sophie's had towards Randal earlier—undeclared love. Did Jane's eyes betray her as well?

As for Sophie, Jane began to wonder whether she had imagined the afternoon. Her friend chattered all the way home about the people she had met, particularly the young philosopher.

"He was able, David, to talk quite coherently. I thought he might be like Mr. Quickly at home—the parson, Jane—who is generally held to have a superior mind but rambles on about the dullest topics as if his listeners were stone statues with nothing to say to the matter at all. Mr. Wetherby and I discussed the possibility of there being mermaids, and whether an English child brought up in China would speak Chinese. I still think it would speak *some* English."

Lord Wraybourne laughed at this but refused to be drawn into the debate, though Jane and Sophie discussed it all the way home, agreeing in the end that the child would probably speak Chinese, but with an English accent.

Lady Harroving was still out, and Lord Wraybourne sent Sophie to bed but ordered the footman to light the candles in the red saloon. Jane preceded her betrothed into this elegant room, with its rich Turkish carpet and red velvet curtains a pointed contrast to the saloon they had occupied the night before. A germ of excitement was building in her. He would kiss her again. Instead, he put the width of the room between them.

"I hope you enjoyed this evening, Jane. I look forward to the time when we will spend many such together."

"It was delightful."

"Good. But I must ask your indulgence. As you know, I have to go out of Town again tomorrow."

Jane stiffened, and she saw from his face that he had noticed. She was not sorry if he felt uncomfortable. His neglect of her was scandalous.

"I do regret it, Jane. It is a commitment I cannot avoid. I have to see someone in Exeter for my uncle, Mr. Moulton-Scrope. I wanted to remind you to be careful while I am away. You and Sophie both."

It was not a very satisfactory explanation. Earls did not usually act as messengers, even for their uncles. Jane turned away from him to study an elegant piece of Dresden china.

"I see," she said coolly. "Can you tell me exactly how long you will be away? I have so little time left in London."

"Then it is all the sooner to our wedding day," he said. She could hear the smile in his voice. "You cannot expect me to be sad at that, Jane."

She heard his footsteps approaching slowly, then his voice close behind her.

"What is it that bothers you, Jane? Is it the silly talk? I think we have put a stop to that. Or are you already bored by Society?"

He turned her slowly to him. Jane was finding it difficult to keep control of her wits.

"It is more fun when you are here." That wasn't what she had intended to say!

"I will treasure that on my weary journey, Jane. Just think what fun we are going to have for the rest of our lives."

He pulled her to him as if impelled, but though he held her tightly, he did not kiss her. He buried his face in her neck, and she could feel his soft, moist breath there. She turned her head slightly to kiss his hair but, otherwise, they remained so. The longer they stood together, the more impossible it seemed to Jane that they should part, but eventually he pulled away and looked at her with passion-filled eyes.

"It really is as well that I am out of Town so much, Jane," he said gently.

"Are you not going to kiss me?" The question would not be held back, even though she suspected it was better left unasked.

He laughed and rested his hands on her shoulders. "If this is my Jane, all in innocence, what will become of me in the future? Stand still, wanton, and I will give you a kiss."

She stood *quite* still as he leaned and touched his lips to hers. But when she began to press forward and open to him, he moved away.

"Tush, tush." There was such smiling affection in his face that she smiled back. He dropped six light kisses on her mouth. "One for each day I will be gone, Tiger Eyes."

Feeling greatly daring, she kissed her fingers and laid them on his lips. "And one to take with you so you will not be tempted by any other wantons you meet on your way."

Sensing how difficult it was for him to go, she broke away and, with only a smile, left him there and floated up the stairs. As she passed Sophie's door, Jane thought sadly of her friend, feeling much as she did at this moment, yet able to hope for nothing. Whereas Jane anticipated undiluted happiness forever.

Lady Harroving had experienced as satisfactory an evening as her charges in her own way. She had spent her time in a discreet establishment, playing Faro and winning. She also encountered a gentleman who had seen Lord Wraybourne in Yorkshire.

"Saw him about Harrogate a few times, always with the same woman. Had to look twice. After all, wouldn't expect it. Not in Harrogate in June. Full of damned provincials. I was only there myself to visit an uncle. Got expectations."

"Doubtless his great-aunt," said Lady Harroving, more interested in the turn of the cards than in his chatter.

"Doubt it," he chortled. "Pretty filly, if a bit quiet. Looked upset or sickly. Wouldn't surprise me if she was a *chère amie,* but I'm surprised Wraybourne would get involved with her sort. Always better to stick to the knowing ones, my father says, and he's right. Paying her off before the wedding, I suppose. Enough to make any young filly look blue-devilled. Dash it all, you've all the luck tonight, Lady Harroving."

Lady Harroving agreed as she scooped up yet more guineas. "Do I gather you spoke to my indiscreet cousin, Mr. Peel-Saunders?"

"Good God, no. Obvious he wouldn't want a third at those discussions."

"He was fortunate that he was only seen by someone of your tact," she said with a warm smile. It was an excellent opportunity to pursue her course of destruction. "I understand he did have a mistress of that sort. He is forever in the company of lesser folk, artisans and professionals. I quite feared at one point that he would marry such a one, but he has more sense than that, thank heavens. And I am sure he was extremely generous to his disappointed friend. Lord Wraybourne can always be depended on to do as he ought."

She moved away, aware that Peel-Saunders would soon have the story all over Town, and reflected that it could be mostly true. David had no young relatives in Yorkshire. Whatever his business there, it was unlikely to be innocent. She wished she could tell the story straight to Jane, but the girl had become distrustful of late. And she would be the last one to hear the gossip. Lady Harroving felt the fates were with her when Mr. Carruthers walked into the room later in the evening.

"Crossley, I wish to talk with you."

"Talk to me? Dammit, Maria. I've come to play," said the gentleman. He was flushed with drink.

"The night is young. You can play later. I have better sport for you."

She dragged him off to a quiet corner. "I am disappointed in you, Crossley. The wedding is only weeks away, and you have made little impression on Miss Sandiford."

"It's my opinion you were out in your facts, Maria," he protested. "The whole Town is talking of their goings-on at the Faverstowes'. If they weren't in love before, they are now."

"The town knows nothing," she said in a hard voice. "They came back to Marlborough Square afterwards and quarreled dreadfully. It is all a sham." Seeing that he was willing to believe her lies, she continued. "They would both be well pleased to be free of their entanglement. Jane merely needs a reason to break the engagement, and you could give it to her. David has a mistress, at present residing in Harrogate. He was seen with her recently."

He considered the matter with a pout. "She wouldn't be such a fool as to break the match over that. She can't be so naive."

"Consider, Crossley," Lady Harroving said with patience. "Not only does he have the mistress, but he has abandoned Jane in Town to be with that mistress *since* the betrothal!"

Light dawned. "Yes indeed. That is different. But will she believe it?"

"If you put it well, yes. You can tell her that Matthew Peel-Saunders saw them together. It's the truth."

He thought for a moment. "Might be worth a try. But what's the odds she'll just cry off and run home to mother."

"It is obvious you have not met Lady Sandiford. The last thing Jane wants to do is to return home. It is the only reason she is still betrothed to my cousin, and that is why she will elope with you."

He nodded, eyes bright and greedy. "I'll do it, and I'll soon make sure she has to marry me. You're sure she has money coming that can't be touched? It may take a while to win her parents around."

Maria Harroving lowered her lashes to hide the humor there and lied again. "Of course I'm sure. There is a substantial sum from an uncle. And when there is a grandchild, I'm sure they will part with the unentailed property, which is a large part of the whole."

You poor fool, she thought as she watched him walk

away. I wish I might be present when you try to soften the heart of that walking icicle, Amelia Sandiford.

Lady Harroving licked her lips with satisfaction. She had primed a weapon and pointed it at target. That weapon might not achieve its full potential, but she had great hopes of it wreaking considerable damage on its way.

❧ 13 ❧

THE ATMOSPHERE IN the Harroving household became very strained. Lady Harroving had resumed a degree of good humor, but there was a brittle quality to it. Jane sometimes caught the older lady watching her with malicious anticipation. Whether he was also disturbed by this unpleasantness in his wife, or for other reasons, Lord Harroving was particularly surly. Sophie had recovered superficially, but Jane detected a melancholy in her friend which gave her natural high spirits an hysterical edge.

Jane herself alternated between worry about Sophie and dreamy anticipation of Lord Wraybourne's return. At times the dreaminess was supplanted by an overwhelming burst of energy, and she dragged Sophie out for rides and long walks. One such morning, Jane was frustrated to discover that Sophie did not wish to ride in the park.

"Sophie, it is a beautiful day," she protested. "You know how much you enjoy these rides before the world is about."

Sophie was in one of her disconsolate moods, however. Lord Randal had attended the Matlock rout the night before at his glittering best. Jane had known at the time that Sophie would suffer today for the pleasure of the evening, so was saddened rather than surprised when her friend buried herself deeper in the bedclothes and ordered Jane away.

She decided to ride anyway. It would not be improper, merely a little unusual, to do so with only a groom in attendance, and the groom would protect her from the whisperer. She was surprised at how free she felt and realized that she had never been outside the door of the Harrovings' house without Lady Harroving or Sophie as companion and maids and footmen in attendance.

Riding along the almost deserted paths with the groom a discreet distance behind, Jane could imagine herself alone for the first time in her life. Tigress—that was the name she had given her beautiful mount—sensed her mistress's high spirits and shook her head, asking for the chance to gallop.

"Very well, you darling creature," said Jane with a laugh. "But only a canter. I am resolved to be good. Stay here, Stinson," she called to the groom. "I will go just to the end of the ride."

When she'd done so, Jane wheeled the mare to return to the groom. She was aglow with exhilaration and reflected on how she had changed in these last weeks. She had learned to cope with the whims of Society. She had made friends and handled some difficult situations. She remembered herself as the nervous girl who had arrived at The Middlehouse and knew that was a different person. For the first time, Jane wondered if her mother had been mistaken in Lord Wraybourne's intentions, if he had been attracted to her from the start. With her new self-confidence it did not seem so absurd a notion. She was certain by now that he had no need of her money, and plenty of other well-raised young ladies were eager for his attentions.

She remembered with a smile how she had feared his *disturbances*. She could look back now to that day at The Middlehouse and laugh at the game he had played with her. He had been remarkably kind, she realized, and must have known how nervous and unsure she was. Now she wanted nothing more than to be disturbed as frequently as possible.

This beautiful morning would have been perfected by the presence of her betrothed by her side. However, it was not Lord Wraybourne but Mr. Carruthers who appeared to accompany her. She was not surprised. He frequently rode out in the morning and had often joined herself and Sophie. But though he was a pleasant companion, Jane could well have dispensed with his presence on this particular morning.

"Miss Sandiford!" he exclaimed, doffing his hat with his usual elegance. "Fortune smiles on me today. Permit me to accompany you."

Since he had already guided his horse alongside, Jane

could not easily refuse him, and though she found him silly, he was an easy companion now that he seemed to have abandoned his embarrassing pose of thwarted lover. She supposed that a fortune hunter, which she knew him to be, must by nature be amusing and agreeable if he was to have chance of success. He was a fribble but an amiable one, and so she gave him good morning.

He asked solicitously after Lady Sophie and expressed warm satisfaction on hearing that she was in excellent health. He went on to converse about the weather, the prospects in the park, the upcoming delights of the Season and the most recent *on dits*. Jane, finding that her part in the conversation was easy to uphold, remembered her mother's comments about the Art of Conversation. Here was another master of it of whom that lady would not approve.

"I hear great talk of you and Lord Wraybourne, Miss Sandiford. You appear to be the latest Romeo and Juliet, the latest Abélard and Héloïse."

"I hope not, Mr. Carruthers," she said with raised brows. "I am anticipating a happy ending."

"A happy ending. Of course!" he replied with a laugh. "But how difficult it is to think of a pair of happy lovers. Othello and Desdemona, Antony and Cleopatra, Tristan and Isolde were tragedies all. Perhaps," he added after a short pause and in a serious tone, "this is because love is so full of traps for the unwary."

"Well," she declared, "I do not think that is the tone to take with one who is soon to be a bride."

"A bride, yes. I am sorry," he said with a speaking look.

"It is probably a reflection of my own poor state. You see before you a man with a broken heart."

"I feel for you," she said sincerely, but surprised.

She had not thought he had the capacity for suffering in the cause of love. She did wonder, however, who was causing him to pine. She cast about in her mind to think who he had been attending since he had ceased to pester herself.

She was somewhat disconcerted by his turning to her and declaiming in passionate tones, "Oh, sweet lady, I value your words of kindness!"

"Then you may have as many as you want," she said lightly. "Words are free, and I try always to be kind to my friends."

"A friend. Is that all I am to you, Miss Sandiford?"

She was suddenly uncomfortable and glad of the stolid groom, sitting on his horse within sight. "What more *could* you be, Mr. Carruthers?"

His smile was sad. "Once you gave me to hope, dear lady, that I might be more. You said . . . but I realize now that I took too seriously a few playful words. You young ladies like to play games with the hearts of men."

Jane was upset at being seen as thoughtless, particularly since she suspected it was true in this case. She attempted to smooth the matter over, hoping all the while that he was not going to become a bother again.

"I never meant to play games, Mr. Carruthers. When I came to Town it was all new and a little frightening. I welcomed your company. I am sorry if I misled you. I was, after all, already engaged to Lord Wraybourne. You knew that."

"Yes," he sighed. "I knew. But since when has love followed sense? Francis Bacon wrote, 'It is impossible to love and be wise.' I am afraid he had the truth of it."

"I am sorry, Mr. Carruthers," Jane replied bracingly, to hide an uncomfortable degree of embarrassment, "but I really cannot believe you to be as smitten as you pretend. I am nothing out of the ordinary, and it is certainly unwise of you to cast your heart towards one who is already bespoken."

"Nothing out of the ordinary! With your beauty, Miss Sandiford, and your kind heart and clever wit, you are a *rara avis* among all the pretty blossoms we call debutantes."

Jane suppressed an urge to point out to him how he had mixed his metaphors. She could not deny there was a grain of pleasure to be had at being the object of such strong devotion, and she felt she should be kind to him. All the same, she did not quite believe his protestations and found the whole scene most uncomfortable. Even if he was passionately in love, he had no right to embarrass her in this way.

"Mr. Carruthers, I must ask you never to speak of this again," she said firmly.

He sighed. "As you wish, sweet lady. I am, after all, unworthy. I realize that. Even were you free, I could not lift my eyes to you."

Jane suddenly realized he was sounding like Sir Tristram again and had to turn away to hide her twitching lips. Such protestations no longer seemed appealing, merely silly.

Mr. Carruthers mistook this reaction for encouragement. "You are touched! Dear Miss Sandiford, I knew your

heart could not stay hard. I have no hopes of true felicity, but if only I could be sure, at least, that you would be
happy in your fate!"

Jane turned in surprise. "Then you have your wish, Mr.
Carruthers. I am very happy and expect only greater joy. I
love Lord Wraybourne."

It was the first time she had spoken the words aloud.
She was caught up in the magic of the moment, savoring
them, repeating them in her mind . . . then came to herself to realize the dratted man was still speaking.

". . . too late. Is he truly worthy?"

She had tried to be kind. Now it was time to be firm.
"I beg your pardon, I missed what you first said, Mr. Carruthers." He looked quite flushed and agitated. Heaven
knows what new embarrassment he had been spewing
forth. "I am sorry. I must go. Good day." With that she
urged Tigress forward and ignored a shouted comment
behind her.

On the way home she rode slowly and allowed herself
to relish once more the thought of love, like a lamp glowing within her. She was, quite simply, different because of
it. When would she tell Lord Wraybourne? Should she wait
for him to say the words to her? He could not love her
yet, or he would not be busying himself elsewhere even if
it was innocent business for his uncle. Feeling as she did,
she would not willingly part herself from him for a second.
Still, that hardly mattered. He was hers, love or not, and
she could soon count on his presence day by day. That was
enough happiness, for now.

Jane wondered how she would find Sophie upon her

return, but that mercurial lady was once again in spirits, assisting Lady Harroving, herself in one of her better moods, to settle details for the masked ball. As Lady Harroving hurried off to consult with her staff, Sophie showed Jane the designs for the decor.

"Maria is turning the ballroom into a veritable forest with trees in pots, and there are to be fireworks at midnight, Jane. These are the drawings. There will be groves and grottoes and only a few lights."

"It looks lovely," Jane said, "but we will be forever losing track of people."

"That is the idea, goose!"

"But what of the whisperer?"

"Jane, you allow that pest to upset you too much. He is an unpleasant worm but not dangerous at a ball. Even if he were to get you alone, you would only have to scream. As he seems too cowardly to ever show his face he can hardly do you harm. The secluded areas will be ideal for lovers. I would have thought you would be in favor. Just think what fun you and David will have."

"I am sure he would not approve." Jane was aware of sounding stuffy and, of course, Sophie laughed.

"Maria says he has attended all her previous balls and enjoyed himself immensely. If *you* don't slip off with him to a bower you can be sure there will be plenty of other ladies to oblige him." Jane could not hide the hurt she felt, and Sophie blushed. "Oh Jane, I am so sorry. My wretched tongue again. Of course, David will not want to be apart from you for a moment. So you need never fear the whisperer again."

Jane had to seek reassurance. "Do you really think so?"

"Of course I do. I have seen the way he looks at you. I am sure he hasn't thought about another woman since he first met you."

"Oh Sophie," Jane protested, the scene in Clarke Street coming to her mind, "that is coming it too strong. When we first met, Lord Wraybourne and I were strangers and even though we became betrothed, we were strangers when we parted. I do hope he has come to like me, but I hardly expect that he is *bouleversé*. After all, he has been gone so much of the time I have been in London."

Suddenly, she remembered what he had said, that it was better he be away from her until they were married, and she felt her face warm.

The color must have shown, even on her creamy skin, for Sophie said, "Why, Jane. What is there in that to make you blush?" She did not wait for an answer. "I envy you, Jane. Even though you will not tell me what has been going on, I am sure David has been making love to you. And here I am, innocent of all but a few daring pecks on the cheek from young men in Bath. I have been careful not to encourage familiarity since I came to Town, and what has it achieved? Exactly what one might expect—nothing! Even your dratted whisperer hasn't found me worthy of his taunts."

She was silent a moment, then as if on a different topic went on, brightly this time.

"Do you know what I heard today? A delicious piece of gossip. Jennifer Witherspoon, who was the most prissy piece imaginable at school, is marrying Jimmy Fentress in a hurry because they were caught in an *incriminating* situation."

"The one with spots and no chin?" Jane exclaimed.

"Which one?" giggled Sophie. "Good heavens, both of them!"

At that, they both burst into laughter, only interrupted by the butler with a note for Jane, who took it, wiping her eyes. She hoped it would be from Lord Wraybourne, but it was not his hand.

She could hardly have been more shocked to read:

> *My dear Miss Sandiford, I felt it Imperative you be told that Lord Wraybourne has spent a Considerable Time in* recent weeks *with a Young Lady who resides in Harrogate, a Young Lady of whom rumor says she has been sent to Yorkshire to be away from her friends while she awaits the Consequences of her Imprudent Behavior with a Gentleman in London. A well-wisher.*

Jane read the words through twice, then started to read them a third time as if they might change into something less horrifying. Sophie took the note from Jane's hand.

"What is it? You look quite pale." She read the message and exclaimed, "This is utter rubbish, Jane. Pay it no heed. I doubt if David has ever been to Harrogate."

"Oh yes he has," said Jane calmly. "He told me so."

The woman from Clarke Street, she was thinking. He sent her to Yorkshire and then went to be with her. No wonder she seemed upset if she was telling him she was expecting a child.

"How extraordinary. But even so, any acquaintance there would be chance-met."

Jane looked at Sophie. "Tell me. If David had a mistress—and it would not be so unusual, even I know that—and she was expecting his child. What would he do?"

Sophie had turned quite pale herself. "Well, he would arrange something, I suppose. Perhaps find her a husband or a place to stay until the child was . . . born." She stared. "Oh, Jane!"

Jane licked her lips, unaware that she was also clenching and unclenching her fingers nervously. "I do not mind so much the mistress," she said in a wavery voice. "And I suppose a child would be mischance. But why has he been with her so much? I suppose he has returned to her now. He *said* he had business for your uncle in Exeter."

"Uncle Henry?" queried Sophie with enough surprise in her voice to make Jane sigh. "What will you do, Jane?"

Jane already knew the answer. Her heart gave her no choice. "Why nothing. I am marrying your brother. It will be up to me to make sure he does not stray."

"I think you should show David this note. It must be nonsense. It sounds so unlike him, and I am sure he really cares for you."

"Oh no." Jane was proud of the command she had regained over her voice. "I have reason to believe that there may be some truth to this. And if your brother was the cause of this poor woman's predicament, I am sure he would take care of her. I would prefer to ignore it, though I do wonder who my well-wisher is."

"Yes." Sophie studied the note again. "I did suspect

for a moment that it might be Maria, but this is far from her hand, which looks more like the tracks of a clumsy spider."

"Would she really write something like this?"

"Certainly, if it suited her ends. What of Phoebe Danvers?"

"No. I think she is content with Dromree, and I cannot see her stooping to anonymous notes. Had she wished to inform me of something like this she would simply walk up to me and say it."

"I think you may be right, and I like her the better for it. Who else?" She saw an expression on Jane's face. "Who have you thought of, Jane?"

"Crossley Carruthers! He was behaving very strangely this morning when I met him in the park. I missed part of what he said, but he could have been trying to tell me this. I have never seen his handwriting."

"Well, I wouldn't put anonymous notes beyond him, but what does he hope to gain by it? If he thinks to make you elope with him, he's lost his wits. And what would it gain him? You have no money of your own, have you?"

"No, and my parents would see me in rags before they acknowledged such as him as my husband. Could he be so foolish? He declared that he knew his love was hopeless—"

"His what?"

"Love. He claimed to be dying of love for me."

"Well, that is twaddle! He is the most shallow, self-centered creature alive. He loves nothing but his own comfort. Do you know, he chooses which invitation to accept according to the quality of the food or the comfort of the beds."

"But even a hedonist can love."

"Oh let us forget him and the foolish note," said Sophie abruptly. "But I will have a word with Mr. Carruthers when next I see him."

The occasion presented itself that very evening at a reception, where Mr. Carruthers found himself the nervous target of Sophie's interest.

"So many weeks of the Season gone by, Mr. Carruthers," she said sweetly. "So many pairings, not to speak of the couplings."

"Lady Sophie!" he exclaimed with a strangled laugh.

"And, alas, I have not found the man of my dreams, and you have not found your fortune."

"Really, I—"

"Of course, you have foolishly wasted so much time at Marlborough Square. What can you have been about? You must know you are not up to my weight, and Jane has not a penny at her own disposal, besides being spoken for. Maria! Do not tell me you are smitten with my cousin?"

She turned laughing eyes on him as he absorbed her words, and could not help but say, "I believe Miss Sandiford to bring a handsome dowry."

"Oh certainly," she replied. "But it will not go willy-nilly, only to a target of Lady Sandiford's choosing. If Jane were so foolish as to marry to disoblige her parents, she could die in poverty and they would not raise a finger."

He had recovered his composure. "Then we must all

rejoice that she will wed with their blessing," he said and sauntered off.

Sophie's spirits were lifted by this encounter, and she was amused to see that Mr. Carruthers spoke briefly with Lady Harroving, then left. A glare across the room from her cousin was quite pleasing as well, for it confirmed her suspicion that Lady Harroving had something to do with Crossley Carruthers' strange pursuit of Jane.

Jane summoned a smile when Sophie related the incident and was truly relieved to think she did not have Mr. Carruthers' broken heart on her conscience. Whether he was the author of the note or not, however, the fact remained that the contents probably contained a germ of truth. Thus, she found it impossible to be in high spirits. If only she had not seen Lord Wraybourne that day in Clarke Street, she could have laughed off the whole thing as Sophie was inclined to do. But in that knowledge, Jane could only console herself with the thought that he was impelled by duty and not by love of the lady in question.

Jane was further distressed to see Sophie move off to join a group which included Lord Randal and his sisters. Knowing how she herself felt, Jane could guess Sophie would not be able to stop such behavior even if she realized how harmful it might be in the end. Perhaps, Jane really ought to find the courage to speak to Lord Wraybourne or to Lord Randal. However, the mere thought of doing the latter gave her a *frisson* of horror, and the former seemed too disloyal.

The Harroving party moved on to Almack's, and Jane entertained a faint hope that the Ashby party would go elsewhere. But, of course, they joined the cream of Society at the Marriage Mart. Jane wondered whether the patronesses had entertained doubts about giving vouchers to Lord Randal. He was hardly a pattern of propriety, but then there were a number of other gentlemen present, and not a few of the ladies, whose private lives would not bear close scrutiny. Birth could outweigh a great deal, after all.

Promenading with Mr. Brummell, Jane found herself discussing, in what she hoped were general terms, her predicament. She had always found the Beau a pleasant companion, and he was very shrewd as well as surprisingly discreet.

"I discover myself in a quandary, Mr. Brummell."

"If it is a matter of how to hold your gloves or the color for your stationery, I am sure I will be able to assist you, Miss Sandiford."

"Nothing so simple, I am afraid, Sir."

"Simple! Miss Sandiford, I thought you to be one of my most promising pupils. Such details are complex and crucial."

She smiled, aware that he was playing his part, not speaking seriously. "I am afraid, Mr. Brummell, that it is more a question of scruples and, perhaps, etiquette."

"Ah, etiquette." The Beau waved an elegant and perfectly manicured hand. "There, Miss Sandiford, I am an expert. Inquire away."

Jane found it very difficult, now the moment had come, to put her problem into words without revealing too much. "My question is, would it be proper for me to approach a gentleman of my acquaintance in order to discuss matters personal to him and a friend—a lady friend?"

"Proper? Most definitely not. But, perhaps, desirable. I cannot tell."

Jane met his smiling, heavy-lidded eyes. He was being quite sincere for once. At times, she had observed, he was the kindest of men. She understood why so many people were devoted to him despite his annoying ways.

"I do not think I can say more . . . ," Jane admitted after a moment. "But, a year or two ago, if I had been acquainted with Lord Byron, would it have been desirable for me to have asked him to stay away from Lady Caroline, for the lady's sake?"

He smiled delightedly. "What a wonderful hypothesis, Miss Sandiford. If you had been a fortune-teller, yes, I believe it would have been desirable, but I fear you would have been renamed Cassandra. They would both have laughed at caution. My dear lady, if you are attempting to manage matters of the heart, I say to you, desist. Not for reasons of propriety, but because you might as well stand on London Bridge and tell the Thames to stop flowing."

Jane sighed. "Must we stand and watch our friends hurtle towards disaster then?"

As she said it, she thought the words could apply to the Beau himself. From all accounts, he was following a disastrous course of gambling and debt, and his friends were unable to turn him from it. Maybe it was the same thought that caused his famous smile to twist slightly.

"That, or turn away. But it is the fate of true friends to stand and watch, Miss Sandiford. A painful experience, though sometimes there are pieces to be rescued after the debacle."

If this conversation gave Jane little consolation, she would have been even more distressed to realize that Sophie had drawn Lord Randal apart into a small salon off the refreshment room.

Lord Randal was not best pleased, either. "This is most improper, Sophie."

"Randal. Don't tell me *you* are going to start preaching at me too," Sophie said with a laugh.

He extracted a delicate snuffbox and took a pinch. "*I* choose where and when I go beyond the bounds of propriety. If you wish to speak to me privately, can it not wait until tomorrow? I will call on you."

"And Maria will insist on sitting with us. You are wasting time. Listen to me. Jane has received an anonymous note saying that David is off in Harrogate with a pregnant mistress."

His hand was arrested midway to his nose. "The devil you say!"

"She is trying to make light of it, but I can see it has hurt her. Is it true?"

"Of course it ain't. He was in Harrogate, but it was on business for your uncle."

"Uncle Henry! What kind of business can he have that would involve David?"

"Never mind. But you can reassure Jane that he is now in Exeter, or quite likely on his way back. So, unless she cares to think that he has *enceinte* convenients all over England, she can put her fears to rest."

"Could you tell her, Randal? She would believe you, I think."

He shrugged. "Very well. Now let us leave this room before someone finds us here."

"Would it be so terrible?" Sophie asked archly, leaning against the door to prevent their exit. "After all, we are behaving with total propriety."

"But no one would believe that, minx, as you well know. Stop fooling, Sophie, and move. You've no more desire to create a scandal than I have."

"Have I not? What could happen? They would all fuss and go red in the face. It could be amusing. Perhaps," she said with a grin, "they'd say you had to marry me."

"It's more likely that David would run me through. What mad idea have you got into your head now?"

"Might it not be fun for us to marry, Randal? You wouldn't be always preaching at me and improving me."

His eyes had hardened. "A few minutes ago you complained of just that. If that was a proposal, Sophie, the answer is no," he said flatly.

Sophie moved away from the door and reached up to touch his cheek, feather light. Then her fingers ran over his lips in a caress. He stood quite still, eyes locked with hers.

"Why no?" she asked softly.

But she had made a strategic mistake. He sidestepped her and opened the door, then glanced outside to make sure that all was clear.

"Because you'd have me gray before my time. Go and find Jane. I'll wait here for a few moments and won't be surprised if she doesn't lend herself to this kind of improper behavior."

"Being much more of a lady than I am, I suppose!" snapped Sophie. She took a breath and smiled, with her lips, at least. "Sometimes, my friend, I fear you are growing sober. It must be old age."

With that she swirled out of the room. Slowly and thoughtfully, Lord Randal took a pinch of snuff, carefully dusting off his jacket afterwards. His thoughts were obviously far away. He was still standing there when Jane came hesitantly into the room. She had been reluctant to keep this tryst, not just for sake of propriety, but because it went against Lord Wraybourne's advice to avoid being alone with any man. Though Lord Randal was surely safe.

"Very strange behavior for Almack's, is it not?" he said with a reassuring smile as he closed the door. "But this will only take a moment." He quickly recounted his conversation with Sophie and his reassurances.

"Thank you," Jane said, feeling suddenly as if a cloud had moved to allow the sun to shine through. "David told me that he was going to Exeter, but I let that silly note throw me into a panic. So if he was meeting a woman in Harrogate, it would be for his uncle?"

"Yes. I cannot go into more detail, but I am certain he could have no personal interest in her."

This made Mr. Moulton-Scrope seem a little peculiar, but that was no concern of Jane's. She suddenly realized she could now speak to Lord Randal if she had the courage. Though it might achieve nothing, she knew she had to try.

"Did Sophie say anything else, Lord Randal?" she asked.

She knew, from the flicker of emotion in his eyes, that something had indeed occurred.

"Nothing of importance, Jane. We really should leave here." He went to open the door again.

Gathering desperate courage, she said, "Sophie loves you!"

He stopped abruptly, and Jane noticed that, sudden as the arrest of motion had been, a sculptor could have taken the lines of his body and made of them a masterpiece.

"She is playing games," he said simply.

"No. She loves you. I know this is an embarrassment to you, but I felt you should know. If you could see less of her, perhaps the feelings would pass and she would be able to fix her affections on someone who can return them."

He turned to her, a half smile on his lips. "Dear Jane. Are you implying I am unable to feel the tenderer emotions?"

"Good heavens, no!" Jane was heartily wishing she had held her tongue. "But if you were going to fall in love with Sophie, you would have done so long ago. And Lord Wraybourne has told me you want to join a regiment."

"What a very simple view you have of love, to be sure. But you are, of course, right in this case. If Sophie has taken a mad fancy in her head to imagine herself enamored of me, then I should by all means avoid her to give her time for a return of sanity."

With that he steered Jane out of the room and back into the glittering company.

↬ 14 ↫

JANE COULD NOW anticipate Lord Wraybourne's return with pleasure and feel the noble satisfaction of having done her best to steer her friend from disaster. It was painful, of course, to watch Sophie's sadness as Lord Randal discreetly avoided her. If they met, he was always in the company of his sisters. On many occasions, Lady Caroline or Lady Cecilia would explain that he was otherwise engaged.

"Poor Randal," said Lady Caroline one day in Hookham's. "He has really been very kind to give up so much time to the entertainment of mere sisters, but now we have many willing escorts." This was said with a delicate coloring on the faces of both twins. "He feels able at last to engage in activities of his own choosing, horrid things such as prizefights and mechanical expositions."

It was true that both sisters were well on the way to finding husbands. The world was expecting Viscount Daubry to make an offer for Caroline any day, and Lady Cecilia was seen to spend a great deal of time with Mr. Jeremy Hythe. To be sure, he was a commoner, but a wealthy man all the same, who was making a name for himself in the business of state and expected to go far.

This further felicity, and that of many other young ladies who were choosing and being chosen, did nothing to lighten Sophie's spirits. In fact, she only achieved her usual animation when engaged in the planning of the masked ball. Jane encouraged Lady Harroving to busy Sophie with this as much as possible.

Meanwhile, Jane received a brief note from her betrothed, telling her to expect his return on the twenty-eighth of May. The missive was accompanied by another gift, this time a charming onyx box, bound with silver. She thought at first it might be a snuffbox, though she could not imagine what she would do with such; but when she opened it, she found the compartment lined with creamy silk upon which rested a faceted ruby in the shape of a heart.

For the next forty-eight hours the household grew accustomed to treating Jane as if she were a sleepwalker, usually to be found wandering around in a daydream. The staff, now working frantically to prepare for the ball, would detour around her with a load of china or a large vase, knowing that to ask her to excuse them and step aside would take far longer. Sophie lost all patience with Jane's constant wish to talk about her brother and snorted in disgust when she found Jane in her room, sitting in dreamy contemplation of her wedding dress, newly arrived from the *modiste* and ready to be taken with her to Carne in a week's time.

Jane's excitement reached its apogee on the day appointed for Lord Wraybourne's return, then slowly evaporated over the long day when he did not arrive. Though Jane's dreamy happiness had irritated Sophie, she could not stand to see her disappointment now.

"Travelling is always a chancy business, Jane," she consoled.

"But what if there has been an accident?"

"Then we will know, sooner or later. Come and help me with these flowers, Jane," she insisted. "It was mad of Maria to invite twenty for dinner only two days before the ball. The staff are going demented."

In one way or another, Sophie kept Jane busy throughout the remainder of the afternoon and evening and bullied her into dressing for the evening when she said she would rather eat in her room.

"David will likely come here as soon as he reaches Town, knowing you are expecting him. How will you like it if he finds you in your working dress?"

Jane was glad of Sophie's wisdom when, as she waited with the glittering company to go into dinner, Lord Wraybourne was, in fact, announced. He was tired and dirty and still in his travelling clothes, but even before apologizing to his cousin for appearing so, came directly to Jane.

"I'm sorry I was not able to keep our appointment," he said softly, with an intimate smile, then added in a louder voice, with a rueful twist to his lips, "I have had the very devil of a day." He turned to include the rest of the group. "Maria, I hope you can excuse my dirt. I stopped at Welwyn last night so I only had a matter of thirty miles to cover. A couple of hours, I thought."

He had the attention of the whole group. They could sense a good tale.

He sighed. "First I was delayed in setting out when the ostler discovered one of the traces to be worn through. Then, only a few miles out, my leader went lame. We un-hitched the team and walked them to the next inn. I left them there with the groom and proceeded on a hired hack."

He was a skillful *raconteur,* and everyone was following his misadventures in smiling sympathy.

"It still should not have taken me all day to arrive here? Of course not. And it wouldn't have done if I had not come across an overturned stage."

He acknowledged the disbelieving laughter. "I assure you! Wailing women and cursing men all over the road. No fewer than three children, though it seemed more, all screeching.

"I could hardly ride by with a wave. Fortunately, there were no serious injuries but many minor ones, and one man had been knocked unconscious. I restored what order I could, then sent a young fellow off to the next village for help—on my horse.

"There was a long wait but help did come in the form of a couple of old gigs which conveyed those unable to walk. Eventually, we came to the village of Hadley. There I

discovered the messenger had continued on his journey—
on my horse!"

He interrupted his story to address his cousin. "I hope
you are going to feed me, Maria, even though I am in such
a disreputable state. I am not sure that food has passed my
lips since breakfast."

"Of course I am, David," she said gaily. "We are all wait-
ing for more of your adventures. I am sure there *are* more.
But you seem to be a jinx today. If this house burns down,
I will expect you to recompense us!"

"At this moment I would pay you the cost of this house
for a square meal," he announced.

Choosing his time to a nicety, Nuttall announced the
meal, a discreet nod of his head assuring Lady Harroving
that he had anticipated the need for an extra place at table.

Lord Wraybourne offered his arm to Jane. "I expect
you have waited in all day for me and are justifiably cross,"
he said softly.

"It would serve you right if I had forgotten you were
expected."

When he first entered she had been overwhelmed by
her emotions and doubted she could have been coherent,
but the interlude had allowed her to regain a superficial
composure, beneath which her nerves hummed and she
felt bubbly and light, like champagne. She was proud to be
able to converse in an everyday manner.

"I am not cross, however," she went on. "I have been
busy with my costume for the masked ball."

He was startled. "Good Lord, I had forgotten that would
be coming up!" It appeared he would be angry, but he sud-

denly laughed. "I find I am too weary to care. Only tell me your disguise."

"No, My Lord," she replied with a mischievous look. "That you will have to discover for yourself at the time."

Once the party was seated, Lord Wraybourne continued his story.

"I will be brief, or I will never get to eat. It was now two in the afternoon and there was no riding horse in the village. The locals were most helpful, suggesting a lad be sent to various houses in the area in search of mounts. Someone even recommended the doctor's cob but I was spared that as he was found to be elsewhere that day.

"I resisted the urge to collapse in that place." He flashed a meaningful look at Jane. "Which was not difficult as the only inn was full of the aforementioned wailing women, cursing men, and screaming children—all still doing same. I bought—*bought,* mind you—one of the broken-down gigs and continued my journey.

"Being on a busy road, I expected to soon find another village where a suitable mount would be available, and I did. I was within sight of London by five o'clock"—he paused—"when the horse lost a shoe!"

The whole company burst into laughter.

Lord Wraybourne regarded them plaintively. "I gave up. I hitched the nag to a nearby bush and walked, leaving word at the next habitation of where he was to be found and a few coins for the trouble of bringing him into town. And here I am."

"But surely you did not walk to this very door, Wraybourne," said one of the men. "You took a cab."

"A cab?" said his lordship in horror. "After today I was going nowhere near the equine species, nor will I until the day is over." He then applied himself hungrily to his food.

All present were very pleased with this saga and began to contribute their own tales of travelling mishaps. Jane was content to listen. He was a wonderful man. She watched him unself-consciously, not bothering to eat or converse with the gentleman on her other side.

Eventually, he turned to her. "I am a dreadful partner, Jane. But I was truly famished. How have you been?"

"Very well," she said. "I must thank you for the gift. It is delightful."

"I bought it because I thought it beautiful, but it is intended to be set. I will have it done."

"If you please, I would rather not," she said quickly.

He looked inquiringly at her and she explained, "It is a personal treasure at the moment. I would not like to exhibit it."

His eyes met hers, and he raised his glass slightly in a silent toast. She responded in kind, smiling gently.

Lady Harroving's voice broke into their moment. "Come, you two! Why are you forever billing and cooing at the table?" With a malicious glint in her eyes she added, "David, tell us what you have been about on your journeys. We are all agog."

There was a stirring of interest, for a number of the guests had heard Peel-Saunders' Harrogate story.

Lord Wraybourne raised his brow slightly and looked around. "My business is boring routine, Maria, I assure you, of no interest to you except for the strange misadventures I suffered on the way back."

He rose from the table. "Forgive me, cousin, but I must leave and seek my bed. I would not have called here except that I had engaged myself to visit Jane and felt she should have an apology in person.

"And of course," he added, "I have now to walk home."

This caused fresh laughter and shouted suggestions that he beware of runaway horses. He bowed ironically and left. The whole company was delighted with their evening's entertainment. This late in the Season it was rare to come across anything so fresh and unconventional.

Later, Jane was given a note by the butler.

> *Written in haste! I would offer to make all good by riding with you tomorrow, but the weather is threatening rain. I will call, David.*

The scribbled note gave evidence of his exhaustion, and she thought how tempting it must have been earlier for him to go straight to his home and send a note of apology. Such thoughtfulness was so typical of the man she had come to love. She folded the note up small and placed it beneath the ruby heart in the onyx box.

∽ 15 ∽

As LORD WRAYBOURNE had predicted, the next day was cold and wet and there could be no riding out for pleasure. He called, as promised, but there was no excuse for him and Jane to seek privacy so they joined in the household activities, even playing a lighthearted game of Commerce, which Sophie won.

The next day was the Harrovings' masked ball. Along with the rest of the household, Jane was busy helping with arrangements and preparing her costume. Sophie was in high spirits, so high that Jane felt uneasy. Lord Randal would be at the ball. What did Sophie have planned?

The grand ballroom of the Harrovings' house had been transformed into a sylvan glade. Lady Harroving had not copied Countess Lieven by spreading grass upon the floor, but artificial trees and thousands of plants transformed the surrounding area into leafy grottoes, ideally suited to private encounters. As the weather had recovered and the evening was warm, the terrace doors were open to the small garden where more discreet corners were available.

Jane and Sophie had explored during the afternoon. Sophie declared that she had chosen the most suitable grottoes for private moments. Despite Sophie's arguments, Jane was still nervous about the whisperer and did not think that she could bring herself to slip away into one of the corners with anyone except Lord Wraybourne, but felt deliciously excited at that prospect.

She hoped he shared the fashionable fascination with the medieval. Her gown was of deep green velvet. The bodice hugged tight down to the hips and then swirled out into a full skirt. Since all her other gowns had high waists, the form-fitting dress seemed very bold. The neckline was low so the swelling of her breasts was revealed, and a gold cord was cinched about her hips, seeming to emphasize her womanly curves. Even though Sophie had called medieval dress nunlike, Jane knew that the style revealed more of her shapely body than her usual gowns. She felt a tremor of nervousness, as if her mother might be peering at her from the shadows, but shook that off. She was sure Lord Wraybourne would approve.

She had originally intended to wear her hair in two long plaits but decided that this would give away her identity too easily. She had chosen instead to coil it over each ear and to cover the whole with a filigree net, cleverly lined to suggest that the hair beneath was golden.

When she was dressed and ready for the ball she applied a delicate touch of rouge to give her skin unusual color and placed a pearly mask over her eyes. When Sophie came to her room, she clapped her hands with delight.

"No one will know you!" she declared.

Sophie herself was not so well disguised. Her page's costume of black silk was comprised of knee breeches and jacket with foaming lace at neck and cuffs. The feathered hat sat jauntily on her curls, but they were as clear an identification as her name. Not even her slim black mask could disguise her. But Sophie, of course, had no particular desire to be unknown. She was able to enjoy the daring pleasures of a masquerade without disguise.

Full of excitement, the two young ladies went down to slip into the ballroom. Because it was a masked ball, there was no formality, no receiving line. They found it easy to mingle, and Jane was amused at the fact that she was not recognized. How liberating it was not to be the Sandiford heiress or Lord Wraybourne's betrothed, but an unknown. She wandered among the Romans, the knights, the Arabians, and the yokels. Thank heaven no one had chosen to come as Adam, which had happened not so very long ago. She recognized a few of the guests. Some, like Sophie, had hardly tried to hide their identities at all. But she was surprised how many people appeared as strangers when she knew she had probably met them all during her time in London. Jane wondered if she would recognize Lord Wraybourne and if he would recognise her.

The highest sticklers had stayed away, of course, but a

large proportion of Society was only too willing to disport itself in daring and permissible circumstances, and the event was obviously a success.

Lady Harroving, dressed as Venus in supposedly classical and very revealing draperies, glowed with triumph. She had temporarily abandoned her vendetta against Jane, and as she had an interesting Austrian diplomat in her sights, she was inclined to let the matter slide. She had belatedly realized that it might be unpleasant for her if David became aware of her machinations. Still, when she came across Crossley Carruthers in Elizabethan elegance, she could not resist telling him of Jane's disguise.

"That's of no interest to me, Maria. And I damned well don't believe you were mistaken about the chit's circumstances."

"Of course I was, Crossley. But even if she is no longer marriage material, she is a handsome piece. Wait until you see her in her clinging gown. Do you not feel you deserve a little taste of her charms after all your labors?"

He wet his lips but was hesitant. "I wouldn't want to cross Wraybourne."

Diverted, she asked, "Whatever did you think you were going to do when you ran off with his bride?"

"He's such a stiff-rumped one. He'd wash his hands of her. No use crying over spilled milk and all that."

She couldn't repress a little titter. "Oh, Crossley, you do amuse me. But my cousin isn't here yet, and in this setting, I'm sure you could find a discreet corner. She's such a sweet girl and quite fond of you. I don't think she'd set up a screech if you went about it the right way."

"Protest my undying love, hopeless longings, that kind of tripe?"

"Exactly," she approved. "You have a wonderful way with young things, my friend."

"If my wonderful ways don't bear fruit soon, Maria, I'll be all rolled up," he said disconsolately. "I would have probably starved to death this Season if I hadn't discovered that the arty fellows set a damned good spread at their open evenings." He nodded. "Yes, the chit owes me something." And he went off on his search.

Jane, meanwhile, was watching the behavior of some of the guests and wondering what her mother would say. Merely to picture Lady Sandiford in this company made Jane giggle. It was beyond her powers of imagination. She, however, was not finding the event unpleasant. She enjoyed dancing and had many partners, some of whom she recognized and some she could only guess at. She was fairly sure that none had identified her. A few gentlemen flirted rather more than would normally be allowed but in the most harmless manner. She decided that unless one was unwise enough to wander off into the more secluded grottoes, the tenets of society still held, and a young lady was safe from incivility—and whispering voices.

Although she was enjoying herself, Jane scanned the room constantly, seeking Lord Wraybourne, sure that he would never find her unless Sophie was to describe her costume. But before Jane discovered her betrothed, she was detected by Sir Marius, who knew her at once and claimed not to have had help. He could not disguise his height and so wore only a domino. He had a mask but swung it from his fingers.

"It's as well you didn't live in medieval times, Jane," he said. "There would have been wars fought over you."

Jane was delighted. "I never thought to receive a compliment from you, Sir Marius."

"I must be growing addled with age," he sighed with a humorous look.

She suddenly became aware of him as a desirable man. Over time they had developed a kind of friendship, and she had learned to be at ease with him. Now she was shocked to find herself wondering what it would be like to be kissed by him and felt natural color adding to the rouge on her cheeks. She had never been kissed by any man other than her betrothed. On later reflection, she would decide she had been led astray by the free-flowing wine and the air of licentiousness. For the moment, forgetful of all her good intentions and the threat of the whisperer, she looked at Sir Marius with new eyes.

"A word with you, Sir Marius," she said and drifted around some potted ferns into a secluded area.

"What are you about, minx?" he asked, following.

He sounded stern, but she could see the light of amusement in his eyes and that reassured her. This was as she imagined a game with a brother might be.

"I would request a favor of you, kind sir."

"And what would that favor be, sweet maid?"

Now the moment had come, her nerve almost deserted her and she swallowed hard. "A kiss," she said, breathlessly.

The humor glowed brighter in his eyes. "Why?"

"Let us call it a scientific study," she got out, her heart choking in her throat.

What was she doing? He'd tell Lord Wraybourne, for sure. But that did not seem to be Sir Marius's inclination.

He laughed. "The Royal Institution would not approve," he remarked and raised her chin with one long, strong finger.

"I don't suppose many people would approve," she whispered, mesmerized by his face above hers.

"David would probably call me out," he said conversationally, bending until his face was just inches from hers.

Panicked, she slipped away from him. "That would be dreadful," she said quickly.

She would have left immediately, but he caught her hand. "I will be around all evening," he said with a grin.

He had never really intended to kiss her, had known she would turn tail. She fled the grotto to the sound of an understanding chuckle. She knew he had been kind in a way, but she was ashamed of her flight nonetheless. Having once started the adventure, she should have had the nerve to go through with it. This surely would be the last chance for such experiments. In two days she would leave for home to prepare for her wedding. She wished she had the courage to return and surprise him by taking up his challenge. She wished Lord Wraybourne would arrive and take his position by her side so she would not be tempted to such foolishness.

When she emerged onto the dance floor she was claimed by her next partner, Sir Edwin. He did not wear a mask and was dressed as Shakespeare. The costume was tolerably successful because of his half-bald head and a false beard. Unfortunately he felt obliged to quote from the Bard, not always appropriately.

" 'Your azure veins, your alabaster skin / Your coral lips, your snow-white dimpled chin,' " he murmured to her. "Is not that appropriate, sweet miss?"

"I have no dimple, Sir," she replied as she curtsied to begin the dance.

"But you have golden hair. How about this, my dear. 'Her hair like golden threads played with her breath. Oh modest wantons, wanton modesty.' "

"My hair is most suitably confined," she remarked as she passed under his arm, a little startled by the tone of his words. "Does that absolve me from wantonness?"

"Would that I could loose it," he whispered hotly, making her glad the dance separated them at that point.

The whisper reminded her horribly of her tormentor, though of course it was ridiculous to think of Sir Edwin lurking in corners to distress young ladies. But no matter how trustworthy he was, the atmosphere of the masque had obviously had its effect on him. She had no wish to dare a kiss with Sir Edwin, whose lips were probably as clammy as his hands.

When the dance brought them together again he declared, " 'Frailty, thy name is woman.' I feel I know you."

"Not if you think me frail, Sir Edwin," she said sharply, causing him to miss his step and confuse the other couples in their set.

"All women are frail," he said crossly, "in mind if not in body. The Bard says, 'For men have marble, women waxen minds / And therefore are they formed as marble will.' "

"If you expect women to shape themselves to your liking, Sir Edwin, I wonder at your pursuit of Lady Sophie."

"Good God!" he said suddenly. "It's Miss Sandiford. You always had too forward a tongue."

Again the dance separated them before she could answer, but this time she was not thankful. She longed to give Sir Edwin a sharp retort.

The time spent moving through the set from partner to partner cooled her irritation, however, and when they met again she merely said, with genuine curiosity, "Pray tell me, Sir Edwin, if you feel so about women, why have you been so much in our company? There are many more waxlike ladies around Town."

"I do not seek the easy way," he said with fervor. "It is my task to save Lady Sophie. Her brother is too lax. I would have prevented her from so imprudently displaying her limbs this evening. But I forgive. She is merely poorly governed. Consider her ruinous course, however, if she does not marry a man capable of forming her afresh."

Jane could think of nothing to say after this diatribe. She was thankful that there was no possibility of Sophie accepting his suit. She found him slightly frightening, and as soon as the dance was over she slipped away.

She had a mind to search for Sophie to relate the incident. She thought her friend should be on her guard. But Sophie was in the refreshment room amid a large, noisy group, so Jane decided instead to go to the entrance to see if the footman there had noticed Lord Wraybourne enter.

As she came to the top of the steps, however, she saw Lord Wraybourne entering below. Like his sister he had made no great effort to disguise his identity. He was dressed as Robin Hood in a medieval tunic of green and brown. A knife and hunting horn hung from his belt. The outfit suited him remarkably well, and she could not help but notice how the strong muscles in his legs were revealed by the green hose he wore.

She suddenly felt quite warm and dry in the mouth. How appropriate his costume was. She, after all, could be Maid Marian. She wondered with a smile whether she should make herself known to him or wait until she was recognized. The next moment she received a great shock. He turned to the lady who had entered with him and gave her his arm.

The lady was dressed as a Dresden shepherdess in a lacy and beribboned gown. She wore a charming villager hat, decorated with more ribbons, and carried a crook. Her plain mask was really no disguise, and Jane was sure that she was not a relative of her betrothed or even a close friend in Society. Jane tried to tell herself that the lady was merely chance-met, and yet there was something in the way they walked and talked together that said otherwise. Suspicions she had believed put aside crept to the front of her mind again. Unhappily, and guiltily, Jane stepped back a little from the door and prepared to spy on them.

Lord Wraybourne stopped at the top of the stairs and tied on his own mask. He pulled the hood of his tunic over his auburn curls and was suddenly well-disguised.

"Ready?" he asked, smiling fondly at his companion.

She nodded but then asked, "David, are you sure this is wise? If anything goes wrong it could cause a great deal of talk."

"It is our only chance," he said and dropped a quick kiss on her cheek. "Be brave."

With that they entered the ballroom.

Jane stood frozen with disbelief. She realized that this could be the woman he had embraced on Clarke Street. Had he brought his mistress to the ball? It seemed unlike him to do anything so outrageous. And was this the same woman he had been seen with in Harrogate? Her waist was too small and trim for one with child. The shepherdess had made free with his name, which Jane had not yet brought herself to do, and that seemed the most terrible thing of all. The hurt that had been building in her was suddenly swamped by anger. She would not be duped, if that was their plan, nor would she give him up. How dare he. She would face them both, and if it caused a scandal, so be it!

However, by the time she had come out of her place of concealment and entered the crowded room, there was no sight of them. She angrily circled the dance floor, refusing a number of partners, and eventually spotted the shepherdess dancing with a Red Indian Jane suspected to be Lord Marchmont. There was no sign of her betrothed. Had she been wrong in her suspicions? And yet, there was that conversation, which was *not* open to misinterpretation. Jane wondered if she could be losing her mind. As she passed a thicket of potted bamboo, however, she heard his voice.

". . . if you could keep an eye on Jane for me."

There was no opening on this side. Trying to appear calm, Jane hurried around to the grotto entrance, but found no Robin Hood within, only a sinister-looking Renaissance gentleman all in black. She recognized Lord Randal.

"Where is Lord Wraybourne?" she demanded.

"He just left," he said calmly. "It is Jane, is it not?"

As she turned to go, he caught her hand and said rather plaintively, "Are you too going to desert me? Alas, all the ladies seem to be out of kindness tonight."

"Perhaps you should not look so evil, Lord Randal," she said, not resisting his restraining hand. She would make herself ridiculous, scouring the room for her betrothed. He could not avoid her all night. "You make me think of those Venetian stories where someone is always slipping a knife into someone else's back."

He gave her a hug. "Delightful child! That was precisely my intention. It is tedious to be always seen as decorative."

Within the impersonal embrace Jane looked up at him. Her anger and bewilderment focussed. "Kiss me," she said. It was no longer curiosity which drove her but the desire for revenge. She just wished she could force David Kyle to watch!

With mischievous humor, Lord Randal dropped a kiss upon her lips. Jane shook her head.

"No wonder the ladies are unkind if that is your best kiss."

Fire suddenly danced behind the black mask as he grinned at her. "You didn't say that you wanted my *best* kiss. . . ."

His arms enveloped her as his head bent down, and she

found her body shaped and curved to his. Off balance and breathless, she would have fallen if he had not supported her and yet she was secure in the strength of his arms. His lips played upon hers with such sureness and pleasure that she gladly responded. It stirred a kind of excitement, and yet she had to accept there was none of the devastation her betrothed could arouse in her. At last Lord Randal withdrew his lips. He said nothing, merely smiled at her.

"That was a very nice kiss," she said truthfully.

He gave an elegant bow to acknowledge the compliment, but his eyes told her he guessed something of her motives. "Do you mind telling me what you are about?" he asked.

Jane felt unable to confess that she had been using him for revenge and so she summoned up a light manner. "Oh, despite my undeservedly *risqué* reputation, I have led an unexciting life, my friend," she said airily. "I decided I should have a few little adventures before I become a dull married lady." But she forgot her act and spoke seriously as she added, "Once I am wed I am determined to be completely faithful, even if Lord Wraybourne proves not to be."

"I am sure he would never be so uncourteous," he said quietly and with equal sobriety. "Are you still bothered by that letter? I assure you, he is not much given to wickedness."

"Then why," Jane demanded, irritated into honesty, "has he brought another woman to this ball?"

Lord Randal was surprised. "Has he, begad? He merely said he had some business to take care of. Let us go and investigate."

He would have no argument and guided Jane in search of her betrothed. The crush on the dance floor had thinned, as many people had decided to go in to supper. Lord Wraybourne was spotted across the room, talking to his sister.

"So," said Lord Randal. "Where is the lady?"

Jane looked around. Had she imagined the whole? But then she spotted the woman. "There," she said. "The shepherdess."

"My, my," he said softly. "How intriguing. Let us go and talk to David before your imagination runs away with you."

Despite Jane's demands for elucidation, he would say nothing more until they reached the brother and sister.

Sophie looked out of temper. "Here is Jane now," she said crossly. "I suggest you pay attention to her and leave me alone. I don't consider breeches indecent."

She imperiously commanded Lord Randal to take her into the garden and swept away while her brother shrugged and appeared to put her costume out of his mind. Jane could detect only warm appreciation on his face when he turned to her.

"May I congratulate you on the costume, Jane," said Lord Wraybourne. "It is very becoming and a cunning disguise."

"Yours also becomes you very well, David," she said, forcing herself to use his given name.

If some strange woman could use his name, then she could too. He noted it with pleasure but with some degree of curiosity as well. Jane waited for a comment or a voluntary explanation of the strange matters at hand. None was forthcoming.

Abandoning a number of subtle approaches Jane asked outright, "Who is the shepherdess?"

He looked at her in puzzlement for a moment and then snapped his fingers. "Of course, you were the lady behind the pillar by the stairs. I didn't recognize you at the time."

"Are you going to tell me?" she persisted, disconcerted by his lack of alarm.

"There isn't time," he said in a preoccupied manner.

His eyes scanned the dance floor. A couple emerged, giggling, from a nearby bower, and he swept her into it and took her in his arms.

"Have you any idea how much havoc you have caused in me, Jane Sandiford? I should have insisted on an early wedding. I love you to distraction."

Jane knew that she needed to breathe but she seemed to have forgotten how. There was no doubting the sincerity or the need, glowing in his eyes. His mouth met hers, and they seemed to melt together. Although it was not as dramatic a performance as Lord Randal's, she found it much more stirring. She made free with her hands to feel the long muscles of his back and felt him do the same. Distant lilting music made their embrace seem like a dance.

Abruptly, he broke away and cradled her face in his hands. His thumbs teased her lips and she turned to kiss one, marveling at herself. With a choking laugh he held her close.

"Our marriage cannot be a moment too soon for me," he whispered in her ear. "I doubt I can control myself much longer. Perhaps it is as well that I cannot spend the night in dalliance with you. I have to play a little game out on the dance floor," he continued. "The shepherdess is involved, but she is not my mistress. In no way does she threaten you. Trust me."

"I trust you," she said, conscious of his body pressed to hers.

All doubts and questions had been swept away. It was not possible that this feeling they shared could be founded in deceit.

"You could help me if you wish," he said.

"Anything," she answered.

"Can you find Crossley Carruthers and persuade him to dance with you?"

"He will take little persuasion once I reveal my identity," she replied. "Sophie said he has been seeking me out."

"He has better taste than I thought," he remarked with a warm smile, then dropped a quick kiss on her lips. "Later," he murmured and propelled her on her way.

She had spotted Mr. Carruthers earlier in the evening and used the knowledge to avoid him. Now she approached where he stood alone, glowering at the company. She realized with disgust that he was drunk but summoned her resolution and went up to him.

"Mr. Carruthers," she said teasingly. "You have been ignoring me."

"Who the devil are you?" he asked.

"Fie on you, Sir," she gushed, trying to be as silly and coy as possible. "And I thought we were so well acquainted!"

He studied her for a moment, and she suspected that his eyes did not focus as well as usual.

"Could it be Miss Sandiford?" he asked at last. "Those yella eyes. Well, well, well. I didn't think you'd come around."

Jane took an involuntary step backwards as he pushed his face towards hers.

"Not surprising I didn't see those eyes till you got close up," he said with geniality. "But I should have known those curves." He seemed to recollect his role of lover. "You are too beautiful to be wasted on an ungrateful lecher like Wraybourne."

Jane felt disgusted, but she summoned a flirtatious smile. "Really, Mr. Carruthers!"

"He's deserted you again, eh?" he leered and caught her in his arm. "Let's find a cozy grotto, and I'll convince you I'm the better man."

"Good heavens, no," she said sharply. "I have been told most expressly not to go into such places."

"Rules were made to be broken," he whispered.

A shudder passed through her. Was it the same hoarse voice?

"Not a soul will know. They are all too engaged with their own pleasure."

To her horror he dragged her close and pressed his lips to hers. In public! Fumes of wine, both stale and fresh, almost overpowered her. His lips were soggy and moist against hers. She thrust him away without effect, but then suddenly he was gone.

Sir Marius had him by the ruff. "I think it is time you left," he said formidably.

Pale-faced, Mr. Carruthers seemed ready to agree.

Jane looked round and saw Lord Wraybourne and the shepherdess close by. She could tell from the conflict on his face that he heartily supported the action Sir Marius had taken and yet was concerned for the ruination of his plan. She summoned a smile and turned back to Sir Marius and his captive.

"Please, do not be cross, Sir Marius. It was merely a little game."

She gave him a meaningful look, hoping he would realize that there was more to the business than he first perceived. A look of disgust crossed his face, and too late she saw that he thought she was referring to their earlier encounter. He thought she had asked Crossley Carruthers to kiss her.

"Nevertheless," said Sir Marius stonily, "I am sure that Mr. Carruthers would prefer to be on his way."

"Quite!" squawked the victim, half strangled by the hand at his neck.

"Nonsense!" snapped Jane, genuinely angry at the situation in which she found herself. "Mr. Carruthers was just about to lead me out to this set."

She stretched forward her hand, and Sir Marius could do nothing but let the gentleman go. He scowled quite dreadfully at Jane as she walked away, and she could not resist giving him a saucy look over her shoulder. He would know soon enough that she was innocent, but, goodness, he looked angry enough to crush rocks! She had best avoid him until David could set the matter straight. Meanwhile, her partner's arm trembled beneath hers.

"Do not think me ungrateful for your aid," he said hoarsely. "But I would not have much minded leaving, and I had lief not be in Sir Marius's bad books. He could knock me out with one blow!"

"Be bold," she said bracingly. " 'Faint heart never won fair lady.' "

This and the increasing distance between themselves and the scowling Corinthian enabled him to recover his spirits. Unfortunately, this meant that he once again became amorous, and Jane wondered what he was about. Had he forgotten she was not a rich plum for his picking? Jane took solace from the fact that Lord Wraybourne and the shepherdess were one of the couples in their set. But when Mr. Carruthers realized who the Robin Hood was, he gave Jane a very knowing look and positively smirked with triumph.

The dances were lively country ones which did not favor long conversation. Unfortunately, the Sir Adrian's Passage involved the ladies passing from one gentleman's arms to the next. Mr. Carruthers was inclined to hold closely and managed to intrude his hands into the most unlikely places. To offset this, however, there was the advantage of the passages with her betrothed. During one of these he took the opportunity of their closeness to whisper a thank you and a promise to set matters right with Sir Marius.

At their last pass together he told her she could dismiss Carruthers as soon as she wished. However, Mr. Carruthers had become bold under her earlier encouragement and tried to hustle her over to the leafy shade, promising a variety of delights that disgusted her.

"If you do not let me go I will scream," she hissed.

"Why so coy now?" he queried hotly. "You showed how much you like my kisses and how much you want more. Bet Wraybourne's never given you more than a kiss on the cheek."

"You're drunk and disgusting," she snapped, wondering how she was going to get rid of him without a scene.

"Bet he's given more to Stella Hamilton," he continued. Seeing her bewilderment he went on. "That pretty shepherdess he has. Long-time friends they are. How many mistresses are you willing to allow him before you pay him back in his own coin?"

Panicked, she looked around and saw Sir Marius watching sardonically. She cast him an appealing look. He either did not see or chose to ignore it. She tugged at the hand which Carruthers held in a surprisingly strong grip. He was turning nasty.

"Or are you merely using me to get back at your neglectful fiancé? Taking advantage of my devotion? Not nice, Miss Sandiford," he sneered. "I am nobody's dupe. You'll come with me and pay your dues."

He broke off because someone had tapped him on the shoulder. It was Lord Wraybourne. The lecherous fortune hunter's eyes popped.

"My dear Carruthers," said his lordship pleasantly. "I fear for your health."

Jane found herself released and moved gratefully to stand beside her betrothed.

"My health is fine, My Lord," said Mr. Carruthers, with an attempt at boldness.

Lord Wraybourne smiled at him. "You think so, my dear man, but the atmosphere here is positively poisonous. You must leave immediately."

Mr. Carruthers spluttered, but there was something particularly menacing in such *bonhomie*. Lord Wraybourne was an expert with the sword and the pistols, while Mr. Carruthers was competent with neither.

"I was leaving anyway," he said with bravado. "Miss Sandiford, I will see you another day."

"But your health!" protested his lordship plaintively.

"What about my health?" demanded Mr. Carruthers, confused by the whole business.

"You must travel, my dear man," said Lord Wraybourne earnestly. "Country air. I hear Cheltenham has much to offer such as you. I assure you it is the only way to avoid disaster."

Crossley Carruthers glared, but after a moment he spun around and left the room.

Lord Wraybourne shared a smile with his betrothed. "I trust that will remove the menace."

"I am sure it will. I never thought him such a coward."

"I would not exactly call it cowardice," he remarked pleasantly. "More properly, prudence. He knows I will kill him if he touches you again."

Her startled gaze flew to his, and they shared a look as intimate as an embrace.

"I should not ask it of you," he said after a pause. "But are you able to face another encounter? I would not expect it to be so uncomfortable for you."

"Of course," she said. "As long as you are near I am safe. I did wonder whether Carruthers was the whisperer."

"No. I wondered too but it appears not. I will explain everything very soon," he said. "To enlist your help was a last-minute inspiration or I surely would have told you everything before. Now, can you get Sir Edwin to dance with you?"

"I am sure I can if I can find him. At least he will not force himself upon me. He is a bore but a gentleman. I will merely have to endure more of his Shakespearian quotations."

Lord Wraybourne laughed. "Hamlet's soliloquies, I suppose."

"Oh no," she said as she searched the room for the Bard. "Strange stuff. I would have thought that he had made it up except that he is no poet. My introduction to Shakespeare is recent so it is not surprising that I did not recognize his passages. Except, of course, 'Frailty thy name is woman,' which I thought rather insulting."

"I am surprised you didn't box his ears!" said Lord Wraybourne, laughing. "Can you remember any more of his gems? Were they all misogynistic?"

She concentrated for a moment, "I don't think so," she said at last. "I know he said something about my 'snow-white dimpled chin,' which I thought weak for I have no dimples."

Lord Wraybourne was thoughtful. "You have coral lips, though," he remarked.

"Yes, that was part of it!" she declared. "How clever you are. What is it from?"

"It will come to me," he said absently. "Any more?"

"Something about 'wanton modesty.' I was not sure whether he was being insulting."

"Not in context, no."

"Do you know that passage too?"

"It comes from the same piece, unless I am mistaken."

"And what piece is that?"

"*The Rape of Lucrece.*"

Jane could feel herself grow hot. "It sounds most improper."

"In fact it is not," he said. "But it fascinated us as schoolboys because it hinted at all kinds of wickedness. That is why I recognized those passages."

"What a strange choice of study for a ball, though," she remarked.

"Is it not?" he replied with a rather unpleasant smile. "There he is in that group around Sophie. We could have guessed. But a less likely pair is hard to imagine."

"Sophie would never be interested in Sir Edwin," she said as they began to thread their way around the room. "He apparently wants to save her from her folly. She needs a strong and upright man, he told me."

Lord Wraybourne hissed a violent oath, and she giggled with nervousness. Everyone was behaving so out of character. She was not sure that she liked costume balls, after all.

"Oh yes!" she exclaimed. "There was something else he said. I cannot remember the words but it was about women having minds made of wax, ready to receive the impression of their husbands' stronger intellect."

"I don't recall that, but it is very sound," Lord Wraybourne said, having recovered his equanimity. "I am sure you are as a blank tablet, ready to take my impression."

Jane glanced up and was reassured by the teasing twinkle in his eyes. "I am already impressed by you, My Lord," she returned with a naughty look and then continued with an air of innocence. "I am sure I will always be happy to learn. Are you confessing, however, that your mind is set in stone, never changing?"

"You are a wicked wench and my greatest delight," he murmured as he left her.

She continued on towards Sir Edwin alone. The group about Sophie was gay and witty, but the beauty herself was out of spirits. Jane suspected that was because Lord Randal had once more disappeared. Sophie's time with him in the garden must have been very brief. Sir Edwin, who was being pointedly ignored, was easily persuaded away.

"Something ails Lady Sophie," he complained. "She hardly heard my words, when I had selected some passages from the Bard especially for her."

"There were so many people talking there, Sir Edwin," said Jane soothingly. "Have you not sought her hand in a dance?"

"She will not dance," he replied peevishly. "She says she feels foolish doing so in her costume. She should have thought of that before she chose such an unsuitable garb," he added sharply. "Women should never expose the outline of their lower limbs."

"Why not?" asked Jane directly, irritated even though she agreed with him.

He spluttered with outrage but was lost for an answer. At last he said sternly, "They tempt men!"

"Men who have a mind to be tempted seem able to be so by any number of unlikely pieces of anatomy," Jane replied dryly. "Feet, ankles, legs, hips, waists, bosoms, shoulders, arms, necks, chins, lips, eyes, hair. What are we poor ladies to do? Go covered in a sheet as do the women in the East?"

"I believe you must have been indulging in wine, Miss Sandiford," Sir Edwin said icily, thin lips pressed. "Your sentiments are forward and immodest. Pray be guided by one wiser than yourself, in the absence of your betrothed. It is not for women, particularly young women, to criticize men."

Jane suppressed the urge to argue, as it would hardly lead to them participating in the set about to form. Sir Edwin was pleased by her silence, which he interpreted as contrite humility. Actually, she was searching for a conversational topic which would last until the set was formed and would not raise any controversy between them. She was saved the trouble when everyone's attention was caught by an amazing late arrival.

The lady was dressed in the extreme magnificence of Versailles fifty years before. Her gown of ruched ivory silk, heavily embroidered, must have been eight feet across at the hem, if not more. She only just managed to pass through the large double doors without brushing them. The tight bodice was encrusted with jewels, as was the fan she waved before her face with a gloved hand. Her powdered hair was swept high and topped by two doves in flight. As she was not a short lady, this gave her the impression of great height. She seemed altogether on a different scale to the rest of the company.

Jane could not guess who it might be and was amused when the lady drifted over to Sir Marius and persuaded him to give her his arm around the room. Sir Marius was the only man present who would not be dwarfed by her. How did more ordinary-scaled gentlemen and such ladies go on in the past? Jane wondered.

She and Sir Edwin discussed changing fashion amicably enough until the set was formed and the dancing started. Jane was surprised to find that the music to Sir Adrian's Passage was being played once again and saw a number of dancers look puzzled and annoyed. She guessed that Lord Wraybourne had made the request of the musicians and wondered why.

At least Sir Edwin did not repeat his behavior of earlier by pestering her with quotations. But he also ceased to be interested in the Versailles lady, seeming to have his attention on Lord Wraybourne's partner, instead.

"Do you know the shepherdess, Sir Edwin?" Jane asked. "I admire her costume."

"I? No!" he said sharply and then added, "Perhaps I do. It is difficult to say." Jane thought there was definitely something strained in his manner and wondered at it.

"I believe she is a Miss Hamilton," she said helpfully before she stepped to the middle to join hands with the ladies. She noted that the shepherdess was rather pale.

"Are you unwell, Miss Hamilton?"

The lady denied this, but she too looked very strained.

Could there be a connection between Miss Hamilton and Sir Edwin? Jane's imagination leapt to deserted wife, abandoned mistress, betrayed maiden.

As the dance continued, she was aware of a tension in the air. When she swung round with Lord Wraybourne, she could feel that he was wound up like a spring. Suddenly, the shepherdess, swinging in the arms of Sir Edwin, seemed to trip and fell with a scream. The dance stopped as everyone gathered around the lady, who moaned that her ankle was twisted.

"She must be got out of here," said Lord Wraybourne. "Bring her this way, Hever."

As he turned and began to clear a way through the crowd, Sir Edwin had little option but to gather up the lady and follow. He looked strangely distressed by the task. Jane picked up the lady's hat and slipper and followed, most eager to see what was about to happen.

⤜ 16 ⤛

To Jane's surprise, Lord Wraybourne passed by a number of doorways and led the way to a small anteroom to the library. There, he directed Sir Edwin to lay his burden down on the lounge. The baronet turned to leave, but Lord Wraybourne detained him.

"Do not rush away, Hever. You may be of service."

"I was intending to seek out the housekeeper or another person who might be able to offer Miss Hamilton some assistance."

Lord Wraybourne was at his most charming. "I knew I could depend upon you, Hever, for practical measures. But I feel Miss Hamilton should rest a moment and then she will be able to tell us how seriously she is injured. Jane is here if she needs female assistance."

A decanter and a number of glasses stood on a sideboard, and Lord Wraybourne poured wine for them all.

"I had forgotten that you were acquainted with Miss Hamilton, Hever," he said.

"I have that pleasure," said the gentleman with a small bow. "I am a great admirer of her brother's work. As they are kind enough to keep open house every week, I have frequently taken the opportunity to mix with minds more gifted than my own."

"Ah yes. You have a taste for the company of artists and intellectuals. I appreciate that inclination, for I share it. I too find a concentrated diet of Society can stultify the mind."

Both the ladies were quiet, watching the progress of this civilized dialogue. Jane was frankly bewildered, but Miss Hamilton looked very pale and tense. That could merely be the effect of her injury, of course. Sir Edwin had become his usual reserved self, but he seemed ill-at-ease. Lord Wraybourne was the most pleasant and genial of hosts, and yet Jane felt she could still detect that tension she had noted during the dance.

When Sir Edwin did not return the conversational ball, Lord Wraybourne spoke again. "I understand you also visit the Morris household and Sir William Stone's. A brilliant physician, is he not? His daughter is quite a beauty. A loss to the town now that she has gone to live in the country."

Jane saw Sir Edwin pale and his prominent Adam's apple jogged.

"Have you visited the house of Ashley Stanford?" continued his lordship. "Such wonderful music! Miss Stanford has one of the truest voices. It is a pity, I think, that she cannot be persuaded to sing professionally. Do you not agree, Hever?"

"She has a lovely voice," replied Sir Edwin, his own rather strained.

Lord Wraybourne smiled warmly at him in approval of his return to the conversation. "There are so many gifted ladies," he continued. "Mary Youngman is a very talented miniaturist. She is not so foolish as to hide her gift and is beginning to be in demand. You are acquainted with her, are you not?"

"Yes."

"Ah," said his lordship sadly. "I see what it is. You disapprove of young ladies who seek to make a living from their talents."

"As a matter of fact, I do," said Sir Edwin stiffly. "It is unbecoming of a lady to deal with business and to put herself forward as she must if she is to make a living from her art."

"But what are they to do, Sir Edwin?" demanded Miss Hamilton forcefully. "Not all young ladies are blessed with a fortune."

"If they cannot remain under the protection of one of the men of their family," was the cold reply, "then they should seek a post which places them in a household where they will be protected from a cruel world."

"If they need protection, Hever," said Lord Wraybourne, his voice no longer genial, "then it is from you."

"What do you mean?" squawked Sir Edwin, spilling some of his wine.

"Miss Hamilton has identified you as the man who assaulted her recently."

"What?" The baronet jerked as if he would flee but then he regained a modicum of control. "She is deranged, and so are you to believe her!" he exclaimed and stood, showing the intention to leave the room.

Lord Wraybourne calmly opened a drawer, took out a pistol, and pointed it at the baronet. He was pale but his hand was steady. "As you see, I am prepared. Please sit down, Hever."

"Even you would not shoot me here in your cousin's house," declared Sir Edwin, looking ready to defy the order.

"You think not?" was the gentle reply. "It would solve so many problems." There was such honesty in Lord Wraybourne's tone that Sir Edwin blanched and sat again.

"You are quite mad," he protested.

"I am certainly very angry," replied his lordship evenly. "But as for mad, no. Your victims noticed enough about you to make me fairly certain and though that valet of yours seems truly devoted, I know he drove your carriage for the attacks. He will break when we put full pressure on him. There have even been a few strange occurrences close to your estate which would bear investigation. I had a little suspicion of Crossley Carruthers, but I think there I was merely prejudiced. He is a fool, but you are a sickening example of humanity. If you could not control your needs, why could you not at least have used the women who will serve a man for pay?"

"A common harlot!" hissed Sir Edwin. He was in a fury.

"That may be your taste, My Lord. It is not mine. Let me leave this room or I'll have you clapped in bedlam!"

"Then why not an uncommon one?" pursued his lordship. "There are many high-class Cyprians who would be honored by your patronage."

"A harlot is a harlot," Sir Edwin snarled. "It is a pity you do not know the difference. I pity your wife." He cast a sneering look at Jane, where she sat, quietly appalled.

Lord Wraybourne seemed taken aback when reminded of her presence but then returned his attention to the attack.

"You should have married, Hever."

"I will," was the cold reply. "I thought to ally myself with your family, but nothing could bring me to do so now."

At this moment the door to the corridor opened. All four people in the room turned, stunned, to see Sophie enter and stand back as a page would, to admit the elegant lady of the *ancienne régime,* who had to sidle to work her panniers through the doorway. Lord Wraybourne looked nonplussed. Sir Edwin gaped as if this merely confirmed his opinion that the world had gone mad.

"Do we intrude?" asked the lady in a soft and husky voice.

Familiarity tugged at Jane's mind, but she could not grasp the connection.

"We came to see how the invalid was, being of a period with her, as you see."

She seemed totally oblivious of the pistol still in Lord Wraybourne's hand, though Sophie was staring at it and at Sir Edwin.

"Miss Hamilton is recovering," said Lord Wraybourne evenly. "We were conducting some private business, Madam."

The upper half of the lady's face was covered by a visor mask and the lower by her silk fan but blue eyes flashed amusement. "At a ball? How quaint."

Jane happened to be watching her betrothed and knew the moment he recognized the lady. Unwilling amusement twitched at his lips.

"A trifle unusual, I grant you," he said. "Perhaps you could oblige me, Madam, by escorting the other ladies back to the ballroom."

"Most unwise," said the lady and subsided onto a chaise longue, taking up the whole of it with her skirts.

Sophie walked to her proper place behind. Sir Edwin had taken the opportunity to move towards the door but hesitated indecisively when Lord Wraybourne raised the pistol again to point at him.

In a clipped voice, Lord Wraybourne said, "Sophie, you and Jane will leave now." After a moment Jane rose to obey. Mutinously, Sophie began to walk to the door.

"David, really—"

She broke off with a squeak as Sir Edwin seized her and dragged her backwards, one-handed by the hair. Lord Wraybourne moved to rescue her but was stopped by Sir Edwin.

"Come any closer, and I'll break her neck. I know how. Put down the pistol."

Lord Wraybourne did as he was instructed. Jane marvelled at the control he had over his voice as he spoke, though his skin was bleached with strain.

"Let me appeal to your logic, Hever. There is no way you can escape your guilt. Though I found you an unlikely suspect when the evidence began to point to you, I had to try this experiment to test out my hypothesis. Miss Hamilton was sure she could identify her assailant if she could be close to him. She has identified you. And you have now obligingly admitted your guilt. Let my sister go."

"I have done no such thing," retorted the baronet, his eyes flashing around the room.

Jane could see his whole body trembling with fear or rage or insanity, she knew not which.

"I am defending myself from an armed madman!" he cried.

"We are not alone," remarked Lord Wraybourne. "Do you really think I would murder you before so many? If that is your fear, it is pointless. Let Sophie go!"

There was command in his voice, but Hever's hand only tightened more compulsively on his captive's hair. Jane saw Sophie swallow a scream. Jane had to force herself not to call out or leap to some pointless action. She could imagine how much worse it must be for Lord Wraybourne.

"Who knows what a madman might do?" Hever yelled.

He must have relaxed his hand a little, for Sophie twisted her head and sank her sharp teeth into his wrist. The next moment, she screamed as he yanked her head back at a vicious angle.

"Vixen! Whore!" he spat into her terrified face, seeming to forget for a moment the other people in the room.

Lord Wraybourne took a step then halted as the movement brought the baronet's attention back to him. Jane perceived a stir of movement from the corner of her eye and she saw the Versailles lady rise smoothly from her seat. "Sit down, Madam!" Sir Edwin snapped.

"You poor man," said the husky voice as the lady disobeyed and drifted closer to the center of the room. "No wonder you are distraught. But you should be kind to little Sophie. She has done you no harm."

Sir Edwin's face contorted with rage, and spittle flecked his mouth. Jane suddenly realized that he *was* insane, and real fear for Sophie chilled her.

"She has sneered at me!" he choked. Horrified, Jane recognized the hoarse voice.

"I would have married her, saved her, but she laughed at me! Now she prances before the world, showing her body. But would she give me one kiss?"

Hever's eyes never left Lord Wraybourne, but Jane noticed that the lady was slowly edging towards the table upon which Lord Wraybourne had put the pistol. But what could she do with it if she reached it?

"She is a filthy whore," Sir Edwin whispered, spittle drooling down his chin.

Jane no longer had a fragment of doubt. Sir Edwin had been her whispering tormentor.

"She is not worthy of the love of a decent man!" he snarled, with a gloating look at Lord Wraybourne, whose eyes glared murderous rage.

A thunderous noise filled the room, and it seemed to Jane that everything moved in slow motion for a moment as Sir Edwin let Sophie go. Jane, horror-struck, saw the elegant lady with the smoking pistol in her hand. Then the pistol was thrown down, and she raced, along with Lord Wraybourne, to Sophie, who had fainted. Jane, suspended in shocked disbelief, recognized Lord Randal and realized he had shot Sir Edwin.

The next thing she clearly knew, she was standing in the breakfast room with trembling, white-faced Miss Hamilton and Lord Wraybourne, who was not in much better condition. Jane supposed, with objective calmness, that she must look the same herself. They were huddled together, both giving and taking comfort from the embrace. Jane had the strange notion that shots were continuing to sound somewhere and wondered if it could be an echo in her mind of that dreadful, thundering moment.

Lord Wraybourne pulled away. "I must go, Jane. Randal will have got Sophie out of sight, and there were no servants close by. But something must be done before Hever is discovered." He ran a shaking hand over his face. "I never intended . . . You should not have seen that. . . ."

Jane quieted him with a hand on his. "We will manage," she said. "Go and do what you must. He was the whisperer."

"Yes." He kissed her roughly. "My dear delight. You have reserves I never dreamed of. If that had been you, instead of Sophie, I think *I* would have risked the shot."

She touched his cheek gently. "Remember that, David."

He was caught by the intensity of her voice. "What do you mean?"

"I know it isn't what you would want, David, but Sophie loves Lord Randal. I believe now that he loves her too. I think they may be each other's only chance for true happiness."

"No," he protested. "Randal would just lead her into further imprudence."

Jane said nothing, merely looked at him. He sighed and rubbed at his face again, as if attempting to draw blood back to his pallor. "Stay here. I'll return as soon as I can."

Stella Hamilton was trembling with shock. Jane, marvelling at her own calm, rang the bell repeatedly until a harried maid answered the summons. She then ordered tea.

"And, Riddle," she asked, "can I hear banging noises?"

"Bless you, yes, Miss. It's the fireworks. Such a bang there was a while ago. The staff are watching from the side, Miss."

Jane correctly interpreted this as a hint of complaint against people wanting tea in the breakfast parlor when there were such exciting goings-on but she hardened her heart.

"Miss Hamilton is not well. She must have a restorative, Riddle, as soon as may be."

As the door closed behind the disgruntled maid, Jane let herself go and sat down on the nearest chair with a thump, to sink her swimming head in her hands.

Lord Wraybourne returned to the anteroom to find it deserted except for Sir Edwin's corpse. Randal had carried Sophie away. The urge to follow them and protect his sister was very strong. Yet, David knew he had to handle matters here first. He locked the door from the inside, then went to open the second door which led into the library.

Mr. Moulton-Scrope looked up from the study of his brandy. "Not quite the *dénouement* we planned but satisfactory."

"I fear Maria is likely to be a trifle cross," agreed his nephew as he helped himself to cognac and took a healthy gulp. His voice was normal but the golden liquid shivered in his hand. "Thank heaven Randal is a dead shot! The man was completely unhinged. God knows what he would have done."

"Must have been a pretty shot. I could only listen, of course. What in the name of Hades was Lord Randal doing in a dress, by the way? Part of the plan?"

"Oh God, no. Just his mischief. I could have throttled him when he waltzed in to upset everything, but as it happened it saved the day. Ironically, it was only because Sir Edwin despised women that he ignored Randal until it was too late. What the hell is that damned banging? I thought it was my ears."

"Fireworks. Opportune, I must say. It's the only reason I've been sitting here waiting for you. They must have disguised the sound of the shot."

"What do we do now?" asked Lord Wraybourne.

Mr. Moulton-Scrope heaved himself out of his chair and walked into the other room. "Suicide, don't you think?"

He then placed the pistol by the corpse's hand and continued to chat in a calming, natural voice. "Ashby insisted on carrying Sophie off before she regained consciousness. I didn't interfere, though you know my opinion of the scoundrel. You *did* say you trusted him," he added when he saw the tightening of his nephew's face.

"I only wondered whether he had anything on under the dress," said Lord Wraybourne with a slight smile.

Having assured themselves that the scene was set, the two men returned to the library. Lord Wraybourne saw his uncle lock the door and place the key in his pocket at the same time as he became aware of the relative silence that signalled the end of the pyrotechnics.

"No need for you to be involved in this at all, my boy," said Mr. Moulton-Scrope amiably. "I am sure that you have other matters to attend to." Which was one way of looking at things, thought Lord Wraybourne as he went to the door. He hesitated a moment but saw that his uncle was waiting until he had left before pulling the bell to summon the servants.

Outside, David waited in concealment for a little while to make sure that all went off well, but he should have known that his uncle was equal to the task.

David heard his authoritative voice. "Get a spare key, Nuttall. Hurry. I heard a shot and both the doors are locked!"

Within minutes the door was opened and the exclamations of horror told him the "tragedy" had been revealed. When Maria had arrived and started screaming and a number of domestics followed their mistress's example, David decided that he could make himself scarce.

He hesitated in the hall. He wanted to go and assure himself that Jane was coping adequately with the evening's events, but he also needed to find his sister and Lord Randal. Reluctantly, he ran upstairs to his sister's room. Outside her door, he paused for a moment. What would he do if he were confronted with something improper? He ran tired hands through his hair. The last thing he wanted was to have to call out his friend. The temptation to walk away from the door was enormous, but Lord Wraybourne resolutely turned the handle and went in.

A lamp softly illuminated the scene. Lord Randal was sitting in a large winged chair with Sophie wrapped in a blanket in his arms. His upper body was bare, silky smooth as a Greek statue, but at least, noted Lord Wraybourne, he had on the black tights which had been part of his first costume.

Sophie started and, seeing her brother, would have sat up but Lord Randal gently stayed her and she relaxed again into the protection of his arms. No one spoke as Lord Wraybourne quietly closed the door. His eyes took in the evidence of the room. The blue damask bed-cover was smooth and untouched. Randal's head rested on the high back of the chair, and there was a slight smile on his lips, rueful and self-mocking. His eyes met his friend's unflinchingly.

Shock and suffering had marked Sophie's face. Yet there was a tranquillity to it which struck Lord Wraybourne with considerable force. Not only did he know that he could not bring himself to take that peace from her, but he realized that it would not be in Jane's eyes at this moment. For all that she had coped so marvelously, she would need him now.

He took a deep breath and suddenly understood, with

surprise, that he was happy with the situation overall. The feeling of lightness was so strong in the room that he could almost see it hovering in the air around them. When he spoke, his own voice sounded improperly loud.

"Hever committed suicide. Uncle Henry is handling everything. I must go to Jane."

A gentle smile curved Sophie's lips, and the two in the chair seemed to relax and blend even closer together. Without further words, Lord Wraybourne left them that way.

❧ 17 ❧

LORD WRAYBOURNE MANAGED to slip into the break-fast room without being noticed by the guests and servants milling excitedly in the hall outside the library. He found Jane and Stella apparently composed and sipping delicately at tea. It was only as he came close and the aroma assailed him that he realized the tea was strongly laced with brandy. Jane saw his lips twitch and wondered how he could be amused at such a time.

"How is Sophie?" she asked, surprised that it seemed to take some effort to form the words correctly.

"Doing well," Lord Wraybourne replied, sitting down beside Jane at the table. "But I think I should send up some of the brew you are imbibing. It seems highly effective."

"Oh yes," she agreed, happily. "Riddle suggested it. She said her grandmother used it in times of difficulty, and it

does seem to make problems a great deal less unpleasant—
as well as being delicious." She looked around, noticing
that it also took some effort to focus her eyes, or perhaps it
was only that the candles needed trimming. "I believe we
only have two cups or I would offer you some."

Stella Hamilton spoke suddenly, enunciating very
clearly. "I am most pleased that Sir Edwin is dead."

"So am I," said Lord Wraybourne, leaning back and re-
laxing for what seemed like the first time in hours. "It was
not quite as we planned it, but he had to die."

"We?" asked Jane and Stella together.

"Uncle Henry was in the library, listening to everything. We couldn't let the thing go to trial, so the idea
was that we would convince Hever that he had no hope
and then leave him alone. Ideally, he would shoot himself but if he didn't—and I had no faith he would have
the courage—then Uncle Henry was going to go in and
do it for him."

"Mr. Moulton-Scrope?" squeaked Jane. He had always
seemed a pillar of society.

"Orders from the top. As soon as we were sure Hever
was the man, he had to die. Like a mad dog. For a while,
despite the evidence, it seemed so unlikely. As it was, he
was so near the brink of insanity that I think any little thing
would have pushed him over. But Sophie was the ideal last
straw, as it happened, though I would never have used her
as a weapon. He hated all women, I think, but he had come
to see her as the epitome. I suspect his affronts to you,
Jane, were as a substitute for Sophie. Since he hoped to
make her his wife, his twisted mind would not allow him to

insult her directly." He sighed. "I must escort Stella home, Jane. Where will I find you when I return?"

Jane was disinclined to move. "Here, I think. I do not wish to join the ball again."

"Everyone will be leaving soon, now Sir Edwin has been found. I will come back here, but I think I should take away your magic potion if you are to be coherent when I return."

Jane stared at him. "Am I drunk? Good heavens. What would my mother say? But I can quite see why so many gentlemen do it so often," she added with a giggle.

Her betrothed shook his head and took charge of the brandy bottle as well as Miss Hamilton, who moved with slow and careful dignity as he escorted her from the room. Jane enjoyed the solitude. She watched the play of the candle flames and the curl of the smoke. She was aware of distant noises but no one came to disturb her privacy. She really should be more upset, she thought.

She wondered what David had done about Sophie and Lord Randal. Should she go to find her friend? The effort was beyond her and David had said everything was in order. She would have to persuade him to let them marry. She wondered what had been going through Randal's mind as he decided to make the shot. Perhaps he had had no choice. Even she had been able to see that it needed only a little more of the maniac's strength to bend Sophie's slender neck further than any neck was meant to go.

The euphoria was slipping away. Jane jumped up and began to pace the room. She was shocked, when she glanced into the mirror, to see a stranger looking back.

She had forgotten her disguise. She had taken off her mask after the shooting. Now she dragged the lined filigree from her hair and worked and teased at the coiled braids until her hair was hanging heavily around her. Then, using a napkin from a drawer and the cooled water from the tea tray, she scrubbed at the cosmetics on her face. At last, Jane Sandiford looked back at her. When the door opened, she turned to greet her love. He seemed to stop breathing.

"I love you," she said softly across the room.

"As I do you," he replied. "But I am not sure I should touch you, I need you so."

Joyful awareness of her power surged within her and, unafraid, she walked slowly forward and stood before him. She raised her hands to his face and then gradually stretched on tiptoe, teasing out the moment, to taste his lips. He crushed her to him. Their mouths and bodies seemed to be seeking ever closer union when, suddenly, he stopped and held her away with rigid arms.

"No," he said, breathing hard but smiling. "I will not be seduced by you, Jane, not here, not now. Save your tricks till we are wed."

After a moment Jane did not oppose him. There was an aching sweetness in this postponement of delight.

He pushed her gently into a chair and finger-combed her tangled hair, then divided it in two and began to braid.

"What are you doing?" she asked, mischievously trying to twist her head to kiss his fingers.

"I am confining your hair so that it cannot bewitch me."

"Do you know how to plait?" she asked, tilting her head back to look at him.

"It is done to horses' manes, you know."

She sat still under his ministrations. Tiny shivers went through her at the movements of his fingers in her hair and their brushing at her nape.

"You never asked about my golden flowers," she said. "I suppose you have fulfilled your part of the bargain."

"I no longer feel any jealousy," he replied. "If I wonder who gave them to you it is only because I admire his taste. They are exquisite."

"*Merci du compliment, Monsieur!*" she said, glancing up at him with a grin. "I purchased them for myself."

That necessitated a kiss, but they made it a gentle one. Their eyes kept touch long after their lips had parted. Then, he gently turned her head and continued his work on her hair. At last he finished and laid the two fat braids on her shoulders.

"There," he said. "Now you are tamed." He saw the glint in her eye and, laughing, added, ". . . if I get you into a public place very quickly. I think it is time to go and find Maria."

That lady was delighted to have a new audience for her wailing account of the horrible happenings, and Jane and David were suitably horrified and amazed, while behind her back they exchanged small smiles. It was obvious that Lady Harroving, despite her supposed anguish, could not believe her luck that Sir Edwin had chosen to enliven *her* ball with his scandalous demise.

After Jane's love had left, she went to her bed. She first looked in on Sophie but found her tucked under the covers like a child, fast asleep. Jane smiled when she saw, on her friend's pillow, a pair of doves in flight, the ones which had ornamented Lord Randal's headdress. Perhaps something good was to come out of this horrible affair after all.

EPILOGUE

THE WEDDING DAY dawned in perfection on Carne Abbey. The sun burned away wisps of mist from the river. Nature was at its peak. Even the austere stone house could not remain bleak in the midst of such midsummer glory. Nor had it been able to resist the advent of Lady Sophie, who had decided to flee town and its pressures to help Jane survive her return home.

This was a Sophie as sparkling as ever, yet deepened by her experiences and by the fruition of her love. Every day she and Jane wrote to their fiancés, and every day they received notes, usually accompanied by gifts. Even the fact that Lord Wraybourne had insisted Sophie and Randal wait until the autumn for their wedding did nothing to quench her spirit. She floated about Carne, singing, flinging back draperies, and arranging flowers.

It was not at all clear what Lady Sandiford felt about all this. Her eyes noted every change, yet she said nothing. Jane concluded that her mother had decided to live with what must be only a temporary aberration.

The basic arrangements for the wedding had been made. Sophie now began to embellish them with complicity, Jane was amazed to find, from her father, who gave Sophie permission to order what she wished. The cook was delighted to elaborate upon the wedding breakfast. She was even more delighted to be told to prepare a special feast for the servants later in the day. A considerable quantity of flowers, ribbons, and garlands was ordered from Cheltenham for the decoration of the church, and musicians were hired for the Abbey and the village, where the tenants would feast in the couple's honour.

Jane and Mrs. Hawley watched in amazement. The years which had conditioned them to expect the place to be gloomy had no power over Sophie. As a result, the gloom ceased to exist. Occasionally, one could even hear a servant singing at her work.

"I wonder if Carne will ever be quite the same again?" said Mrs. Hawley as they checked off lists of provisions for the house guests.

"I should think it will revert," replied Jane, "like a cleared bit of ground is soon retaken by the forest."

"Well, I will not be here to see it," said Mrs. Hawley cheerfully. "These last weeks when you have been in Town have been unutterably dull, Jane."

"I wish you had been with me," said Jane, and her eyes twinkled. "Well, perhaps not, for you would have stopped me doing a great many things and I think, however silly they seem in retrospect, I had to do them to arrive where I am now."

"Someday," said the governess, "you must tell me what you have been about—if you think my poor nerves can take the strain. The change in you in a few short weeks is amazing."

They laughed and Jane asked whether Mrs. Hawley had found a new position.

"Well, I have decided, for the moment, not to seek another post. I have a small pension from my husband, you know, and your parents, whatever else one may say about them, have paid me well. My brother works for Forsham's Bank in London, and he has invested the greater part for me these last twelve years. I have enough to live on. It only remains to see whether I can bear the idleness."

"Where will you live? In London?"

"I think so, near my brother."

"Then I hope you will come and visit me in Town but also come and stay with us at Stenby."

"I do not think that would be proper," said the governess gently.

"Beth, you are my friend. I know how much I owe you. Believe me, David will have no objection. He has spoken admiringly of you a number of times."

"If your husband is pleased to invite me, then I will be delighted to visit you," said the governess happily. Jane was already searching her mind for a gentleman suitable for her friend.

*   *   *

Jane awoke on her wedding morning and reflected on the change in her life in a few short months. Tonight, the change would be complete. She still had no clear understanding of the secrets of the marriage bed but on an instinctive level, she was aware. She had thought for a moment of asking Mrs. Hawley for advice but decided against it. David would understand. Before she slept tonight, she would be his wife in every way.

In no time at all her room was invaded by Prudence Hawkins, Sophie, and Beth. Jane bathed and had her hair dressed in an austere coronet. Her wedding dress was beautifully cut white silk, without ornamentation except for embroidered silver flowers around the hem. The same silver flowers decorated the edge of a silk gauze veil. White kid slippers and gloves completed her toilette, and she carried a pearl-bound prayer book, a gift from her mother. Jane took a moment to thank Sophie for her support.

"I dread to think what today would be like without your efforts."

"It would still be your wedding day, Jane," Sophie replied with a warm smile.

"Yes, nothing could spoil that. I hope to help make your wedding day as perfect."

"How could it not be?" said Sophie simply. "I will be marrying Randal. He should be here soon, with David."

Jane was suddenly aware that Sophie was strung tight with anticipation and felt the same vibration in herself, waiting for a footstep, a voice, a presence. They would neither be satisfied, for their lovers would wait at the church. Still, the knowledge that they were near was in Jane's blood and her friend's . . . like the sweet, brandied tea had been.

When it was nearly time for the party to go to the church, Lady Sandiford entered the room and dismissed the others. She had dressed for the occasion in a rich, blue silk and looked very much unlike her normal self. She was still unsmiling, however.

"You look very beautiful, Jane," she said after consideration. It was more an adjudication than a compliment. There was silence while austere mother and stately daughter considered each other. "I do not believe you are unhappy with your lot, Jane."

"No, Mama. I am not unhappy."

Lady Sandiford gave a little nod. "I am mother enough to be glad of that," she said. "I will not give you any advice about the marriage bed. I judge Lord Wraybourne to be a man who handles himself with care."

With no further word she turned away, leaving Jane little the wiser about the woman who had given her life.

Jane walked down the aisle of the village church. Lord Wraybourne stood before her at the altar. It was a week since they had seen each other, and neither could suppress a spontaneous smile. Lady Wraybourne, a gaunt and sad-eyed woman, was seen to dab her eyes.

When the ceremony was over, Lord Wraybourne lifted the veil and touched Jane's lips with the briefest of kisses. The look in his eyes went much farther. They moved through the celebrations that followed, full of anticipation, their attention always on their friends and relatives while little touches and stolen glances made promises for the night.

Jane saw Randal and Sophie float in each other's orbit as if strings connected them. Less the focus of everyone's eyes, they could be more together. Jane could sense how difficult the waiting was for them.

Sophie, as bridesmaid, came to help Jane change into a travelling dress scarcely more practical than her wedding gown, being of buttercup-yellow silk with deep ruching around the hem. An enormous high-poke bonnet was trimmed to match.

As the two friends returned downstairs Sophie whispered, "I wish I were you."

"But I thought it was Randal you loved," teased Jane.

"Idiot!" laughed her friend. "I'm tempted to slip into his bed tonight."

"Will you?" asked Jane, worried.

"No," sighed Sophie. "He'd probably beat me. He has become dreadfully *righteous.*"

Jane smiled. "Love does the most amazing things. Only see how it has tamed you."

"How tedious that would be. I have my work cut out to persuade Randal not to give up his wish to buy a commission. I'm sure if I apply myself I can marry off stuffy Chelmly, and then the duke can have no objection."

"Would you want to follow the drum?"

"I wouldn't mind. I don't want him hurt, of course. But I want him happy more."

Sharing an understanding of the pleasures and pains of love, they embraced once more before Jane climbed into the handsome new travelling chariot with her husband.

"It is a pity you had to take off your wedding dress," he said. "I think you looked more beautiful in that than I could ever have imagined."

"Am I so ugly now?" she teased.

"You'll do," he said, but his eyes said more.

"Are you not going to kiss me?" she asked, leaning towards him.

"In that bonnet?" he declared with mock horror. "Anyway, we do not have far to go."

"I can take it off," she said, raising her hands to the ribbons. "Where are we headed?"

He stayed her hands. "I have borrowed Randal's estate at Fairmeadows. It is not very far away. Let us wait a little longer."

They rode for an hour, chatting as if they were an old married couple, never touching except with eyes and thoughts. Jane felt every nerve ending tingling in anticipation.

When the chariot finally turned between curlicued wrought-iron gates, Jane saw that Fairmeadows was not a large house, but was a charming Jacobean manor built of soft golden brick covered in places with climbing roses that looked to be as old as the house itself. The cottage-style gardens were full of flowers and humming insects.

The couple was welcomed by the small staff, declined the offered food, and was soon in their chamber. Jane looked around at the comfortable furniture, old and well-polished, and breathed in the mixed perfume of the pinks in a vase by the window and the lavender in which the bedding had been stored.

"This is a beautiful house," she said.

"Yes," he agreed, leaning against the door and studying her with loving eyes. "Perhaps I shouldn't have brought you here. Stenby is going to seem a barbaric pile after this."

She turned to smile at him. At the look in his eyes, soft color crept into her cheeks. "A cave would be heaven with you, David."

"You are my precious jewel, my perfect flower, my dear delight. But I am still afraid to touch you in case my need overwhelms my caring."

With a sweet and radiant smile Jane reached up and slowly untied the silken ribbons of her bonnet to take it off. The great mass of her dusky hair swung free and loose around her. She saw his breath catch and a flame leap in his eyes.

She walked slowly towards him until they were barely touching and his breath was warm on her face. He smiled down into her eyes, and the flame burned into her. She took his face in her hands, then stretched slowly upwards to taste his lips.

He gathered her gently to him and buried his head in the dusky cloud of her hair. As his arms tightened, she felt the tumultuous beat of his heart in counterpoint with her own. His voice shivered across her ear as he murmured, "My wonderful Tiger Eyes."

Then his fingers began to work slowly at the long length of fastenings on her dress.

Dear readers,

I hope you've enjoyed my very first book. Yes, *Lord Wray-bourne's Betrothed* was the first book I sold, and I can still remember the thrill, especially of holding the first copy in my hands. I threw a party and had all the guests sign it, so it makes a lovely keepsake of a special moment in any author's life.

I wrote six Regency romances in the early days of my career, and they've become expensive and hard to find, so I'm delighted that NAL is reissuing them, and with such lovely covers, too. For complicated reasons, it was the last of those six books—*The Fortune Hunter* and *Deirdre and Don Juan*—that was reissued first in a collection called *Lovers and Ladies*, which came out last year. Their publication together approximately coincided with my twentieth anniversary of publication.

Yes, it was early in 1988 when I received that magical phone call to say that Walker Books of New York wanted to buy *Lord Wraybourne's Betrothed*, and by late in that year, I had a copy in my hands. The wonderful Melinda Helfer of

Romantic Times magazine gave it a rave review, saying, "The sky's the limit for this extraordinary author." I think I've been trying to live up to that ever since.

Now, beginning with this story, the remaining four will come out in order.

These books don't form a tight series like my Company of Rogues or the Mallorens, but Lord Randal Ashby forms a link. He's a handsome young devil nicknamed the Bright Angel in school, largely in contrast to his friend the Dark Angel, Piers Verderan—a troubled boy who would turn into a dangerous man.

You've met Randal now, and seen how he becomes entangled with Lady Sophie, Wraybourne's sister. The next book, *The Stanforth Secrets* (February 2010), takes us back a few years to when he helped his cousin Chloe cope with murder and mayhem and find her own true love.

In *The Stolen Bride* (June 2010), the date for Randal and Sophie's wedding is coming close, but all is not well in their Eden. Sophie thinks Randal is behaving strangely, and fears it's because he's been trapped into marrying her. She wants him for her husband more than anything in the world, but she knows an unwilling groom will be disastrous. Into this fraught situation comes an old enemy.

As those problems work out, we meet the Dark Angel himself, and see exactly why people are always warning Randal to stay far, far away from him. However, in *Emily and the Dark Angel* (October 2010), Verderan meets no-nonsense Emily Grantham in a cloud of violet-scented talcum powder and his life will never be the same. This book won a RITA award.

I hope you'll enjoy all these classic stories, for the first time or again.

If you visit the page for these books on my Web site—www.jobev.com/tradreg.html—you'll find more about the books, plus a place to sign up for an e-mail reminder when the books are arriving on the shelves. Those are the only e-mails you'll get from there, so don't worry about spam. You can also sign up for my occasional e-newsletters. There's a separate sign-up box for those, but again, no chat, no spam.

All best wishes,
Jo Beverley

Please read on for an excerpt from

THE
STANFORTH
SECRETS

Available from Signet Eclipse Trade
in February 2010

With a sense of premonition, Chloe heard the sound of wheels and hooves on the coast road behind her. She allowed herself to hope, however, that they would sweep past and be on their way to the vicarage or Troughton House, anywhere but Delamere. After all, fate could not be so cruel as to have her meet Justin again for the first time in four years when she was covered in mud. Half an hour before, a silly young horse had unceremoniously dumped her onto the damp sands of Half-Moon Bay and then taken off for the stables.

There was a clear word of command, however, and the vehicle stopped. With resignation Chloe turned to confront not one but two smart equipages with grooms already at the horses' heads and two equally smart young gentlemen laughing at her as they leapt down from their seats. Hands on hips, Chloe glared at her cousin Randal, looking beautiful as always, and her cousin-in-law, Justin, thinner, darker, tougher-looking, but still handsome. Still heart-tuggingly like her dead husband.

"Chloe?" Justin said in surprise. More surprise than just at seeing her trudging along the road. Had she perhaps changed too?

With some notion of showing him she was no longer a hoyden, she dropped a curtsey. "Welcome home, Lord Stanforth."

His brows went up and he grinned as he bowed. "Thank you, Lady Stanforth."

This appealed to Chloe's sense of the ridiculous and she burst out laughing. "I warn you there's a plenitude of Lady Stanforths these days. Two a penny, we are." Chloe wanted to use his name. Once he'd been Justin to her, but now she felt . . . shy? Surely not.

She turned quickly to her cousin, and Randal swept her up for a hearty kiss. "You're looking very fetching, Chloe. It must be the smears of mud which are the finishing touch."

"Regulation wear in Lancashire," she remarked and rubbed her dirty gloved finger down his elegant nose. "Can one of you take me up back to the Hall?"

As she was standing by his side, it should surely have been Randal who made the offer, and yet somehow she found herself handed up into Justin's curricle. She caught a glint of familiar amusement in her cousin's bright blue eyes. What was Randal up to now?

Justin took up the reins and sent his groom to ride behind the other vehicle. "I do hope you're going to tell me how you came to take a toss, Chloe. It must be an unheard-of event."

"Very nearly," she agreed as she arranged the skirts of her ruby-red habit and took control of her agitated nerves. "But everyone gets thrown now and again. I was on a young horse and woolgathering when a seagull chose to fly at us. That is the sum of it."

"Is the horse likely to be hereabouts? Perhaps Corrigan could find it."

"Oh, Mercury will be home by now, I'm sure, the dis-courteous beast."

"How is everything at the Hall?" Justin asked. "I find it difficult to think of it as my home, even though I spent many happy times here as a boy."

He spoke so casually, thought Chloe. As if it wasn't four years since they had last met, since that moment . . . They had never spoken of it, that flash of awareness, and so she couldn't be certain he had felt it as much as she. She had told herself over and over it had been imagined, and yet here she was, within moments of meeting him, her senses disordered.

It would not do. She had meant every word when she said she would not bind herself again to a Dashing Delamere.

She sternly controlled her thoughts and addressed the businesslike subject. "Everything is running smoothly. Scarthwait, who was Stephen's manager, has carried on, and he is very efficient. You'll find the land in good heart."

"I was a little surprised to find how well-to-do I am.

After the estate had been through Stephen's hands, and then Uncle George's, I expected to inherit nothing but debts."

"That is unfair," said Chloe sharply. "Stephen may not have been organized, but he left everything to Scarthwait. And he was not terribly expensive. He didn't gamble, you know."

"Except with his life," said Justin quietly and drew the horses up again, waving Randal to pass them and go ahead. He turned to Chloe. "My wits and manners must have both gone begging. I'm very sorry, Chloe, for speaking like that. I wrote, after I had the news, but I'll say again how sorry I was to hear of Stephen's death. It has been a year, so I suppose the first pain must have faded but . . ."

"Oh please don't, Justin," said Chloe, looking away, for he was bringing tears to her eyes. "As you say, it is so long ago now. My mourning is past, and there's no point in going over the ground again."

He covered one of her hands with his for a moment. Chloe felt the warmth of it through two gloves, a warmth which swept through her. Her breath caught. Then he clicked the horses to a walk. They drove in silence a little way.

How would he feel if he knew her hypocrisy? That the tears had come from sadness at not feeling more bereft?

"How long have you been in England, Justin?" she asked, to break the silence. It was only then she realized she had used his name twice without the heavens falling in.

"Three weeks. I wrote as soon as I reached London."

"Yes, I received it," said Chloe, summoning up a lighter tone. "With relief and prayers to the Lord, I assure you. I cannot wait to drop the responsibility for Delamere in your lap and flee to a more comfortable place. What with the Dowager wandering the place scaring the servants, and the problem of quite how to treat Belinda, particularly when there was a chance she would be the mother of the next viscount. . . . I have been disturbed in the night by ghosts, and have had to handle a stream of tenants complaining about the sudden influx of soldiers. Some imbecile in London sent them because of rumors of smugglers hereabout. Smugglers! In Lancashire! If it wasn't for Grandmama, I think I would have gone mad."

Justin had tried to interrupt at various points in this tirade but now he only said, with a frown, "Ghosts? Delamere Hall has never been haunted to my knowledge."

"Or to mine," said Chloe, her mood lightened by having released some of her annoyance. "But there have been strange noises in the night. Disturbances to furniture and particularly to the cellars. As the chimney of my room passes down by the storage rooms, I have been awakened sometimes by noises. It isn't only I who hear them, either. I usually find Grandmama, who is a light sleeper, there ahead of me. Twice the pantries were found in disarray and," she said forcefully, "I assure you we do not have rats."

He looked sharply at her, but his voice was casual as he said, "I didn't know ghosts were interested in turnips and potatoes."

"Nor did I. This one seems mainly interested in apples. Shades of Adam and Eve?"

"I think I would be more likely to look for a dishonest servant than a spirit," he suggested. "Are any of the servants new?"

"No," said Chloe. Then added, "Well, Matthew, the footman, has not been with us long. Delamere had been without a footman for a while, since Stephen was so rarely in residence and never entertained here. Uncle George hired him. I think Matthew was recommended by George's old friend Humphrey Macy. Macy spent a lot of time at Delamere after George inherited. I was very grateful for it. For one thing he has a normal share of sense, and George would listen to him."

The road had swung away from the coast, and ran now between hedges. Soon it would pass the driveway to the Hall.

"And what sort is this Matthew?" said Justin. "Honest?"

"I think so, or I would have dismissed him. He seems to have settled in here very well, and I have no reason to think he sneaks around the pantries stealing fruit. For one thing, the staff are well fed at Delamere. Now, however," Chloe added with satisfaction, "it is entirely your problem, thank goodness, and you will do as you think best."

She saw his lips twitch with amusement.

Chloe felt a surprising spurt of satisfaction to have made him smile. He was too solemn for a Dashing Delamere and there were shadows in those warm brown eyes. She remembered the Justin of six years before, bubbling with light-hearted enthusiasm for life, just like Stephen. In the short time before she left to make a new life for herself, it wouldn't hurt to brighten his spirits.

Justin swung the curricle between the gates of Delamere Hall and sighed.

"It must be strange for you," Chloe said softly, "coming here like this."

"Yes it is. I can't accept yet that Stephen is dead. He was always so full of life. But then I sometimes feel a hundred years old. At least I've had this year to accustom myself, though it must have been an awkward time here. Was George's wife distressed to give birth to a girl?"

"Belinda is not given to drama but she was disappointed, I think. As mother of the viscount, she could have ruled at Delamere. She thinks little Dorinda gives her a right to live at the Hall, and I suppose she may be correct—Oh dear."

The last two words were caused by a figure which had just stepped out from the rhododendrons into the middle of the drive—an elderly lady in the flowing skirts of the last century. Justin reined in his horse and glanced at Chloe.

"That's your aunt Sophronia," she said quietly. "It must be one of her bad days. Wherever is her companion?"

Justin looked at the Dowager Lady Stanforth with astonishment, and she glowered at them.

"What are you doing that is evil?" she asked fiercely.

"My God," muttered Justin.

Chloe leapt down from the carriage. "Oh dear. Why don't you drive her up to the house?"

"While you walk?" he said in consternation, and then shrugged. "If you can persuade her up here."

The elderly lady greeted Chloe with a sharp, "Hussy!" and made as if to pull away from her hands. Then she recognized her daughter-in-law and her mood changed. She happily allowed herself to be hoisted up into the curricle. Justin looked over her head at Chloe.

"I feel terrible at leaving you here."

"You feel terrible at being alone with her," she replied quietly with a grin. "Don't worry. She's harmless. And no, I am not driving your team even if they are tired. It's no distance. When you get to the Hall, they'll take care of her."

He accepted his orders and drove on.

"A very pleasant gel," said the Dowager in the best manner of a Society Lady. "Niece of the Duke of Tyne, you know."

Justin looked at her and found that, apart from her clothes, she seemed completely normal. Many elderly ladies clung to the styles of their youth, not liking the high waists and straight skirts of fashion. He was shocked, however, at the deterioration in her since he had last been at Delamere. Aunt Sophronia looked to be well over sixty and yet he doubted she had reached fifty yet. He remembered when he had first visited Delamere at age ten. Then his aunt had been a plump and pretty woman with a merry sense of humor.

"Yes, I know," he said in reply to her comment, and got no response. He remembered the lady's hearing had been failing for years.

"How are you, Aunt Sophronia?" he shouted.

"Very well, thank you," she said. "But I am your mother, Stephen. Try to remember these things. I am sure I don't know where you have been recently but you are far too brown. I have a lotion. . . ." Her voice trailed off. After a bewildered pause, she said, "*Potpourri* is quite delightful."

Justin stared at the Dowager, wondering what response to make. As the lady was looking ahead and humming a little song to herself, he decided to make none. He had to confess, however, that the thought that he was now responsible for her terrified him more than enemy fire.

They arrived in front of the house and servants came forward. As soon as someone was at the horses' heads Justin went around to assist his aunt to the ground. "I'm not Stephen," he shouted, feeling more than a little foolish, "I'm Justin."

The Dowager looked at him. "I suppose you are," she said with a frown. Then she smiled sadly. "First Stephen, then George, now you. You see," she said, with a smile which hinted at the teasing beauty of her youth, "I do know what is going on. Do you want an apple?"

Justin looked at her with close attention.

"Why?" he said loudly, wishing he could whisper as seemed more appropriate. "Do you have one for me?"

She looked at him with well-bred astonishment. "Why would I have an apple with me? I haven't the teeth for one. But Stephen was coming here to pick apples, and George kept laughing whenever anyone asked for an apple. I don't think eating apples is particularly humorous, do you? George was dicked in the nob, though, and greedy. Even the Duchess is always asking for apples. Personally, I like a grape. Remind me to give you that lotion, dear. . . ."

With a fond tap on his cheek, the Dowager Lady Stanforth allowed herself to be led off by her anxious companion, leaving Justin staring after her.

He thought about driving back to pick up Chloe but saw she was already in sight, walking at her usual brisk pace. She had never been a dawdler.

JO BEVERLEY is widely regarded as one of the most talented romance writers today. She is a *New York Times* bestseller, a five-time winner of Romance Writers of America's cherished RITA Award, and one of only a handful of members of the RWA Hall of Fame. She has also twice received the *Romantic Times* Career Achievement Award. Born in England, she has two grown sons and lives with her husband in Victoria, British Columbia, just a ferry ride away from Seattle. You can visit her Web site at www.jobev.com.